MERGERS & ACQUISITIONS

AMANDA RADLEY

MERGERS & ACQUISITIONS

CHAPTER ONE

"A SPORTS CAR?" Kate repeated. She furrowed her brow at the idea.

"Yes, silver and red and really, really fast," Yannis said.

He stood up and paced excitedly around the meeting room. Yannis was tall, over six feet. His lanky frame seemed at odds with his constant need to bound around.

Kate suppressed a chuckle as she watched him pace. She appreciated his enthusiasm, no one wanted to work with a miserable client. But Yannis was almost too enthusiastic. He switched from one major project to another without stopping to catch his breath.

"Why a sports car?" Kate queried.

"We build engines, sports cars need engines. This is fantastic," he announced.

Kate suspected that Yannis felt his high-intensity enthusiasm would wear off on those around him. Bouncing around meeting rooms with excitement and informing people that things were fantastic were his way of injecting passion into a project.

Yannis was certainly a successful businessman, but he also was primarily an ideas man. Leaving the details to others. Like her.

"It's… different," Kate allowed.

"Different is good. Exciting." Yannis paused in front of the windows that overlooked the sprawling City of London. "We need to be different. We need to move, grow, change, adapt." He leaned closer to the glass and peered out of the window. "You can see my house from here."

Kate rolled her eyes good-naturedly. She stood up and walked around the meeting table to join him by the window. This wasn't the first meeting she had spent chasing after the excitable man, and it probably wouldn't be the last.

"This is east, yes?" He pointed out of the window. Before she could reply, he was staring intently into the distance, looking for landmarks.

"Yes," she replied. "Yannis, let me just get this straight in my mind. Atrom are going to build a sports car—"

"Ten," he corrected, still gazing over the city to get his bearings.

She felt her eyebrow raise. "Ten?"

"Ten," he repeated. "Selling for a million pounds. We'll only sell ten. I'm having one, of course."

Kate looked skywards. "Right, okay. Atrom are going to build ten sports cars, each priced at one million pounds, and you will buy one for yourself?"

Yannis looked at her. He smiled and nodded his head. "Yes, that's it. And this is big news, so I need my favourite marketing guru to tell the world for me."

"And we'll be more than happy to help," Kate assured. "I assume you want the works? Press releases, websites, viral campaigns, video campaigns, news slots?"

"Everything. International," Yannis said. He looked at her seriously. "It is very important to me that this is international news."

"That's definitely something we can do." Kate mentally put together a quick marketing brief. While she considered Yannis an idiot for investing in a project that was a glorified toy for himself, she welcomed the money the project would bring.

"It's a big job," he said.

"It is," Kate agreed. Huge, in fact. Atrom Engineering was by far their biggest client, in terms of size and profitability. The introduction of a new product, and all that went with it, meant a huge amount of income for Kate's agency, Red Door.

Yannis Papadakis was the kind of CEO that Kate adored. He was rich, eccentric, and didn't think twice about spending a small fortune marketing his already successful engineering company.

"I had lunch in New York last week," Yannis continued. "With Georgina Masters, you know her?"

Kate tried to control her grimace. "I've met her a couple of times. Award ceremonies, conferences. That kind of thing."

"Mastery is considered to be the best advertising agency in America." Yannis walked back to the meeting table. He sat down and opened his MacBook. He hunched over the small machine and typed in his password. "Georgina really knows her stuff."

Kate hummed noncommittally at his mention of the woman. If life were a cartoon, Georgina Masters would be her arch nemesis. The two women were constantly compared within the industry and by the media. They were both businesswomen in their forties, give or take, who had set up successful marketing companies in a male-dominated sector. Of course they were often compared. But comparisons are rarely kind; they certainly hadn't been between Kate and Georgina.

Kate had come to loathe the very mention of Georgina Masters. She was sure Georgina felt the same way about her.

"She is very interested in the sports car industry," Yannis was saying. He turned his MacBook around so Kate could see the screen.

She stepped away from the window and walked towards the table. She wasn't particularly interested in whatever Yannis was about to show her, but she knew she had to make an effort.

"This car was built by some guys in California, they are trying to go for the world land speed record. Georgina is representing them."

Kate picked her glasses up from the table and put them on. She peered at the website. It was garish. She had no doubt that many would think it was a fantastic example of modern web design. Flashing images, unclear navigation, lightboxes popping up. To Kate, it was gimmicky and crass. Just what she had come to expect from Mastery.

"It's a bit... flashy. Don't you think?"

Yannis grinned. "Yes," he agreed.

Kate removed her glasses and tapped the arm on her lip. "If this is the style you like, we can definitely follow this example. Maybe tweak it a little so there's not quite so much… visual noise."

Yannis spun the MacBook around to face him again and started to type. "I want you and Georgina to work together on this. Red Door and Mastery working together. Hand in hand. Then, this project would have the best marketing minds in America and in Europe. Together, the three of us can make something really exciting."

Kate blinked. She stared at Yannis, but he was again lost in his computer screen and oblivious to her reaction.

"You want us to work together?" Kate couldn't shake the shock from her tone. "Georgina and me? Working together?"

"Yes, isn't it perfect?" He didn't look up.

"Perfect isn't quite the word I'd use," Kate confessed. The last thing she wanted was for Georgina Masters to swoop in and take all the glory. And, potentially, the entire Atrom contract. "Yannis, we've worked together for years. I like to think we have a good working relationship?"

Yannis was focused on his screen. "Yes, yes, of course."

Kate knew he was only half-listening to her. "And Atrom and Red Door have always worked well together, haven't we? We can directly attribute the twelve-percent sales growth Atrom experienced last year to Red Door's advertising campaigns. Bringing in another voice, it could be tricky."

Yannis patted the seat next to him, still focused on his screen. "Look at this."

Kate rolled her eyes and shuffled around a couple of

seats at the round meeting table. She put her glasses on again. Yannis gestured to a presentation chart on the screen.

"We need to get more social," he explained to her as if she were a child.

The presentation bore the Mastery logo. Kate pursed her lips. Clearly Georgina had presented this to Yannis and convinced him to take a new direction. Upon closer examination, it was clear that Yannis had been enticed by pie charts and line graphs that showed upward trends.

Competitor agencies pitching to existing clients wasn't a new thing. Any marketing director worth their wage would use any opportunity to speak to decision-makers. Subjectivity was not just the beauty of the marketing industry; it was also its curse.

In other businesses, a job may be a simple predefined product. The business makes widgets, a widget has set parameters. The business decides its success on widgets produced.

But marketing involves so much more. Marketing can be good or bad, or good *and* bad at the same time. A logo can be loved and hated within one focus group.

The individuality of marketing allowed seeds of doubt to be planted by competitors. A magic formula could be proposed, fancy charts could be distributed and buzzwords deployed. All business owners want to recreate the success of other businesses, so a marketing agency promising such success was a potent thing.

Kate looked at the presentation with interest. As she thought, it contained all the generic statistics regarding social media success rates—the standard lure marketing agencies used to hook new prospective clients.

"Engineering firms can only benefit from social media to a point," Kate explained. It was a conversation they'd had several times before. Each time she explained it, Yannis agreed and understood. But within a few weeks, his flighty mind had forgotten and she was left to repeat herself. "The average person on the street doesn't care that the engine on a train is made by Atrom."

"We need to be a part of the conversation," Yannis insisted, clearly repeating the buzzwords he'd recently heard.

"There is no conversation about your sector, Yannis," Kate replied. She took off her glasses and let out a small sigh. Competitor interference in marketing was a common thing. One day a client would be happy, the next they would have read an article and would be explaining what they felt her agency needed to do.

Kate spent most of her days explaining to clients that she knew their market better than the competition. The difficulty was, this was Yannis. The phrase *bee in his bonnet* might have been created specifically with him in mind. Once he had an idea, nothing could make him let it go.

"Georgina has more information on this," Yannis explained. He gestured to the screen. "You understand all of this better than I do, anyway. But the thing to take away here is that this is exciting! We are going to build sports cars, and I want everyone to know about them. We can work together and make this the best campaign ever. Between us, I'm positive that we can make The Bolt something that everyone is talking about."

"The Bolt?"

"I'm thinking of calling it The Bolt." Yannis closed the MacBook and placed his fingers on top of it, protecting the secrets within. He leaned close to Kate. "I am still working out all of the details, but I can feel this is going to be a huge success." He smiled at her, willing her to join him in his excitement.

While his passion for the project radiated from him, Kate felt utterly unable to join in. She didn't want to work with Mastery. The whole point of running her own agency was that she didn't have to work with anyone.

"Yannis," Kate said carefully, "while working with Mastery would be wonderful, I'm not sure how we can work out the logistics. They are based in New York. You and I are based in London. Trying to split the workload, coordinate the teams, that would be very difficult."

"We're a modern world," Yannis told her. "We have video conferencing, Internet, and airplanes." He stood up and started to pack his belongings into his laptop bag. "I need the best, Kate. That's you in Europe. But I need the American market. Do you know how many millionaires are in America?"

"Not off the top of my head," Kate admitted.

"Me neither, but it's a huge country, so there must be a lot. Picture it, my Bolt driving down Sunset Boulevard, maybe driven by a movie star or a pop singer. Who knows?"

Kate knew when his mind was made up. In his head, he was already winning awards and being proclaimed the genius behind the sports car of the decade. Yannis had often explained that his success was borne entirely from his sheer willpower to make success happen. He was dogged in his approach, unwavering in his beliefs. If he wanted Kate and Georgina to work together, that is exactly what he would have.

Any further argument from Kate would just make her sound awkward. As much as she hated the idea, her best course of action now was to play along.

Georgina wasn't a fool, she didn't get to where she was by not spotting an opportunity. There was no way she'd just stumbled upon Yannis. She'd sought him out, presumably armed with enough statistical information on the car industry to put Jay Leno to shame.

It was clear to Kate that Georgina was after the Atrom Engineering account. Now it was up to Kate to do everything she could to hang onto it.

CHAPTER TWO

Sophie Young watched as Kate's assistant Jonathan placed the flowers in the tall vase. He tilted his head to one side and adjusted the longest stem. He moved the vase a few millimetres to the right and then stood back. He regarded the vase with an approving nod before looking back up at her, the agency's newest employee.

"As I was saying, Atrom are our biggest client," he continued. "Over the years, the work we have done for them has grown as they have become more and more successful. Now around two-thirds of the staff here work on the Atrom account. The monthly retainer from them alone pays for this building."

"Wow," Sophie whispered.

She peered through the glass wall into the main office. They were on the twelfth floor; all twelve floors were filled with Red Door staff, making them one of the biggest marketing agencies in London in terms of size and employee numbers. The cost of that much floor space in central London was enough to make Sophie's head spin.

She put her pen to her notepad to jot down the information.

"Don't write that down," Jonathan said. "If you left your notepad on the train and someone found it, Kate would kill us both."

Sophie nodded and clipped her pen to the top of the pad. "And Yannis Papad…"

"Papadakis, Yannis Papadakis is the CEO of Atrom."

Sophie looked at her notebook with uncertainty and then back up to Jonathan.

He smiled at her. "That you can write down."

She felt herself blush and quickly snatched the pen up again. It was her first real day of work, finally moving from being an intern to a paid member of the staff. The nerves were really starting to kick in. Especially being in Kate Kennedy's office, even if the woman wasn't currently there.

The number of photographs on display made it feel like she was, though. Sophie glanced over at the wall of framed images. There were photographs of Kate accepting awards, Kate generally socialising with London's rich and famous. There were even some clippings from magazine articles. Kate hadn't changed over the years: she looked the same at thirty, at forty, and even now at almost fifty. Her emerald green eyes sparkled mischievously, and her shoulder-length blonde hair was always styled to perfection.

"Who were you working with before?" Jonathan asked. He had moved away from the flowers and was straightening items on Kate's large glass desk.

"Tracey, down in accounts on the second floor," Sophie replied.

"Ah, I wondered why I hadn't seen you around

before," he said. He pulled a handkerchief out from his pocket and wiped some dust from the top of the desk lamp. "So, you were an intern in accounts?"

"Yes, I interned there for three months. When my internship ended, Human Resources asked me if I wanted a job up here, with the operations department. I'm on probation." She winced, wondering why she had added that last bit of information. Of course she was on probation. All new employees were. Bringing it up just showed how nervous she was about the whole thing. Specifically about working so closely with the CEO of Red Door Marketing.

Kate Kennedy was a legend. For as long as Sophie could remember, Kate had been the one to watch in the marketing sector. Never in her wildest dreams did Sophie think that she would work for Red Door, never mind on the same floor as Kate. She'd spent the last two weeks of her internship pinching herself and expecting to wake up.

Despite her three months at Red Door, she'd never once seen Kate in person. Her absence had just made her even more mysterious and fascinating. She knew that she had something of an obsession with Kate. When she was a little girl, she would pretend that she owned an impressive marketing agency, a rather specific bit of make-believe that makes her mum and dad chuckle to this day. In high school, she had her hair cut into Kate's iconic style. At university, she'd studied marketing in the hopes that she'd one day be able to follow in Kate's footsteps.

Sadly, life didn't go the way she had planned. Necessity had forced her into the first job she could find, and her dreams of working in marketing had faded. Until recently, that is, when she had seen the internship position advertised. It was too good an opportunity to miss.

Now she needed to get her nerves under control.

"H-have you worked for Kate for long?" She tried to move the topic of conversation away from herself.

"Three years this September," Jonathan replied. He detached the telephone cable and unwound the knots that had formed in it.

"What's she like?" Of course, she had intensively researched Kate. She'd heard rumours about her brilliance. But, as always, there were conflicting stories. Sophie was desperate to get to the truth.

Jonathan chuckled. "She's brilliant at her job. But a complete nightmare to work for. All the rumours you've heard are true."

Sophie swallowed. She'd hoped the opposite would be true. "Even about the intern and the stairwell?" *Surely that was made up,* she mused.

"Yep, all true." He tucked the handkerchief into his trouser pocket. He stood and gave the desk one final look. "She's the best in the biz, there's no doubt about that. But she works hard; her life is Red Door. She founded this company when she was twenty-three, and she's built it into the multi-million-pound empire it is today. We employ four hundred people here in the London office. If you've worked here for a year and survived, you can get a job anywhere."

"That's what I heard," Sophie admitted. She hadn't felt the need to tell anyone about her encyclopaedic knowledge of Kate Kennedy and the Red Door Agency. She wanted to fit in. Even though she had been bumped up from intern to a junior administrator position, she still knew that her employment was fragile. Kate's temper was legendary; she didn't suffer fools.

He looked at her and smiled. "So, what is it that you want to do?"

Sophie nervously adjusted her glasses. She'd only known Jonathan Llewellyn for a couple of hours, but already she felt like she could trust him. He was Kate's personal assistant, her right-hand man. He was kind and considerate, funny and intelligent. It was a relief that she'd be shadowing him while she learnt what her new job entailed.

"Come on," he encouraged. "What's Sophie Young's dream?"

"Well, I… I know it's silly, but I love marketing. I always have. When I was a kid, I used to draw brand logos instead of stick figures of my family. My dad got me a board game just about company brands. When I see an advertisement at a bus stop, I notice the fonts, I notice the colours. I just love it. I want to be a part of it. I want to learn everything there is to know about it."

Sophie took a step towards Kate's desk. Looking Jonathan in the eye, she said, "I know some people think it's just… just a tool to get people to buy stuff they don't want. But I know it's more than that. It's complicated, dynamic. There's psychology and beauty to it. I want to be surrounded by people who feel the same way."

Jonathan smiled and nodded. He opened his mouth to reply and then slowly closed it again, a frown emerging on his face.

Sophie realised he was looking past her and turned around.

Kate Kennedy was storming her way across the office. In all her time at Red Door, Sophie had never seen Kate once. Now the woman was walking towards her, straight towards her.

Sophie felt her eyes widen in fear. Suddenly she felt woefully underdressed. Her baby-blue shirt and khaki-coloured trousers were no match for Kate's fitted light-grey skirt-suit, clearly designer label. Probably costing more than Sophie made in a month.

Kate entered the office and threw her binder onto the coffee table. "I need a team meeting, now. All Atrom account managers," Kate told Jonathan.

As she walked across the room towards her desk, she looked Sophie up and down. "Who is this?"

"I'll introduce you both later," Jonathan replied. He took hold of Sophie's shoulders and gently moved her towards the door. Sophie was glad for the assistance. Not only had she lost the ability to walk, but also the ability to speak.

Luckily, Kate was quick to ignore Sophie and focus on whatever drama was happening.

"Get Jeremy up here, and Colin. And that woman in digital, the one with the hair."

"Alice?" Jonathan asked.

Kate sat at her desk. "Yes, that one. Ten minutes."

Jonathan guided Sophie out of the office and towards his desk.

"What's going on?" Sophie whispered to him.

"No idea, but it looks bad. Can you speak to reception? Tell them we need one of the larger meeting rooms immediately. Block it out for the whole afternoon, just in case." He picked up the phone and held it to his shoulder.

"Sure," Sophie agreed, excited to help. "And then what?"

He held up his hand and turned to speak into the phone. "Jez, big hoopla up here, I need your team for a meeting in, like, ten minutes. Okay, great, great, bye." He hung up the call with his finger and then dialled another number. He looked at her. "Then you can go back to writing those name cards for the party tomorrow night," he told her.

Sophie felt herself deflate at not being more involved. She'd always known it would take some time to be considered a real member of the team, not just the ex-intern. But it was her first day. Something big was happening, and she'd just seen Kate Kennedy. *The* Kate Kennedy. Who presumably thought she was a mute nobody.

She shook off her disappointment and hurried towards her desk. She opened the interoffice messaging system and sent a message down to reception to request the main conference room.

While she waited for a reply, she picked up her mobile. She unlocked the screen and hammered out a text message to her boyfriend, Matt. Her hands were still shaking from the excitement and thrill of seeing Kate.

OMG, just saw Kate Kennedy!

Her computer pinged. Reception had replied and booked the room for her. She sent another message to Jonathan to let him know that the room was available.

The screen of her phone lit up.

Awesome, what did you say? What did she say?

Sophie scrunched up her face.

I froze :(

She lowered the phone to her desk and looked up. Jonathan and Kate marched across the office towards the bank of elevators in the middle of the floor.

The open-plan office was bustling with people. Different departments were denoted by signs hanging from the ceiling. They were split by marketing media, specific accounts, and general departments. When she had been offered a job in Operations, she had been ecstatic.

Operations had sounded important, central to the running of the business. It wasn't until she had received her job description that she realised Operations was a fancy term used for the person who did anything and everything.

It seemed that she would be helping whoever needed it, doing whatever they said. She reported to anyone, and no one reported to her. Operations consisted of one person. Her.

On the bright side, her desk was by a window. The London skyline was breathtaking. On the not-so-bright side, the view within the office wasn't quite as glamorous. She was surrounded by filing cabinets and the photocopier.

Sophie cheered herself up by thinking about how her job seemed to involve helping Jonathan. Which meant she'd be seeing a lot more of Kate, a thought which excited and terrified her at the same time.

She picked up the calligraphy pen and the guest list Jonathan had given her that morning. Writing name cards wasn't exactly her idea of getting involved in the marketing industry, but it was a start. She knew she'd have to start from the bottom.

Luckily, Jonathan was nice. She'd had horrible bosses in the past and knew how difficult work could be with a bad boss. They hadn't had much time together, but at least he was talking to her and showing her the ropes. Even taking the time to ask her about her professional aspirations.

At the memory, she put the pen down and lowered her head and softly banged it on the desk. She couldn't believe she'd come out with that impassioned speech about marketing. She must have sounded like a complete idiot. She took a deep breath and sat back up. The last thing she needed was for the office to think she was weird.

Her phone lit up again, and she looked at the message.

· · ·

Aww, I'm sorry, babe. I'll make you a great dinner tonight and you'll forget all about it.

She smiled.

Thanks, Matt. Best boyfriend award on its way! xx

She put the phone back down.

It's my first day, first days are supposed to be rubbish. I'll just get through it, go home, and have a lovely dinner, and tomorrow everything will look better, she told herself.

CHAPTER THREE

"THIS WHOLE THING is giving me a headache," Kate grumbled.

She folded her arms and waited for the elevator to arrive. Not only had she been forced to listen to Yannis's insane plan, she'd then had to sound interested and convinced of its success. The whole thing was exhausting.

"He's making ten super cars?" Jonathan asked, surprise evident in his tone.

The lift arrived, and they both stepped in.

"Yes, thinking he's going to sell them for a million. Each."

"Why sports cars, though?"

The elevator doors started to close. Kate leaned against the back wall, holding onto the handrail behind her with outstretched arms. "Because he is an overgrown boy. Don't let the bald head fool you, he's actually a child."

Jonathan snorted a laugh. "And he seriously wants us to work with Mastery? Doesn't he know they are based in New York?"

Kate rolled her eyes. "Well, in this world of modern communication, apparently, we can video chat."

It had taken a lot of effort not to laugh at Yannis when he had told her his solution to the three-and-a-half-thousand mile distance between the two offices. As far as Yannis was concerned, the distance would be overcome by technology.

"It's just not going to work," Jonathan said. "Can we talk him out of it?"

She shook her head and stood up straight. "No, he has an idea, and he likes the sound of it. As far as he's concerned, we are the very best in Europe, and she is the very best in America. He thinks that combining our strengths will make us this unstoppable team, and everyone will get to hear about his Bolt."

"Bolt?"

"The car." Kate waved her hand. "He thinks he'll call it The Bolt. I'm trying to get him to change it. He hasn't given two seconds thought to the name, I'm sure."

"Why does he want to go through all this hassle?" Jonathan asked. "He's only making ten cars. Even at a million each they could be snapped up. He doesn't need a worldwide campaign, he just needs a sales team to target the right prospects."

"It's a vanity project. It's the Yannis Show. This isn't about making money, this is about him and his fast, little car being on everyone's lips."

The elevator doors opened. "But we're not going to take this lying down," she said quietly as they stepped out. "We don't want to work with Masters, but we can be sure that she doesn't want to work with us either. This is just a play for the account. We need to give the impression that we're happy to do this, that we think it's a great idea. It's going to be a case of who blinks first."

"Sounds like you have an idea?" Jonathan opened the meeting room door for her.

The room was empty; they had a few moments before the others started to arrive. She tossed her notepad and pen onto the table and pulled out the chair at the head. She was still livid, but she was gradually calming down and seeing a way through the storm.

"The car is being built here, in England," she said, "so I think that gives us reasonable grounds to suggest using this office as HQ. I plan to suggest to Yannis that Georgina and a small team come here. If I can convince him that this is a good idea, she'll have to agree to it. And then we'll have the home team advantage."

"What kind of advantage?" Jonathan asked.

Kate leaned on the high-backed chair and watched as Jonathan made them both tea. He'd clearly noticed her stress levels were on the rise and had taken the initiative to soothe her with her favourite herbal blend. It was times like this that she thanked the employment gods for bringing her Jonathan.

"Just taking Georgina out of her environment will be an advantage," she explained. "She'll be here, using our services, even our team. I can't imagine that she'll want to take many members of staff out of Mastery and bring them here. She won't even want to come here herself. Yannis will push the issue, and she'll come with a skeleton team. But once she is here, we'll see her face-to-face and

23

we can figure out what she's planning. Keep your friends close and your enemies closer."

"You really think she is making a play for the account?" Jonathan placed a cup and saucer on the table in front of Kate.

She nodded her gratitude towards him and sat down. "I believe so. As you know, Georgina and I don't exactly get on. I'm sure she'd be delighted to take the Atrom account from me. It wouldn't take much investigation for her to find out that they are our largest account. But I have no intention of letting her take it."

Kate picked up the teaspoon and slowly stirred her drink. She watched as steam rose, feeling calmed by its indistinct patterns in the air.

"You know," Kate continued, "she actually presented to him. Some ridiculous notion about having a social conversation, as if Atrom are going to be tweeting with Mary in Cardiff about compressor valves. But she presented to him, and now Yannis's head is filled with ideas."

Jonathan winced at the thought. He knew as well as Kate did that clients having their heads filled with nonsensical ideas was trouble. "So, what do we do?"

"Well, first things first. We need to know what she's planning."

"How do we do that?" Jonathan asked.

Kate regarded him silently, conveying her idea in a look alone. She didn't want to be the one to say the distasteful words out loud. She knew Jonathan would catch her meaning soon enough.

"You think that we should spy on her?" he asked.

Kate nodded once. "Exactly."

"Who do you think should do it? It can't be me, she'll see right through that. And the other PAs are drowning in work for the audit."

"I don't know," Kate admitted. "It needs to be someone loyal but unassuming." She sipped at her tea. Finding someone was going to be tricky. She needed someone unimportant, someone Georgina wouldn't be enticed to poach for her own staff. It had to be someone that she could trust, someone unobtrusive, someone Georgina would also trust.

"How about the new girl?"

Kate frowned. "What new girl?"

"The new girl. She was in your office just now."

Kate lowered her cup to the saucer. She tried to recall but came up blank.

Jonathan leaned on the back of his chair. "Long blonde hair, ponytail? Glasses?"

Kate shook her head. Why Jonathan continued to think that she had the ability to remember people after all the years they worked together escaped her.

"Sophie Young," he prompted. "She's the one I told you about. The intern, she was in accounts, showed a lot of promise. She's now on the top floor. We told HR to put her in Operations so you could move her to wherever there was a need."

"It's starting to sound familiar." Kate toyed with the teaspoon. "You think she's the right person?"

"I think she is dedicated to the company. She seems quiet, unassuming. I don't think Georgina would think she was a spy."

While the transfer sounded familiar, Kate couldn't place the girl he was speaking of. It wasn't unusual; people came and went fairly quickly at Red Door. If they couldn't keep up, or they weren't up to the job, they were out. She knew it had earned her a harsh reputation, and that was just fine with her. You didn't get to be one of the top marketing agencies in Europe by being kind and forgiving.

If the girl was new and willing to impress, she might be just what Kate needed.

Kate stared at the email she was trying to compose. Choosing the right words for her first communication with Georgina wasn't going to be easy. She'd been looking at the empty text box for ten minutes, and she was no closer to choosing a suitable greeting.

Her eyes drifted towards the browser window beside the email.

Trust Georgina Masters to have her face emblazoned over the homepage of her corporate website, Kate thought.

She leaned a little closer to the screen.

Either she's had work done, or that photo had a team of Photoshop artists working day and night for a week.

Georgina was flawless: she was approaching fifty and didn't seem to have one wrinkle. Her shoulder-length brown hair looked like molten chocolate; her eyes were the exact same hue.

Kate angrily dragged the empty email window over the woman's smug face. She drummed her fingers on her desk as she again pondered how to start the message.

She ignored the tentative knock on her office's open door. Whoever it was would just have to learn to knock with confidence if they wanted to speak with her. If they couldn't get her attention with a knock, she certainly wasn't about to listen to whatever they had to say.

A soft female cough sounded.

Kate sighed. She slowly removed her glasses and looked up at the door. She didn't recognise the frightened young thing standing in the doorway.

"Yes?" she asked.

"You, um, wanted to see me?"

"Do you, *um*, have a name?"

"Sophie. Sophie Young." The scared mouse took a small step into the office.

Ah, the new girl.

"Come in, close the door, and take a seat." Kate gestured to one of the two visitor chairs in front of her desk.

Sophie edged into the room and slowly closed the door behind her. She had the look of a new starter: terrified, unsure of herself and her role.

The girl was the very embodiment of the term preppy. Her long blonde hair and geeky glasses perfectly matched the style. If Kate was a fan of the preppy appearance, she'd be impressed. Unfortunately, for Sophie, Kate hated the rising trend among millennials. More so, she feared that Sophie wasn't actively going for a certain style. Sophie appeared to be geek chic without the chic.

By this time, Sophie had crossed the room and sat on the edge of the visitor chair. She held a notepad in her hand and looked expectantly at Kate.

"So, you interned for us? Is that right?"

Sophie nodded. "I did. I spent three months in accounts."

"Accounts. Riveting." Kate opened her desk planner and looked at her upcoming appointments. Sophie was going to have to work to get her attention. Kate needed to know what the girl was made of.

"It was the only position available," Sophie said quickly.

Kate glanced up at her. "I see. What brought you to Red Door?"

"You." Sophie fiddled with her glasses. "I… I love marketing, and I wrote about Red Door at university. It was my case study. You were… um, I mean—"

"I see." Kate returned her attention to her desk planner. She'd heard enough desperate wannabes telling her that she was their idol. They were all so keen to emulate her rather than walk their own path. "And now you're working up on the top floor. That's a big step for an intern in accounts."

"I'm a hard worker. And very willing to learn. I came here because I wanted to learn from the best."

Kate smirked to herself. "Well, we *are* the best," she agreed. She looked at Sophie and interlaced her hands in front of her. "Tell me, *Sophia*, what do you know about Georgina Masters?"

Sophie swallowed and bit her lip. "Um, she's… she owns Mastery. The American agency."

Kate rolled her eyes. "Your industry knowledge clearly knows no ends… or beginnings." She picked up her pen and looked at her desk planner again.

She waited. Sophie's worth to the company would make itself known within the next twenty seconds, if she had any.

"Georgina Masters set up Mastery in New York when she was twenty-two. She had one client, a local bookshop, which she got into the *New York Times* within a month. Mastery is the biggest marketing agency in America, they have some of the biggest names on the planet on their books. She's been credited with starting the trend of world leaders having Twitter accounts. She's won hundreds of awards. She's been on the cover of *Life Magazine* three times. And she likes dogs. Beagles, I believe."

Kate lowered her pen and considered Sophie again. "Impressive. But it's Basset Hounds."

"Damn," Sophie muttered and shook her head.

Kate allowed the error. She knew full well that Sophie had just demonstrated more knowledge than most of her staff knew existed.

"Red Door and Mastery are going to temporarily work together on a new project for Atrom," Kate explained. "I'm about to invite Georgina to the London office. I'd like you to be her primary liaison."

"M-me?"

"You," Kate confirmed. "I need someone to keep an eye on her. Make sure she has everything she needs."

"I can do that." Sophie fidgeted in her seat.

She's so nervous, Kate thought. *Georgina's going to chew her up and spit her out. Still, the slap in the face of being assigned an ex-intern will send a clear message. Shame to lose this one so soon, she almost has promise.*

"Jonathan will give you more information nearer the

time." Kate put her glasses back on and turned her attention to her laptop. After a couple of seconds, she looked at Sophie. She raised her eyebrow.

"Oh, I'll... yes, thank you." Sophie stumbled to her feet and scurried out of the office.

Kate watched her fumble with the door before apologising again and rushing out. She shook her head and returned her attention to the opening line of her email.

CHAPTER FOUR

Sophie unlocked the front door and stepped into the cramped hallway of her apartment. She let out a deep sigh. The whole Tube ride home, she had been berating herself for her pathetic performance in front of Kate.

If she was going to work for the woman then she was going to have to get herself together. And she needed to tell her that her name was *not* Sophia. Although, she suspected that the name change was a power play. One that she had allowed Kate to win easily.

She needed to get her nerves under control. Not that having Georgina Masters come to Red Door was going to make that any easier. Georgina was the American version of Kate. Glamorous, successful, famous, and rich. Having both impressive women in the Red Door offices at the same time was going to be incredible. Like a dream come true. A very, very frightening dream.

The fact that Kate had handpicked her to look after Georgina was amazing. And terrifying. Now Sophie had a real deadline to get her nerves under control. She couldn't embarrass herself in front of Georgina like she had with Kate.

"There she is, my marketing genius!" Matt padded into the hallway and helped her out of her coat. "How was the first day?"

"Scary," she admitted.

"It will get better," he promised. He hung her coat up on the long hooks shaped like cat's tails. Sophie looked at it with a small grin. She'd been so pleased when she'd found the novelty coatrack at the market. She looked just above it at a figurine she didn't recognise. It stood shoulder to shoulder with the other collectibles that Matt insisted would one day be worth money.

"I know, it's just I want it to be better now. You know how nervous I get."

"I know." He pressed a soft kiss to her cheek.

She looked at him in surprise. "Hey, you shaved!"

In the three years they'd been together, she'd constantly asked him to shave his beard and moustache. He'd always refused, but here he was, cleanly shaven. "Aw, did you shave because it was my first day? Is this my treat?"

"Of course. That, and a great dinner." He looped her arm through his and walked her into the kitchen.

On the small dining table was a homemade pizza and a bottle of white wine. Sophie grinned excitedly. "You made pizza?"

"I made pizza," Matt confirmed. "And I'm only having one slice, so you can take the rest to work tomorrow."

Sophie sat down and looked up at him in confusion. "Just one slice?"

"Well, one big slice. But, yeah, one slice." He sat

down. "You know I have military fitness tomorrow morning. I don't want to go through all the pain of getting up at five in the morning and going to the park to be shouted at if I'm going to put loads of weight on by eating too much pizza."

Matt had always been overweight. He carried it well because of his height, but he loved food and always ate to excess. Sophie was lucky, she could eat whatever she liked and never seemed to put any weight on.

Recently, Matt had signed up to a fitness group that met in the park at the crack of dawn. It was based on military fitness training and seemed to consist of a chiselled ex-Army officer shouting at people to run faster.

"Well, I like you to be a little cuddly," Sophie reminded him. "But you do what you think is best."

"I just want to be slimmer. For you." He poured two small glasses of wine. "I've already lost quite a bit of weight, but there's a long way to go."

"You know that *I* don't need you to lose weight, right?" Sophie reached out and took his hand. "I love you just the way you are."

Matt smiled. "I love you, too. So much it hurts."

Sophie smiled. She let go of his hand and reached for the pizza cutter. "Mm, pizza." She started to run the cutter through the pizza, creating equal slices.

"So, how was it?" Matt asked. "First day on the top floor."

"Yup. I spoke to Kate, and she told—"

"Oh, it's *Kate* now is it? It's always been Kate Kennedy before," he teased.

Sophie could feel the blush flare on her cheeks. She

knew she talked about Kate a lot, she always had. Matt had joked a few times that Kate Kennedy was the third person in their relationship as Sophie spoke about her so often.

"I work with her now," Sophie defended. "I can't call her Kate Kennedy all the time. It would be weird."

"I know," he said. "I'm just teasing you. I'm glad you're working with your idol. It's cool, you worked hard to get there and you totally deserve this. Sorry I interrupted, Kate told you?"

Sophie placed a slice on her plate. "She told me that Georgina Masters is coming over from New York, and I'm going to be her primary liaison."

She looked up to see Matt staring at her open-mouthed. "Are you kidding?"

"Nope." She took a bite of pizza.

"That's incredible! I'm so proud of you," he said.

"I'm not. You should have seen me speaking with Kate, I sounded like an idiot." Sophie shuddered a little at the memory.

"It can't have been that bad if she asked you to look after Georgina Masters, even I've heard of her. And not just from you."

She shrugged. "There's probably no one else available. There's some kind of audit happening, everyone is super busy. And super unfriendly. No one spoke to me, except for Jonathan, he's Kate's PA."

"What's he like?" Matt asked.

"He's nice. Really nice, actually. Which is a relief because I think I'll be working with him mainly."

"Maybe the others just don't waste their time getting

to know the new person?" he suggested. "It sounds like the HR department at Red Door *has* a revolving door. Maybe they wait a week to see if it's worth their time."

"Maybe," Sophie agreed. "It's just hard, you know. Lonely. Being in a packed office but no one speaking to you."

"At least you have one friend." Matt bit into his pizza.

"Yeah, at least I didn't make a complete fool of myself in front of him." She remembered her impassioned speech about marketing and winced. "Well, not much of one, anyway. I just don't know how I'm going to get these nerves under control. I'm smart, I know what I'm doing. I'm articulate, I have good ideas. Until I need to speak to someone new and then I sound like a complete idiot."

"You need to take a deep breath and calm down. Ask yourself what's the worst that can happen," he suggested.

"I could look like an moron and they could fire me?" Sophie suggested.

Matt chuckled. "Well, I'm no help. You know me, I don't care about looking stupid in front of other people. You just need to find your own path. You'll figure something out that works for you."

Sophie hoped that was true. Her debilitating nerves were holding her back. She knew she was talented and had good ideas, but she didn't know how to convey them to other people. And with the likes of Kate and Georgina around, she felt smaller than usual.

Matt shifted in his seat a little. "Would you mind if I went to the pub tonight? You don't have to come, I just want to try to work on Marcus, I really think I can get him to sign the contract. It's easier to talk to him out of business hours, and you know he's in the pub every night. If I can sign that contract, the commission for this month will be great. We can get the tyres replaced on your car."

Sophie bit her lip. She'd been dreaming about a night in with Matt. Cuddled up together, watching television. But now he was planning to go out and work, to make them extra money to get her car fixed. She felt guilty about wanting to spend the evening in when he was thinking about work.

Matt hated his job in sales. He was reliant on commission for them to make enough money to pay the bills. As the economic situation started to pinch, he had started working evenings and weekends to schmooze more potential clients.

Matt was great with money; he dealt with all their finances and protected Sophie from the depressing state of their financial situation. He assured her that he'd work all the hours he needed, even get a second job if necessary, to make sure she had whatever she wanted.

Not that Sophie wanted much. She lived a simple life with no frills, no extravagant expenses.

Still, Matt was the reason Sophie was working at Red Door. The unpaid internship had taunted her, her dreams almost within reach. She'd practically decided against applying for it when Matt had told her she couldn't let the opportunity go to waste. He'd taken on extra hours, working late as he entertained clients at pubs and clubs, despite hardly drinking anything himself to save money.

Sophie had worked for three months without pay, Matt refusing to allow her to take a second job. He told her he wanted her to be fresh at work in the hopes that they would give her a paying role.

It had worked out, she was now finally earning a salary again. And she was working for the company of her dreams. But she felt guilty that her salary was less than it had been before, and Matt was still having to work late nights to make up the difference.

She blinked back to reality. "Sure. I mean, I'll miss you, but I get that you need to work. If you can get that contract then it will be great."

"Exactly, and I won't be home late. I won't drink either. Well, nothing alcoholic."

"You can drink if you want," she offered. She felt guilty enough that he had worked a full day, cooked dinner, and was now heading out again. They were saving money, but she didn't want him to feel that he couldn't have a small drink if he wanted one.

"Nah, I don't want to be out too long. Then I can get back to you and maybe we can watch an episode of something before bed?" he suggested.

"That would be great."

"Great." He smiled. "Now, tell me all about your day. Don't leave a thing out."

CHAPTER FIVE

"Why is it always so grey in London?" Georgina stared up at the clouds that lay over Heathrow Airport like a patchwork quilt of misery. So much for a sunny summer.

She knew that London wasn't as dark and rainy as people implied. She'd seen gorgeous sunny days in the English city. It just so happened that the dark weather coincided with her mood. She loathed not overseeing her own work schedule. Kate Kennedy had somehow convinced Yannis that it was essential that Georgina come to London. Plus, it was terrible timing, as her personal life back home had just imploded.

She shook the thought from her mind and watched as her luggage was loaded into the back of a shuttle van.

"Be careful with that, it's Gucci," she informed the porter. She watched him meaningfully as he lifted the remaining cases with more care.

"It's as grey here as it is in New York," Michael told her. "Come on, let's get in the car and let this man do his job."

She glared at the porter one last time. She turned away from the luggage van and stalked towards the luxurious BMW that Kate Kennedy had sent to meet them at the airport.

"This is ridiculous, coming all this way when it would be just as easy to talk online. I didn't pay ninety thousand dollars for that video conference suite for fun. If we never use it, it looks like we could only afford half the chairs."

Michael held the door open and gestured for her to get into the car.

"It's ridiculous," she repeated, hoping to get more of a reaction from him.

"It is," he agreed.

She nodded and got in. He walked around the back of the car and got in the other side.

As soon as he sat down, she turned to him. "My luggage is being manhandled."

"Your luggage is fine," he told her. "Are you going to tell me what is happening with Jessica, or do I have to suffer this mood throughout the entire two weeks in London?"

Georgina stared at him for a moment before turning to look out of the window.

"There's nothing to say."

She knew bringing Michael along would be a problem. He was the only member of her staff brave enough to speak his mind. He was practically a friend, which gave him the courage to ask personal questions that she would rather were left alone. Like why she was in a foul mood. And why her girlfriend of the past three years had suddenly, very publicly, moved out of their apartment.

"That's not what Twitter has to say." Michael pulled his phone out of his jacket pocket. "Twitter seems to think that you and Jessica have broken up. I get all my major news from Twitter these days."

"Give me that." She snatched his phone out of his hand. She looked at the screen and scrolled. News articles and speculation about their breakup were everywhere. Candid photographs of herself and Jessica accompanied most articles. She rolled her eyes and passed the phone back to him. "We're taking a break."

"I'm sorry to hear that. Really."

She sniffed and turned away again. "Thank you."

"Do you want to talk about it?" he pressed.

"What is there to talk about? It's what everyone assumed would happen: the forty-seven-year-old woman couldn't hold onto the twenty-seven year old." She stared out of the car window, pleading with herself to stay strong and not repeat the incessant snivelling of the last few days.

"But something must have happened. You two were perfect for each other," Michael insisted. "Well, not when she first came to work at Mastery. Then, you were a beast and scared the living daylights out of her."

She chuckled. "I did, didn't I?"

"Yes, and you loved every second of it." He smiled sadly. "What happened?"

She opened her mouth to voice another denial, another line that she had been using to justify the situation to herself. But then she realised that wouldn't help. If she was to move on with her life, she needed to be honest. If she couldn't be honest with Michael, who could she be honest with?

"I guess I held on a little too tightly," she admitted. "I was afraid that she would find someone who was a better fit for her. Someone closer to her age. We argued about her career. I... I might have tried to hold her back."

The truth was, that was exactly what she had done. Jessica had told her so in no uncertain terms. But Georgina had dug her heels in, refused to budge. She knew she risked losing her, but she'd rather things end quickly and at her own hand than the alternative. The very thought of Jessica slowly drifting away from her was not even worth considering.

What kept her awake most nights were thoughts of Jessica falling in love with another and gradually floating away. She looked for the tell-tale signs and even monitored her movements. Of course, she didn't think that Jessica was the type to cheat. It was the others that she couldn't trust. The ones she saw discreetly watching Jessica at parties. The ones who were waiting for their fairy-tale relationship to break down so they could swoop in and have Jessica for themselves.

Georgina worried about them not waiting. She fretted about Jessica breaking her heart.

Not wanting Michael to see the emotions that were playing across her face, she turned back to look out of the window. Since Jessica had walked out four days ago, Georgina had been bombarded with memories of their time together.

When Jessica had come to work at Mastery, she was meek and unsure of herself. She had no interest in marketing, she wanted to work with charities. But a lull in the employment market and the need for a paying job had pushed her towards a temp agency at the exact same time that Georgina had fired three assistants in one week.

Georgina could still remember the day Jessica walked into her office. Her long blonde hair and earnest expression had irritated her. She looked like a child, wide-eyed and hesitant. Georgina had itched to put the tall, slim woman into a fitted suit and have her hair and makeup professionally styled. There was obviously an attractive woman under that cheap blouse.

They danced around their attraction for the better part a year, each of them convinced that the other was definitely not interested. The fact that a ridiculous episode in a stalled elevator had eventually drawn them together was such a cliché, but it had caused them to finally talk. And for Jessica to find the bravery to go after what she wanted.

"Have you apologised?" Michael's question broke through her reminiscing.

"What do you think?" Georgina asked ruefully. "She's gone, Michael. Let's just get on with our lives."

The driver entered the car. "Your bags have been packed, Miss Masters. We can leave for the hotel now if you like?"

"Please, this airport is ghastly," she replied.

The car started to move, and the privacy glass raised.

Georgina turned to Michael. "I won't hear another word about Jessica. We're here to work."

"Of course, Georgina. Whatever you wish," he said sweetly.

She ignored the tone that indicated he was simply appeasing her now. "Kate Kennedy may think she's won by dragging us over here, but that's not going to last for long. You and I are going to kill her with kindness. She's expecting us to be problematic, but we're going to be veritable angels."

"Angels who throw the occasional wrench in the works?" Michael asked with a grin.

"Precisely. Travelling all this way and not getting the Atrom contract is not an option."

CHAPTER SIX

KATE SMOOTHED down her red sheath dress. She looked out of her office window at the London skyline. She'd met Georgina Masters in the past, but they had never spoken for any length of time. They shared a joke or two about the media's constant comparisons of them and would then move on. Now, they were being forced to work together.

She knew enough about Georgina to know that neither of them would be happy with the arrangement. Kate felt like she had the upper hand, having convinced Yannis that Georgina should travel to London to meet everyone and see the new car in action. Georgina had tried to back out, but Yannis's tenacity soon forced her hand.

Now, Georgina was to be set up in the Red Door offices for two weeks while the project got under way. Two torturous weeks where her lead competitor would be in her office, a fox in the henhouse.

Kate knew that Georgina wanted to take the Atrom account, there was no other realistic reason for her to agree to so much compromise for The Bolt project. As far as

Kate knew, Georgina wasn't interested in sports cars. And, while the project would deliver a reasonable fee, it wasn't exactly lucrative.

Kate couldn't afford to lose the Atrom contract. As hard as she tried to keep her business diversified, Atrom kept hiring Red Door for new projects. As Atrom expanded, they threw more cash into the marketing budget, which Kate was happy to spend. She'd always known that it was dangerous to have a business so heavily focused on one client, but the economic downturn had forced her hand. With no other clients with such substantial budgets, and a reticence to over-expand Red Door, Kate had been left in a bad situation.

A far worse situation, now that Georgina was sniffing around. There was one contract and two bidders. There would be no compromise. Someone would win, and someone would lose.

"Kate, darling!"

She fixed a smile on her face before turning around. Georgina walked into the office with her arms open wide.

"Georgina, it's been forever." Kate stepped into her loose embrace. They air-kissed each other's cheeks.

Kate took the opportunity to look at Georgina's outfit: a simple black skirt with a white bouclé jacket. Very understated. Very not-Georgina.

"I love your office," Georgina announced. "Very… modern, spacious. And such a view." She walked over to the floor-to-ceiling windows and looked at the cityscape. "I'm surprised you get any work done with such a tremendous view."

"I try my best," Kate replied with a small smile.

"Please, sit down." She gestured towards the two over-stuffed armchairs in the corner of the office.

"Such a lovely position. What part of London is this?" Georgina asked as she sauntered over to the armchair.

"Farringdon," Kate replied. "It's become a hub for the up and coming. Can I get you a drink?"

"No, thank you. I had breakfast at a delightful little cafe downstairs. Very… quaint."

Kate kept the forced smile on her face. While quaint may be a good thing for some, it certainly wasn't for Georgina.

"There are several places around, I'm sure you'll find somewhere to your tastes," Kate replied. "I forget, where did we book for you to stay?"

Of course, Kate knew exactly where they had booked for her to stay. It had taken a lot of liaison with Georgina's team in New York, as well as sending Jonathan to a handful of Kate's favourite London hotels to find somewhere that would match up to the expected standards.

"The Rosewood," Georgina replied with a knowing grin.

"Lovely." Kate nodded.

"As you know, I'm booked for two weeks, but of course I can extend my stay if we can't figure out an appro-priate working arrangement. Although I can't imagine why we couldn't." Georgina looked through the glass wall out to the main office. "You seem to have up-to-date tech-nology here."

Kate followed her gaze to the busy outer office. "Oh, we do," she confirmed, "but, as I'm sure you know, Yannis likes to drop in now and then. It's good to be within easy reach. Wouldn't you agree?"

"Absolutely. Although he spends about as much time in New York as he does in London these days."

Kate snapped her head back to look at Georgina.

"Oh, didn't you know?" Georgina almost smirked. "I thought it was common knowledge. He's bought a new business in New York. It's taking up a lot of his time."

Kate knew that Yannis had business dealings in New York, but she wasn't aware of a new deal. If he was to be spending more time in New York, then it might be more difficult to shake off Georgina than she'd thought.

She narrowed her eyes and turned to look back out into the office. Her eyes fell on the tall man talking to Jonathan.

"Ah, I see Michael is with you?" she changed the subject. "I would have thought you'd leave your number two in New York and bring an assistant instead."

Out of the corner of her eye, she noticed Georgina stiffen slightly. Naturally, she knew about her relationship with Jessica and their subsequent breakup. While the young thing hadn't been Georgina's assistant for some time, it was common knowledge that Georgina hadn't been able to hire another one since Jessica left Mastery.

"Only the best for you and Yannis," Georgina replied.

"Well, I had anticipated your needs, and I'm happy to provide you with someone who can help out as an assistant and, of course, a liaison between us." Kate reached over to the phone on the coffee table and pressed the intercom. "Jonathan, could you send Sophie in?"

"Oh, you don't need to do that," Georgina said. "We're fine as we are. Michael and I can muddle through."

"Please, I insist. I know it must be difficult to be without an assistant. I couldn't possibly manage for two weeks without Jonathan. I think I'd starve," she joked.

A moment later, Sophie softly stumbled into the office. She looked a moment away from hyperventilating and held onto her ever-present notepad with a white-knuckle grip. Kate discreetly coughed to cover her growing smile. Not only would Georgina have a spy in her department, she'd also know that Kate had provided her with the most junior team member she could. It was a double win.

"Sophie, come and meet Georgina Masters." Kate gestured to Georgina, deliberately bucking the etiquette of introducing the higher-ranking person first. "Georgina, this is Sophie Young, your new liaison."

Georgina stood up and held out her hand. "Sophie, it's a pleasure to meet you. I'm Georgina."

Kate looked up as the two women shook hands. Irritatingly, Georgina didn't appear to be at all offended by the gesture. Or she was doing a very good job of hiding it. Which was not the Georgina Masters she knew at all.

"It's a pleasure to meet you, too. I-I have prepared your office as per the instructions that were sent over," Sophie replied.

Georgina smiled. "That's wonderful. I know I must seem very particular, but I do like my environment to be just so. I find I work more efficiently that way." She turned to Kate. "If it's okay with you, I'd like to settle into my new office now. We can catch up again at the team meeting after lunch."

Kate stood up. "Absolutely. Settle in and then we can crack on with some real work this afternoon. If you need anything at all, don't hesitate to let Sophie know."

"Oh, I'm sure we'll get on just fine." Georgina took Sophie's hand and looped it through her arm. "Lead the way."

Kate watched as Sophie blushed and inarticulately mumbled about directions to Georgina's office. The two stepped out into the main office.

Kate watched as they crossed the floor. Georgina's office was located on the opposite side of the building. They could just about see each other's office beyond the sea of people between them. It was all part of Kate's plan to keep an eye on the woman, while also keeping her at arm's length.

She felt a little guilty for throwing Sophie to the wolf, but the girl needed to learn to toughen up or find new employment. Kate's little scheme just meant that the decision would be made a lot sooner.

Jonathan entered the office with a cup of tea, which Kate accepted gratefully.

"How was Michael?" Kate asked.

"Sickeningly sweet," he replied. "Georgina?"

"The same. It appears that they are on a charm offensive. Of course, she couldn't keep it up for long. A couple of snide comments snuck out." Kate sipped at her tea and watched as Sophie and Georgina entered Georgina's new office. "We will need to keep a very close eye on them. They are without a doubt up to something."

CHAPTER SEVEN

GEORGINA HUNG on Sophie's arm as she walked across the busy office floor. Of course, she knew the Red Door staff were watching her every step. She smiled and greeted people as they passed by. Anyone could be a spy or a potential ally.

"So, tell me, Sophie. How long have you been working at Red Door?"

Sophie swallowed, and Georgina felt the muscles in her arm constrict. She had a feeling she already knew the answer: not long. It was a genius tactic, supplying support staff in the form of an anxious and timid junior. It ensured that the support was more trouble than it was worth. Georgina would have to add it to her own arsenal.

"In all, nearly four months," Sophie said.

Georgina let out a throaty chuckle. "And, in reality?"

"Three weeks," Sophie mumbled.

Georgina smiled. She wondered if Sophie was the most junior employee Kate could dig up. She was surprised Kate had even remembered Sophie's name. But if that was the game Kate wished to play, Georgina was willing to fight fire with fire. Or, in this case, contempt with kindness. It would infuriate Kate to know that Georgina found Sophie helpful. Invaluable, even. And the girl was probably tasked with spying on her. Showing her some kindness might mean that information turned into a two-way street.

"Three weeks? Well, you have a head start on me. We can learn the ropes together."

As she stepped into her temporary office, Georgina let go of Sophie's arm and looked around the room. It was a reasonable size and seemed well-furnished. A set of armchairs, like the ones in Kate's office, sat in the corner, out of view of the main floor. Her desk was large and white, as per her specifications. Her MacBook stand, plug, mouse, and extra keyboard were all laid out as she liked. Her water, glasses, and fruit sat on the corner of the desk in the usual configuration. The latest marketing magazines were fanned out on the table beside her desk. Everything was set up perfectly.

She turned to Sophie. The girl looked nervously around the room.

This was usually the point where Georgina would dismiss her assistant and slam the door. But these were unique circumstances. She needed to find a way to be kind, to gain Sophie's trust. Being kind to an assistant had started and ended with Jessica, but she was on a mission and allowances needed to be made.

"You've done a wonderful job," Georgina said. Normally, such praise would never pass her lips. It felt strange, eerie but somehow familiar.

She pulled out the office chair and sat down.

"Can I… get you a drink? Something to eat?" Sophie asked. She hesitated in the doorway. It was clear that she had no idea what her job entailed. Her panic reminded her of Jessica's first few anxious days, something that Georgina didn't want reminding of. She needed to help Sophie fast-forward past the nervous stage.

"You can sit down." Georgina gestured to the visitor chair in front of her desk.

Sophie's eyes bugged in fear. She turned and looked out at the main office before turning back and slowly edging towards the chair.

"Unless you have a pressing matter to attend to?"

Sophie shook her head and sat down. "No, no, I—"

"Good. If we're going to work together, we should get to know each other." Georgina leaned forward and snagged a red apple from the bowl on her desk. "Tell me about yourself." She took a hearty bite and waited.

Sophie sat silent for a moment. Georgina could almost hear the cogs of her mind whirring around. She was about to prompt the girl with a specific question when she took a deep breath and began to speak.

"I have worked as an Operations Junior Administrator for the last three weeks. Before that I worked in accounts for three months as an intern—"

"An intern?" Georgina couldn't help but interrupt.

"Yeah." Sophie squirmed in her seat. "I just really, really wanted to work in marketing, and no one was hiring. I was working in a law firm, but I hated it. I saw the intern role and thought it was a good opportunity. I'd written it off because it was unpaid, but my boyfriend convinced me to go for it. He's supported me, and now I have a real job, in marketing."

"I see. And what does an Operations Junior Administrator do?"

"Um, well, I help with the Operations team… which is mainly me. And Jonathan, kinda."

"I see, you're a gopher." Georgina understood.

Sophie balked. "'Gopher'?"

"Go fetch this, go fetch that. Gopher."

Sophie sadly nodded. "Yeah. I guess that's me."

"We all have to start somewhere," Georgina reassured her. "You must be passionate about this new career to leave a paid job to become an intern?"

"I am." Sophie looked at her seriously. "I really am. I love marketing. I want to learn everything there is to know about it. That's why I wanted to come here, I wanted to learn from Kate. Learn from the best…" Sophie's eyes widened as she realised what she had said.

Georgina chuckled. "No offense taken," she joked.

"I'm so sorry, I didn't mean—"

Georgina held up her hand. "It's okay, Sophie. I know what you meant. Kate is excellent at what she does. We'll agree to disagree on her being the best, though." She winked.

Sophie giggled. Georgina took another bite of her apple and regarded the girl. She fidgeted with her thick-framed glasses, a nervous tic that Georgina nearly found endearing. Almost. She made a mental note to look out for the tic in the future; it could lead to clues about what Kate was up to.

"So," Georgina said. "I presume you know where to find a decent coffee around here?"

Sophie beamed. "That I can do."

"Wonderful. You won't be surprised to hear that I'm very particular about my coffee—"

"Large, hot caffè latte with almond milk and an extra shot," Sophie recited.

Georgina regarded her for a second. "Sophie, you and I are going to get on just fine."

CHAPTER EIGHT

KATE HELD her hand to her forehead to stop the sunlight from blinding her. Yannis had been talking without pause for the last ten minutes. She had a lot of experience at pretending to look interested in various engine types, information on horsepower, and the pros and cons of different air intake systems. But she was fast losing her patience with this particular speech. Why he had seen fit to drag them all out to a racetrack was beyond her.

He was clearly having the time of his life. He stood in his racing outfit, emblazoned with the Atrom logo, and a crash helmet resting casually in the loop of his arm. They had yet to see the car itself; Yannis wanted the grand unveiling to be just that. Grand.

Kate would have been just as impressed seeing the car for the first time in a showroom. Or a garage. Or in a photograph. The sweltering heat and the noise of the race-track was not appreciated. The longer they stood in the intense heat, listening to him yammer on about throttle control, the more intense her need became to throttle him.

Of course, Georgina was encouraging him. Every time he stopped for breath, she asked him for more pointless information on the technical aspects of the engine, the aerodynamics, or the material the car was built out of. The heat either didn't bother her, or she didn't show it.

Michael and Jonathan had both divested themselves of their suit jackets and their ties, even rolling up their shirt-sleeves as the midday sun beamed down on them. Both looked on excitedly as sports cars powered noisily around the track beside them.

The noise, the heat, and Georgina's incessant questioning were giving Kate an almighty headache. She hoped that her illness wasn't flaring up, she didn't have time to be sick.

"Can I get you a water?"

She turned to look at Sophie who had softly whispered the question to her. Why Georgina felt it so important to bring Sophie on the outing, she didn't know. Kate's plan to insult Georgina by assigning her Sophie seemed to have backfired spectacularly.

Georgina had only been in the office for two days, but it was already clear that her strategy was to kill them all with kindness. Not that Kate was falling for it, not for a second. She knew Georgina's game, she'd played it herself once or twice over the years.

"Kate?" Sophie repeated.

Kate glanced at the furrowed brow of the young girl and shook her head. She turned her attention back to Yannis. She wasn't about to miss an opportunity to shine, or to pull the rug out from under Georgina. Yannis and Georgina were getting on a little too well for her liking. In fact, everyone was getting on a little too well with Georgina for her liking.

Georgina was famous for going through members of staff as if they were hot dinners. Her temper was legendary. And yet, all Kate had seen was a friendly, forgiving, smiling face which could only belong to Georgina Master's little-known twin sister, the one that didn't breathe fire. The one that appeared to be made of sweetness and light.

Kate ground her teeth in frustration. Her own temper was also legendary. However, she'd always prided herself on the fact that she wasn't as bad as some in the industry. Sure, there was the time she deliberately ordered three back-to-back fire drills, just so the chubby kid in IT would get to walk up and down the twelve floors of the building. And she was known to shout. And fire people. Yes, Human Resources had taken to emailing her snippets from the Employment Law handbook every Monday morning. But she'd always told herself that she wasn't as bad as some. She certainly wasn't as bad as Georgina Masters.

Except Georgina was about to be anointed a living saint. The problem with judging yourself against someone else was that the other person could have a drastic personality transplant and leave you looking worse for wear.

"I was actually thinking about that very point," Georgina said.

Kate tuned back into the conversation. Bugger Georgina's delightful temperament. It couldn't last. If she was going to attempt to depose Kate, she'd have to show her true colours. She'd have to make a move at some point, and this might just be it.

"Yes?" Yannis asked excitedly.

"You obviously have the prototype, and now you're going to build the real deal," Georgina was saying. "I think we need to set up cameras so we can record the build. That footage would have so many uses. Sped up, it would make a wonderful minute or two of time-lapse footage. Let people see The Bolt come to life in front of their very eyes."

Yannis's own eyes shone at the prospect. "Yes, yes! That is what I'm looking for. Fresh ideas that will bring this project to life, ideas that will make everyone feel like they have a part to play."

"Well, of course we'd record the build," Kate said. "The real key will be choosing what to do with the footage. We need to maximise its impact."

"What do you think, Georgina?" Yannis asked.

Kate felt her annoyance level spike.

"Oh, I think that's something that Kate and I need to discuss in more detail. Don't you, darling?" Georgina looked at Kate expectantly.

Kate smirked. "Absolutely." She felt like Georgina had kicked her in the shin and then offered to clean the wound.

Yannis seemed oblivious to the tension in the air. Instead he announced that he was ready to retrieve the prototype Bolt from the pits and give them a demonstration. Kate watched him walk away and shook her head. Yannis was too caught up in his project to see that Georgina was manipulating him.

"What are we going to do about the name?" Georgina asked Kate as soon as Yannis was out of sight. "We can't call it a Bolt. I know what he's going for, but he's forgetting the other connotations associated with bolt. Bolting away, through fear. Escaping."

Kate nodded. "I know, it conveys the speed, but not the control. No one wants to think about a sports car that's out of control."

"Exactly. Bolt doesn't portray safety. That's going to be a problem," Georgina mused. "You should bring it up with him, he trusts you."

Kate regarded the woman for a moment. "Why don't you bring it up?"

"I can, if you don't want the conflict?"

Kate bit her lip. She was trapped either way. If she brought it up, Georgina could defy her and side with Yannis. If she didn't bring it up, Georgina could and would take all the credit. Not to mention the fact that the gauntlet had been thrown down right in front of her.

"I'll do it," Kate said through gritted teeth.

"Sophie, be a darling and take some pictures." Georgina handed Sophie her phone. "In case I need inspiration later."

Sophie put her notepad under her arm and took the phone. She pressed a button and then looked shyly towards Georgina.

"Um, it's locked."

Georgina grinned. "Oh, silly me." She stood beside Sophie, slightly pressing her side into the young girl as she leaned forward and pointed her finger towards the screen.

"You'll have to memorise my code so you can access it whenever you need."

Kate rolled her eyes. Georgina was taking the whole act a step too far. It almost seemed that she was cosying up to Sophie just to prove a point.

Georgina stepped away from Sophie to stand in front of Kate.

"Kate, I think we can agree that working together on this project is essential and yet... impossible. Neither of us wants to have to explain the ins and outs of our every thought to the other. And integrating the teams like that is going to be extremely difficult."

Kate was surprised by Georgina's admission, but also cautious. "What do you suggest?"

"That we split the tasks down the middle. We already know the basics of the campaign, so we can take the different elements and assign them to either the best team, or, where the teams are equally matched in experience, we can divide them up equally. We both work with other agencies from time to time on certain projects, this will be no different."

"That certainly sounds like a good idea," Kate allowed. Of course, she had her reservations. In some ways, she relished Georgina returning to New York. In others, she wanted to keep her where she could see her.

"Fantastic. We can explain that to Yannis, split the tasks, and then I can return to New York. I think it would be best for everyone involved, don't you?"

"Absolutely." Once Georgina was back in New York, Kate knew she could spend some quality time massaging Yannis's ego and securing the account. Though there was a niggling feeling at the back of her mind that she was falling into a trap.

Her thoughts were interrupted by the roaring of a loud engine. She looked up to see a silver and red car tearing out from one of the pits.

"If you were going to call it Bolt, wouldn't you at least paint it blue?" Kate chuckled.

"You would have thought so," Georgina agreed.

The Bolt sped past them and entered the main race-track. The sound was deafening. The heat from the engine as it passed them was enough to make Kate feel breathless.

Sophie jogged towards the wall of the pit area. She held up the phone and started to take photos as the car powered around the track.

"Wherever did you find her?" Georgina asked with a lazy grin.

Kate chuckled. "She's a work in progress."

"That dress." Georgina shook her head, clearly displeased with Sophie's style.

Kate looked at Sophie and smiled. "Just wait until you see the burgundy trousers."

Kate knew that Sophie's dress sense would not be to Georgina's tastes. Georgina was known for her fashion sense as much as her business acumen. Mastery worked with several top New York designers, and Georgina ensured that her brand was always in fashion.

"She reminds me a little of Jessica," Georgina confessed.

Kate looked at her. She was staring at Sophie as the girl continued to take pictures.

"Jessica?" Kate played dumb.

"My assistant. Turned lover. Turned ex." Georgina turned her attention from Sophie, back to Kate. "The day she turned up at Mastery, it was like a preppy millennial bomb had exploded. Of course, I saw the potential under the rags she wore. Within a few days it was less polyester, more Gaultier."

Kate recognised the feeling. She'd made her own disparaging remarks about Sophie's clothes. If she was honest with herself, she didn't really know why she did it. Sophie's sense of style was her own business. But something inside caused her to constantly pick at Sophie, especially over the last couple of days. Which led Kate to wonder if she was taking her dislike of Georgina out on Sophie.

"Maybe you can work your magic on her," Kate commented. "Though I doubt it. She's quite stubborn under the mousy exterior."

"So was Jessica. And while she may have changed her wardrobe at the office, at home… well, she wasn't about to be changed. It's funny, as much as I hated her sense of style in the early days, I came to appreciate it once we were together. It showed that she was her own individual, there were things about her that she wouldn't change. Things about her that *I* couldn't change. That was something I didn't realise was important until I met Jessica."

Kate nodded. "Contrast is important. In a relationship, I mean."

"Absolutely, if you're dating someone like you, then you'll never grow. You need someone to tell you when you're being ridiculous. Even if it means your partner sometimes wears a frankly burnable pink hoodie from the nineties."

"Really?" Kate chuckled at the thought of Georgina allowing such an item into her home.

Georgina leaned closer to Kate, a devilish smile on her lips. "There's something oddly arousing in taking a woman to an awards dinner in a Westwood gown, only to find her in your kitchen the next morning wearing an oversized man's shirt from Walmart."

The women shared a chuckle.

"I never said that, of course," Georgina added.

Kate held up her hands good-naturedly. "My lips are sealed."

Kate peered into the car interior. It was basic: no trim, no extras, just the essentials. The interior cabin had a criss-cross of metal bars to protect the driver in case of a crash. She couldn't understand the appeal, but she hoped for Yannis's sake that the rest of the world disagreed with her.

Yannis had completed a quick lap in The Bolt before returning to the pits. He had monologued for a while about the speed and engine capacity of the vehicle before taking questions. It wasn't long before Jonathan had eagerly accepted an offer to sit in the driver's seat.

"It's an amazing piece of engineering," Jonathan said. He looked around the dashboard of the car, his hand grazing the buttons in awe.

"It's unlike anything ever built before," Yannis told him. "Would you like to drive it?"

Jonathan looked up at him with a grin. "Can I?"

Kate rolled her eyes and took a step back from the open passenger door that everyone was gathered around. She took out her smartphone and took some photos of the car. If Georgina needed them for inspiration, then so did she.

Kate looked at the car and slowly shook her head. The whole project was stirring up bad memories. She pushed them to one side. Now was not the time to dwell on the past.

Everyone was stepping away from the car, and Kate joined them. Jonathan had put on a crash helmet and was revving the engine. A member of the Atrom team was explaining the controls to him.

"Yannis, is the name Bolt set in stone?" Kate asked.

He looked at her with curiosity. "Yes, why?"

Kate flicked her eyes to Georgina before returning to him. "It's just that the word Bolt doesn't give the best feeling when it comes to safety. It's considered a hurried movement, something unexpected."

"But Bolt is quick, nimble. We want it to be compact and powerful. Bolt emphasises that," Yannis said.

"I understand that," Kate soothed. "But I think we should explore other names. I just have a bad feeling about the name Bolt. We don't want to set something in stone so early in the project, especially when it could have negative consequences down the line."

Yannis was becoming agitated with the talk. Kate had seen the signs before. He would sigh, huff and puff, shift his balance from one leg to the other. She'd had her fair share of disagreements with the man. Sometimes she won, sometimes he did. What was always clear was that Yannis had strong feelings about his brand and products.

"Maybe we should focus on reclaiming the word?" Georgina offered. She placed her hand on Yannis's arm softly. "We can focus on the positive aspects and ignore the negative. Maybe even make a play on them? The silver and red is an amazing choice of colours, but how would you feel about silver and blue? Then we would have a central theme and colour for our campaign. A bolt out of the blue."

Kate could feel her jaw dropping. Georgina had stabbed her in the back, stolen her idea, and humiliated her in one quick sentence.

"Blue, I like it." Yannis nodded with enthusiasm. "This is what we need. A theme that we can use at the core of the campaign. A bolt out of the blue. Blue. That's perfect."

Kate could feel the anger swelling up inside her like a tsunami.

"Hey, Marco!" Yannis called out. "We need to go over new paint samples." He walked away from them to talk to his team.

Kate spun around to face Georgina. "What the hell?"

"He was clearly attached to the name," Georgina said. "I was just ensuring some damage control."

Kate blinked. "Damage control? I thought—"

A loud explosion crashed behind them. Kate crouched down and turned around. The Bolt was on fire. The mangled hood landed metres away from the flaming wreckage. People ran from the pit with fire extinguishers, and an alarm sounded loudly throughout the racetrack.

CHAPTER NINE

SOPHIE STEPPED into the room quietly. She bit her lip as she looked at the occupant of the hospital bed.

"It's not as bad as it looks," Jonathan reassured her.

She walked closer. "Are you sure? It looks pretty bad."

Jonathan's left leg was covered in a plaster cast and raised by some apparatus hanging from the ceiling. His left arm was also covered in a plaster cast that joined with the cast around his shoulders.

She swallowed. "They said you broke your neck."

"Hairline fracture," Jonathan said. "Seriously, I'm on so much medication, I can't feel a thing."

Sophie looked him over again. His skin was pale, and there was bruising to his face.

When the engine exploded, she'd frozen. The shock of the blast and the fear had rendered her immobile. All she could do was watch as the pit crew pulled Jonathan out of the blazing wreckage.

"I'm so sorry," she whispered.

"For what?" he frowned in confusion.

"I... I just stood there." She sat in the visitor chair beside his bed. "I just froze. If you were relying on me, you'd be dead by now."

Jonathan chuckled. "Well, I wasn't relying on you. I was relying on that large team of professionals who deal with that kind of thing every day. Don't worry. Accidents happen. I'm okay, really."

"I still feel terrible," she confessed. She knew it wasn't her fault, but she couldn't forgive her inaction. She'd never felt so useless in her life.

That afternoon, Kate had sent out a company-wide email, assuring all staff that Jonathan was recovering from his injuries. But then she had dived back into work, seemingly unaffected by Jonathan's accident.

Sophie had subtly suggested that she would hold the fort while Kate visited Jonathan in the hospital. Kate had been quick to shoot down the offer and announce that she would not be visiting anyone in hospital, ever. Sophie knew she had no right to judge, but Kate's behaviour had annoyed her. Jonathan was a human life support machine for Kate, and Kate had barely registered his departure.

Sophie had been still more surprised to receive a text message from Jonathan asking her to come and see him that evening.

"You'll be feeling even worse soon," Jonathan was saying, "which is why I asked you to come here."

"Am I fired?" she asked.

He smiled. "No, you're promoted. You're going to have to take over my work. There's no one else we can spare. Everyone else is tied up on the audit, and Kate won't have a temp in her office. It will have to be you."

"Me?" Sophie heard herself squeak. "I mean, why me?"

"There's no one else. She knows you. Well, she can put the correct name to your face about seven out of ten times, and that's as good as knowing you."

"She called me Stephanie, like, yesterday," Sophie pointed out.

"That's most of the right letters, she used to call me Steve. Anyway, if someone doesn't look after Kate tomorrow morning, she'll be out of control. Especially with all the extra stress of Georgina. It will be much worse for you if you don't take over for me."

"What does Kate say about this?" Sophie hadn't been working at Red Door for long, but she knew that Kate was extremely particular about things. And by things, she meant everything.

Jonathan laughed. "Kate doesn't say anything. Kate expects her office to be running no matter what."

"But you're in hospital," Sophie pointed out.

"I know, but Kate will still expect things to run normally."

"That's awful."

"No," Jonathan assured her. "It isn't. She's not heartless, just practical. Red Door operates as a well-oiled machine. If anything jeopardises that smooth running, it could be a disaster. Not being able to provide a client with what they need at the right time could cost us a contract. Which would cost us money. Which could put jobs at risk. Kate expects that everyone is replaceable, even herself. If she were in this bed instead of me, she would want to know that the business was running smoothly without her."

Sophie opened her mouth to reply but slowly closed it again. She had to admit; it did make sense. It seemed horrible to just go on as if nothing had happened when Jonathan was injured, but she understood that it was for the greater good, even if it didn't necessarily feel that way.

"What do I need to do?"

"You might want your trusty notepad for this."

She opened her satchel and took out her notepad and a pen. She found a fresh page and waited for his instructions.

"Kate gets into the office at eight o'clock, you'll have to get there around fifteen minutes before then. Fresh flowers are delivered every morning. They come in prepared arrangements by Kate's florist, you just need to put them in the vases in her office."

Sophie scribbled down notes. She wasn't about to make a mistake and get herself fired.

"Make sure her fridge is stocked with bottled water, not the plastic bottles that are in the staff room. There are extra black-label glass bottles in the storage cabinet by the photocopier if you need more. She needs three clean glasses on her desk, upside down and on disposable paper coasters. That's really key. Make sure they are clean as well. Sometimes the dishwasher in the staff room doesn't leave them sparkling. Make sure the cushions on the armchairs are fluffed up and adjust the air fresheners so they are up to level six first thing in the morning, lower them to three in the afternoon."

Sophie slammed her pen down onto her notepad. "Seriously? Fluffing cushions and air fresheners? Is this so essential to the running of the office?"

Jonathan shifted a little, obviously trying to find a more comfortable position. "Yep. Kate likes things just so. When you get to be the founding director of your own marketing agency, then you can request whatever you like in your office."

Sophie wondered if she would ever reach those kinds of dizzying heights. Was she only ever going to be junior administrator? The idea of getting to the top of her career seemed about as likely as winning the lottery.

"She'll want all the newspapers on the sideboard in her office. They are all delivered first thing and will be with reception. Don't fan them out in a circle, she hates that."

Sophie quickly picked up her pen and continued jotting down notes.

"Get her green tea with vanilla for when she arrives, get it from Simpsons in Hatton Garden. Large. Make sure it's hot or she'll send you out again. She'll have another tea around midday when she'll let you know what to go and get her for lunch. Then in the afternoon, she'll want coffee. Plain, black coffee. Get it from Brewers in Kirby Street."

"Okay, sounds easy enough," Sophie said.

"Reception fields most calls, but you'll still get around twenty to forty a day. Take a message for all of them, never put a call straight through to Kate. No matter who they are. You'll see messages on her desk from the last couple of days, use those as a template and make sure you write them in the same format. As soon as you get a new message, go into her office and put it on the edge of her desk. You don't need to talk to her, just go in and drop off the message. She'll decide if it's important and if she wants to call them back."

Sophie was still panicking about the thought of twenty to forty calls a day. Calls for Kate were bound to be from important people.

"She might want you to take notes in meetings, she'll let you know if she does. Check her schedule and be prepared to join her, she'll let you know literally on her way to the meeting. Keep your mobile phone on you at all times. Oh, and change her speed dial one on both her personal mobile and her desk phone to your mobile number."

"Speed dial one? Me? Even on her personal mobile?" Sophie questioned. Her heart broke at the idea of Kate having her lowly intern-turned-assistant as her primary contact. She knew Kate was divorced, but that was years ago. The media often photographed Kate on nights out. As it became more sociable acceptable, Sophie had noticed Kate was seen with more women than men. She didn't know why that had stood out in her mind.

"Yes," Jonathan confirmed. "Work is Kate's life."

Sophie swallowed. She made a note to make the speed dial change. She wondered if it was worth having everything if your speed dial one would be your assistant and not a loved one.

"What about Georgina?" Sophie asked.

Jonathan let out a small sigh. "I don't know. Try to split your time between the two of them. As I say, there really is no one else."

Sophie looked at her notepad and started to wonder how on earth she was going to juggle the needs of the two women. Two women who were clearly beginning to shed the act of friendly competition.

"Just remember, Georgina is only here for a while. Kate is your boss," Jonathan said, as if reading her mind.

"I don't know how I'm going to appease them both," Sophie replied. She held up her notepad. "I mean, how am I supposed to do all of this and look after Georgina's needs as well?"

"That's not even half the list," Jonathan admitted. "You better get writing, I'm feeling these pain meds really kicking in."

CHAPTER TEN

KATE STEPPED from the elevator and strutted across the office. She kept her large sunglasses on to give her the chance to subtly look around the floor. Not many people were in, but the ones who did arrive early were the go-getters. The ones who wanted to be noticed.

Not that it mattered. She'd heard one too many horror stories about women being overlooked for jobs because they didn't work the same hours as their male counter-parts. Often the woman in question had the equally important job of being a mother.

While Kate had never had the opportunity to settle down and raise a family, she sure as hell wasn't going to begrudge anyone who had. Progression at Red Door was down to a complex mixture of personality, experience, skill set, and ability. Not what time you got into the office in the morning.

She walked into her office and removed her sunglasses. Out of the corner of her eye, she saw someone move. She stopped dead.

"Oh, it's you," she said when Sophie gave her an awkward wave. She walked over to her desk and tossed her sunglasses down.

"I'm going to be stepping in for Jonathan," Sophie said. She held a takeaway cup in both hands. "He has explained everything to me."

"Good." Kate shrugged out of her light summer jacket and hung it up on the coat stand in the corner.

"He's doing okay, by the way," Sophie added softly.

Kate smirked to herself while her back was to Sophie. Clearly, the girl thought her heartless. Between the rumours and Kate's insistence on not going to the hospital, she couldn't blame her.

She turned around and looked pointedly at the drink. "I presume that is for me?"

Sophie followed Kate's line of vision. "Oh, yes, sorry." She handed the drink over.

Glancing at her desk, Kate placed her tea on the correct coaster. She nodded to herself; clearly Jonathan had given exacting instructions. Maybe the girl wasn't so useless after all.

"Any changes to my schedule?" Kate asked. She sat down and pulled her laptop from her bag.

"Palmer's have cancelled the two o'clock teleconference," Sophie said.

"As expected," Kate mumbled. "Is the boardroom booked for my three o'clock?"

"Yes, and food and drink have been ordered. There were two calls from the Japan office on the overnight voicemail, they are on your desk." Sophie gestured towards them. "And… Georgina would like to see you this morning, if you have time."

Kate strongly suspected that the polite enquiry as to her availability originated from Sophie rather than Georgina. She leaned to the side to look around Sophie. Georgina's office door was closed, indicating that the woman had yet to arrive.

"I'll see her when she arrives," Kate said. She sipped her tea. "What's she up to? Have you managed to find out any information?"

"Information?" Sophie's brow furrowed in confusion.

She really is as naive as she appears, Kate thought.

"Yes, information. Surely it hasn't escaped your notice that there is something of a competition going on here for the Atrom contract." Kate put her tea down and leaned forward. "What have you heard?"

Sophie's eyes widened with shock. "Um… nothing, really."

Kate pointed to the chair in front of her desk. "Sit."

Sophie quickly sat down.

"I realise you are still new to working in an office, especially this one. But that thick tension you feel in the air? You're not imagining it."

Sophie just stared at her, lost.

Kate sighed and shook her head. "As liaison between the teams, I need you to keep your ear to the ground. Atrom is a very big, very important client. And I will not suffer the humiliation of losing them to Mastery."

Sophie continued to look confused.

"Oh, for goodness' sake," Kate mumbled. "Sally, let me explain this in a way you'll understand. Your role here is to be a double agent. You are going to infiltrate the Mastery team and report every word back to me."

"I-infiltrate?" Sophie stammered.

"Yes. You're so bland and uninteresting I'm sure they feel comfortable talking around you. Whatever you hear comes straight back to me, do you understand?"

Kate watched as Sophie caught up with the plan. The girl's expressive facial journey was almost comical. From fear to realisation, then horror to understanding.

"I'm not sure I can," Sophie whispered.

"Of course, you can. You make them feel at home. Try to weasel your way in."

"Weasel?"

"Yes, make friends. You know, do…" Kate waved her hand towards Sophie. "…whatever it is you do to ingratiate yourself with people."

"I thought we were supposed to be working together on this project? Collaborating?" Sophie asked, seemingly appealing to Kate's better nature. The girl still had a way to go.

"Oh, we are. We're just going to ensure that Mastery will never work with Atrom again as we do it," Kate told her with a smirk.

"But isn't the whole idea supposed to be—"

"Stand up." Kate walked around her desk. She placed her hands on Sophie's shoulders and turned the girl around. "You see that office?"

Sophie nodded. Her shoulders were tense under Kate's hands.

"That office is full of employees. Your colleagues. If Georgina Masters takes the Atrom contract, I will be

forced to make around thirty percent of them redundant."
Kate released Sophie. She folded her arms and looked out
through the window contemplatively.

The office was starting to fill up.

"What do you think?" Kate asked. "Marie and Simon
do the same job, one of them has to go. Who should
it be?"

Sophie flinched and turned to face her, before turning
back to regard the office.

"Come on, we can't spend too much time on each
decision. We need to cut staff by thirty percent, that's
roughly one hundred and twenty people. Time is money.
Who goes? Marie or Simon?" Kate watched as Sophie
panicked at the very notion of making that kind of
decision.

As cavalier as Kate made it sound, it was the hardest
part of her job. Making staff decisions was something she
never took lightly. Every day she felt the heavy weight of
the responsibility to the four hundred staff she employed.
It was something that employees never considered. They
saw the boss, with their large salary and their fancy car and
they wanted to live that life. They didn't see the sleepless
nights at the end of a fraught business day. They didn't
feel the suffocating knowledge that a mistake at work
could impact the lives of people you felt personally
responsible for.

"It's not easy," Kate murmured. "Being the boss comes
with enormous responsibility. Every decision I make, every
single day, becomes part of a series of events that means we
either continue to provide these people with employment
or we have to let them go."

She looked at the young girl. Light blue eyes scanned the office. A deep furrow in her brow showed the weight beginning to bear down on her.

"Luckily for you, those are weights I carry. Decisions I make." Kate turned around and walked back to her desk. "You, you can help by providing me with information I need in order to secure the working future of this company and the people in that office."

She sat down and booted up her laptop. As far as she was concerned, the conversation was officially over. She'd explained that Sophie's role was essential to the business, not just a petty squabble between two grown women who should know better.

She typed in her password, aware that Sophie still stood, silently gazing out of the window. After a few more silent moments, Sophie exited the office.

Kate chanced a look up and saw the dazed girl take a seat at Jonathan's desk. She wondered if her spy was up to the task. Sophie seemed just a little too sweet and innocent to be happy with the whole idea of spying on Georgina. She was perfect for the job as Georgina would undoubtedly trust her.

Sophie would have information; it was just whether she'd be willing to share it. Kate would have to keep up the pressure on her. Sophie may end up hating her, but that couldn't be helped. The business had to come first.

Sophie glanced up, and they briefly made eye contact. Kate quickly looked away. She didn't know why, but the thought of Sophie hating her sat uncomfortably. She shook her head and refocused her attention on her work. She didn't have time to worry about such things.

CHAPTER ELEVEN

KATE SHOULD HAVE KNOWN. In hindsight, it was obvious that Georgina would try to run the show in whichever way she could. The suggestion that they split tasks was a sensible one, but the way Georgina was proposing they do it was not.

"Maybe I'm misinterpreting your notes here," Kate suggested. She slid her glasses onto her face and picked up the presentation pack Georgina had provided. "It seems you're suggesting we cover PR, copy, and video editing."

Georgina picked up her own pack and leafed through the contents. "Yes, that is what we suggest. Your PR connections are sensational. You've been working with the engineering sector far longer than we have."

Kate couldn't help but feel that was a subtle dig at her age. There were only a few years between her and Georgina, but Georgina had clearly made a pact with the devil to retain her youthful appearance.

"That is true," Kate allowed. "But let's be honest, you're assigning us tasks that keep us behind the scenes.

Anything that Yannis would appreciate and find truly exciting, you're keeping for yourself. Website, landing pages, email marketing, social media… all Mastery."

"All of those assets you mention, they'd be nothing without your team's stellar work on copy."

"We have an excellent digital team here," Kate argued.

"That's true, to an extent," Georgina allowed.

"No, it's true, full stop," Kate replied curtly. "You are not the only agency to win digital awards. Yes, you are known for your social media marketing campaigns, but we can design and build websites just as well as you can."

"Oh, I don't doubt it." Georgina grinned patronisingly. "But surely it makes sense to put the whole digital asset collection together?"

"It makes sense if you're aiming to make a play for the account," Kate accused.

Georgina smirked and shook her head. She placed the pack down on the table. "Are you suggesting I have an ulterior motive, Kate?"

"Are you suggesting that you don't?" Kate took her glasses off and placed them on the table to meet Georgina's gaze.

"Would I like the Atrom account for myself? Yes, of course I would," Georgina admitted. "Am I going to engage in some petty subterfuge to do so? Of course not."

Kate didn't believe her for one second.

"You deliberately set me up regarding the name," Kate pointed out.

"The name?" Georgina frowned.

"The name," Kate repeated. "You didn't back me up when I suggested that Bolt was a bad choice."

"Ah. I didn't back you up, but I didn't set you up either. I simply read the situation. I agree with you that the name is ridiculous. But, as soon as you brought it up, which you were right to do, I could see that Yannis had already made his mind up. I didn't want him to feel that we didn't understand his brief. As a team, we need to demonstrate an understanding of his needs. You weren't in a position to do that, not without backpedalling like a Russian circus bear. So, I took the initiative."

Kate laced her fingers together and leaned forward slightly. "Utter nonsense."

Georgina let out a sigh. "I'm not going to stand beside you and make myself look stupid. You needed rescuing from that mess, I rescued both of us. You're welcome."

Kate rolled her eyes. "Excuse me if I don't thank you. I'm having trouble adjusting to this knife in my back."

"If you want to talk about knives in backs, then may I remind you of Pink Blossom?"

Kate laughed. That particular episode had spilled from Georgina's lips awfully quickly; clearly it was a sore spot. Possibly one that had set this whole mess in motion.

"Oh, I see. That's where this is coming from. You lose a client to me six years ago, and you come after me now?" Kate shook her head and let out a sigh. "And I thought we were professionals."

"You stole that client from me, and you know it," Georgina replied heatedly.

"I did no such thing! Rosie is an old friend of mine, I attended her daughter's wedding, and we chatted about marketing. She was disillusioned with your company, but I didn't say anything to poach her from you, she was already lost to you. If I didn't get the contract, someone else would have."

"Bullshit."

Kate saw the anger in Georgina's eyes. Finally, the veneer was falling away, and they could have a real conversation without the fake niceties. This was all a vendetta, a well-planned and malicious one.

"We're going to have to find a way to work together, Georgina. If you can't work with me, I can explain that to Yannis," Kate threatened.

"You think you're the only one who has his ear?" Georgina replied with a scoff. "I have as much sway with him as you do. You know the kind of man he is, always looking for something new and exciting. Well, here's a newsflash for you, that's me. You're *old* news, Kate."

Now, that *is a dig at my age,* Kate thought. "Yannis may be like a magpie, seeking out the new and the shiny, but he also appreciates loyalty and, above all else, family. I have known the Papadakis family for the past twenty years. I have eaten at his table, an act that means something in his family."

"I know that family is important to him. But so is business. He has lofty goals, ones I can help him reach. He wants to be ahead of the curve, not on it."

Kate stood and walked over to the window. She looked out at the busy city as she contemplated the situation. Both of them wanted the contract, but neither of them would get it if they didn't work together. But working together was starting to look completely impossible.

"We have to find a way to work together," she said finally. "Pink Blossom is in the past. This is now. The bottom line is that Yannis would fire both of us in a heart-beat if he felt we couldn't work together. I think we both know that we're embarrassing our gender at the moment. There's enough talk about bitchy, backstabbing women without us making matters worse." Kate turned to look at Georgina. "Do you agree?"

Georgina nodded. "I do. As much as it irritates me, we're defined by our sex. If two men were fighting over a contract, it wouldn't matter. But do you honestly feel that we can work together? You talk about a knife in your back, I still feel the one you stuck in mine six years ago. You don't trust me, and I don't trust you."

Kate knew that Georgina was right. They couldn't work together; there was too much history between them. There was only one way forward.

"We should let Yannis pick," Kate suggested.

"Explain?"

"I propose that we both present to him, and then we let Yannis pick. Trying to split the contract is pointless, we'd still have to work together. If both Red Door and Mastery present to him on everything from PR to brand-ing, video to digital, then Yannis gets twice as many ideas and gets to pick a winner. That way it's fair, and we get as little blood spilled as possible."

Kate sat back down at the meeting table and regarded Georgina, hoping she'd go for the idea.

"Presumably, we'd present a united front and tell him that this is the best way forward?" she asked.

"Absolutely, we'll explain that we feel this is best for him. No need to tell him of our difficulties." Kate had no intention of explaining to Yannis that she'd rather extract her own fingernails than work side by side with Georgina.

"Sounds reasonable," Georgina allowed carefully. "But I'd need time in order to prepare for a full pitch. We'll need to have a timetable in place. You've worked with Yannis before, so you have an advantage on style guides and industry knowledge."

"We'll agree upon a schedule," Kate said. If Georgina was going to agree to the plan, the least she could do was clear the path for her. "As for industry knowledge, we could host a small presentation together. Invite the big names, show them a taster of what we are doing, and get their feedback. It would be hugely beneficial for both of us. Then we'd have the same market research to go away and each build our own campaign presentation."

Georgina nodded. "That sounds like the best way forward. We'll gather our research together and then separate."

"I think that is in everyone's best interests. Then we'll get Yannis to choose, and the losing party will walk away," Kate added. She wanted to be very clear about that part of the plan.

"Absolutely," Georgina said.

Kate regarded Georgina carefully, hoping to uncover whatever she might be planning. But the American was completely passive as she gathered her belongings from the meeting table.

"I look forward to getting back to New York," Georgina said with a smirk as she turned to leave. "May the best woman win."

CHAPTER TWELVE

THE GRINDING noise squealed loudly through the quiet office. Sophie jumped out of her seat and dashed over to the photocopier. It was the third time the machine had jammed that day. She pressed the end button, and the noise stopped.

"Bloody thing," she mumbled under her breath.

She lowered the main flap and jumped back when a plume of black ink dust flew out. She glared at the machine.

Copying the Peterson presentation should have been a ten-minute job. So far, it had taken over an hour. And now the machine seemed truly kaput. She trudged back to her desk and picked up the phone, dialling the number she had quickly memorised.

She shouldered the receiver and sat on the edge of her desk. As she did, she looked down and saw that her light grey trousers had been stained by the black dust cloud. She reached out to wipe the stain with her hand but paused. The last thing she needed was to get it on her hands, then her face.

The phone continued to ring out. She checked the time and realised it was six o'clock. Her jaw dropped in surprise. It seemed only ten minutes ago that she was greeting Kate with her morning tea. Suddenly, the entire day had vanished.

Being insanely busy had the benefit of helping the day fly by. Not to mention that she rarely had time to get nervous around Kate or Georgina, mainly because she only spent thirty seconds at a time with either woman before having to rush to another task. Luckily both women had been busy, often with their office doors firmly closed. Something was going on, but Sophie wasn't interested. She was too busy to take notes on the current state of office politics. She had no idea how Jonathan managed it all.

She slammed the phone down. Asking anyone in IT to stay after five was like trying to stop the tide from coming in. She looked at the photocopier again, the blackened flap still hanging open like a gaping wound. The account management team needed the copies for the next morning. They were coming into the office early to grab the presentations before getting on a train to go to the client's offices.

Sophie slid off the edge of her desk. She undid the buttons on her shirtsleeves and carefully folded them up as high as she could. The copiers on the other floors were out of ink, awaiting spare parts, or in the middle of printing a massive report for the audit. This copier was her only hope.

She knelt in front of the machine and reached her fingers in, plucking out sheet after sheet of concertinaed paper from the innards of the machine. She delicately blew the ink dust from the flap and looked at the unfathomable instructions for how to remove paper jams.

"Am I interrupting something?"

Sophie jolted. She looked up to see Georgina leaning on the wall, looking down at her with a smirk.

Sophie's mind started to spin. Had Georgina been waiting for something all this time? It was her first day being Kate's temporary PA, and already she was struggling to keep up with the relentless pace. Even though she had thankfully not seen much of Kate all day.

"I've not seen you much this afternoon," Georgina spoke again, filling the silence.

Sophie clambered to her feet. "I'm sorry, is there something you need? Did I forget something?"

Georgina pushed herself from the wall. "No, not at all. Is everything all right?" She looked at the copier and raised her eyebrow. "Technical trouble?"

Sophie plucked a couple of tissues from the box on her desk. She tried to clean her fingers.

"Yes, it keeps jamming. The other machines are busy."

Georgina looked at her watch. "At six o'clock?" she asked doubtfully.

"Well, one is out of ink, and one is awaiting a part," Sophie confessed. She hadn't wanted to admit that she'd wasted so much time because of broken machinery. It just didn't sound good, and she didn't want to give Georgina any further ammunition to use against Kate.

"Sounds like shoddy office management to me," Georgina quipped.

"Just bad luck," Sophie defended. "It's not usually like this."

"I should hope not."

Sophie found herself staring at the woman. Not for the first time. Something about Georgina caused her to stop and stare. She'd caught herself doing it a few times lately and was mortified. Georgina had obviously noticed; nothing seemed to escape her attention. Thankfully she seemed to find Sophie's speechless staring amusing.

Sophie blinked and looked away. "I'm sorry, did I... did we have a meeting?"

"Not a scheduled one," Georgina said. "Michael and I were heading out for a drink, maybe a bite to eat. Would you like to join us?"

Sophie found herself staring again. She caught herself quickly and turned away, retreating to the safety of her desk. "Um, a drink?"

She'd never been asked out for drinks by any of the Red Door crowd. The accounts ladies were all in their forties and fifties and keen to get home to their families the moment work ended. Since she'd been on the top floor, no one had really spoken to her. She wasn't technically a part of a team, so fitting in wasn't an easy matter.

Georgina chuckled. "Yes, a drink. It's something work colleagues sometimes do after a particularly trying day. With the pub culture in your country, I would have thought you'd have heard of the concept?"

Sophie didn't like being mocked. "I've been to pubs," she defended.

Exhaustion was making quick work of her nerves. Maybe she'd found a solution for dealing with Georgina and Kate: just be permanently tired. Of course, that wouldn't last long before she was fired.

"I'm certain you have. Would you care to go again?" Georgina replied, Sophie's snappy tone appearing to roll right off her.

"I… I can't," Sophie said. She sat down and looked dejectedly at the copier. "I have to get that report printed. And then I must get home, Matt's expecting me. I'm hoping we can have a night together, he works a lot of evenings lately."

"Ah, yes." Georgina sat on the edge of Sophie's desk. "The boyfriend. Have you been together long?" She picked up the photo frame that contained a picture of Sophie and Matt. It was a couple of years old now, but it was still her favourite picture of them.

"Three years," Sophie replied. Her eyes fixated on the way Georgina's skirt tightened as she perched on the desk. She suddenly realised what she was doing and snapped her eyes up to Georgina's face. "Three years," she repeated.

"Quite a while," Georgina said.

"He's the one."

Georgina raised her eyebrow again. "The one? Congratulations. What does he do?"

"He's a sales executive for a web design company. The money isn't great, but he's really good at what he does."

"So, you're engaged?" Georgina queried. She looked pointedly at Sophie's ringless finger.

Sophie felt her cheeks flush. "No, not yet. We're waiting until we can afford a wedding. We decided that we'd get married about eighteen months ago, but we're delaying the actual engagement."

"If that's the way you want to do it," Georgina said.

Sophie didn't know why she felt the need to explain herself, but something in Georgina's tone had her wanting to clarify the situation. "And Matt wants to lose some weight, before the wedding."

"I see." Georgina lowered the picture frame back to the desk. She picked up a piece of paper and started to read it. "And how is the weight loss going?"

"Really well," Sophie enthused. "He joined a military fitness club a couple of months ago. Since then, the weight has dropped off."

Georgina lowered the piece of paper. "Ah, I see."

The tone was back. And it worried Sophie. "Why... why do you say it like that?"

Georgina stood up and straightened her skirt. "It's not my place to say. If you change your mind about that drink, we'll be in The Crown on the corner of Kirby Street."

Georgina turned to leave. Sophie struggled to ascertain what was on Georgina's mind. Clearly there was something, but she couldn't for the life of her figure out what it was.

"Wait." Sophie stood up. "I mean... please, what did you mean?"

Georgina stopped and turned back to look at Sophie. She regarded her sadly for a moment before she folded her arms. "You say that you decided to get married eighteen months ago. You're putting off the wedding while you save money and he loses weight. But he only started to exercise a couple of *months* ago. And he is working evenings *lately*. As a sales executive for a web design company. A job that is presumably office-based?"

Sophie nervously licked her lips. When laid out in front of her like that, she could see how Georgina could get the wrong idea. "It sounds bad, but—"

"Many couples can't afford a wedding when they choose to get engaged. Some never actually get married. It seems odd to not announce an engagement at all."

"W-well—"

"And he works late?"

"Sometimes, but—"

"Is it happening more often lately? Does it maybe coincide with his weight loss?"

Sophie opened and closed her mouth.

Georgina smiled, sadly but knowingly. "Is he dressing differently? Taking more care over his appearance?"

Sophie thought of Matt's cleanly shaved face. She swallowed.

"He… he shaved," she admitted.

"Is that unusual?" Georgina asked softly.

Sophie nodded. "He said he never would. Said he liked having a beard." She could actually hear the blood rushing through her ears. Surely Matt wasn't having an affair. They were in love. Practically engaged. Sort of.

"He works late?"

"Y-yes, he goes to the pub. He socialises with work contacts, trying to get them to sign a contract. It's a sales thing."

Georgina took a step forward. She put her hand on her hip and fixed Sophie with a sympathetic look. "Is he still affectionate? Passionate? When did you last have sex?"

Sophie felt the heat pouring into her cheeks. "Wow, um, I don't think I'm comfortable answering that," she confessed.

Georgina chuckled. "Then don't tell me, but ask yourself. Don't be blind to what's in front of you, Sophie."

Sophie considered the cheek kisses. She couldn't remember the last time they were intimate, but she had caught him looking at porn on his laptop once. It had hurt her, knowing that he had urges that weren't for her. They hadn't talked about it; Sophie had swept it under the rug along with so many other concerns.

Georgina was still looking at her. Sophie could feel the burn of embarrassment on her face.

"We're... passionate," she argued, even though she knew it was a lie.

Georgina looked at her with pity. She appeared to see right through her subterfuge.

"I see," she said simply. "Well, as I say, we'll be at The Crown if you change your mind."

If Sophie thought she was exhausted at the office, she was practically asleep on her feet when she finally got home. She'd taken the presentation to a twenty-four-hour printers in the end, but not before she'd ruined her clothes and covered herself in printer ink. She'd grabbed a sandwich for dinner and eaten it while running back to the office to cover and bind the presentation.

All in all, it had been a horrific day. Temping for Jonathan wasn't easy. Dealing with Kate was no fun. And Georgina was asking about her non-existent sex life. A few more days like this, and she'd be happy to go back to interning, where the only drama was whose turn it was to make the tea.

She opened the door to the apartment and could hear the television.

"Hi," she called out.

She shrugged out of her coat and placed it on the cat tail hook. She placed her bag on the table by the door and walked into the living room.

Matt was asleep on the sofa, the television playing quietly in the background. He looked adorable, softly snoring, curled up in a ball. During the journey home, she had decided that Georgina was wrong about Matt. How could someone make such wild accusations about a person they hadn't met? Georgina didn't know him like Sophie did.

Sure, there were some strange coincidences. Things that may have looked weird from the outside. And maybe they were going through a weird patch in their relationship. But they loved each other. Matt told her that he loved her every day.

She watched Matt sleep for a few seconds, a smile appearing on her face.

She crept into the room, picked up the remote control from the coffee table, and turned the television off.

I wonder what the time is? She looked at her bare wrist.

She sighed as she remembered that she had taken her ink-covered watch off earlier. She turned around and saw Matt's mobile phone on the floor by the sofa. She picked it up and activated the screen to see the time.

"What are you doing?" His hand snapped forward and grabbed the phone.

"Whoa, calm down," she told him. "I was checking the time." She looked at him in shock. His reaction had frightened her.

He sat up and rubbed his eyes. "Sorry, I was still half asleep. I didn't realise it was you." He looked at his phone. "It's ten past ten."

She looked at him for a few seconds. Georgina's words echoed in her head. This wasn't the first time that Matt had been overly protective of his phone. In the early days, they would constantly use each other's phone to check the time or access the Internet. But over the past few months, Matt had been a little more guarded.

Over the past few months.

A lot had changed over the past few months. Sophie saw Georgina's pitying look in her mind.

"What's up?" He frowned, but quickly pocketed his mobile phone.

Questions swirled around her head, demanding answers. Puzzle pieces started to fall together like paving slabs hammering down into wet sand.

It wasn't the exhaustion. She felt like she was finally waking up.

"How was work?" she asked.

"It was good," he replied. "I'm not quite up to where I

want to be with commission yet. I may need to work a few more nights until we get to the end of the month."

Sophie licked her dry lips. She couldn't believe she hadn't seen what was right in front of her. She'd been too scared to. Something in her brain had prevented her from seeing the obvious. Until now.

"Matt, we need to talk..."

CHAPTER THIRTEEN

A STACK of papers slammed down on her desk, causing Georgina to startle.

"Here's the meeting minutes from yesterday," Sophie mumbled. She turned around to leave.

"Wait a minute," Georgina called after her.

Sophie paused in the doorway. She kept her back to Georgina as she asked, "Can I get you something else?"

"You can turn around and explain why you are throwing papers on my desk and scaring the hell out of me."

Georgina knew she had overstepped the previous day. She'd only invited Sophie for a drink so she and Michael could pump her for information about Kate's plans for the Atrom campaign. When she'd heard about the boyfriend saga, she'd been unable to keep her mouth shut. To her, a delayed wedding was one thing, a delayed engagement was something else. But it wasn't her place to say anything about it.

She didn't want to upset Sophie. Quite the opposite,

she wanted information from her. But somewhere between seeking information and keeping the girl sweet, care had snuck in. Seeing her stressed out, up to her elbows in ink had triggered something in Georgina. She wanted to protect the girl, warn her. Clearly her good intentions had backfired. Now, Sophie was angry with her.

Sophie slowly turned. "I'm sorry for throwing the papers," she mumbled. She seemed to be struggling to maintain her composure.

"Close the door," Georgina ordered. She couldn't leave things the way they were.

"I have to get—"

"Close the door," Georgina repeated.

A tear escaped Sophie's eye and tracked its way down her cheek. "Please," she begged. "Just let me get on with work."

"I'm sorry about what I said yesterday," Georgina said. "I was out of line. It wasn't my intention to upset you."

"You were right," Sophie breathed out. "He... you saw it... everyone probably saw it. Everyone but me."

Georgina felt her jaw drop open in surprise. "Oh. I'm... I'm sorry."

"Can I go now?" Sophie asked, tears falling readily down her face.

"You can, but I don't think you want your colleagues seeing you like this. You're welcome to stay until you compose yourself." Georgina was already up and leaning around Sophie to close her office door. She was no stranger to people crying in her office, but this was one of the first times she cared. She didn't want the Red Door staff to think she had been the cause of Sophie's tears. Nor did she want Sophie to be upset.

"I don't want to be a bother," Sophie sniffed between gulps of breath.

"You're not a bother." Georgina took hold of Sophie's shoulders and walked her over to the armchairs in the corner. "Sit."

Sophie all but fell into her chair, staring directly ahead into nothingness.

Georgina snatched the box of tissues from her desk and placed them in Sophie's lap. She looked at her watch. There was half an hour until her next meeting.

"Would you like me to leave you alone?" Georgina asked.

Sophie shook her head and made a move to stand up. "I don't want to kick you out of your office, I'll go." The tissue box tumbled to the floor.

Georgina stepped forward, blocking Sophie's path with her body. "No, sit down. You clearly need a few moments to compose yourself."

Sophie hesitated before sitting back down. Plucking a tissue from the box, she curled up into a ball in the chair and sniffled. Georgina looked at her. She had no idea what to do, no experience in this area.

"Do you want to talk about it?" Georgina asked softly.

Sophie quickly shook her head.

She wasn't about to push the point. She knew her skillset in emotional matters left a lot to be desired. "Very well. You're welcome to stay here as long as you need. I'll just get on with some emails." Georgina turned away and returned to her desk.

She pulled her MacBook closer to focus on her work. The sounds of her typing and Sophie's occasional sniffles filled the air. Georgina was dying to know what had happened; her guess had clearly been right. How she was so competent with other people's love lives and so incompetent with her own remained a mystery. As did her behaviour towards Sophie Young.

Georgina wasn't exactly known for her kindness towards others. In fact, she was probably better known for her distinct lack of compassion. From an early age, she had decided that she wanted to be successful. People would know her name, and she would never have to worry about money. It quickly became clear that being successful involved making a lot of people unhappy.

The thrill of taking another step on her ladder of success far outweighed any guilty feelings towards anyone she'd climbed over on her ascent. As years flew by, her sensitivity towards others all but vanished. Her ability to suffer fools had always been non-existent, but her ability to suffer anyone at all quickly joined it.

Anyone not reaching her lofty standards was berated, embarrassed, and, often, fired. She'd quickly discovered that giving people even the slightest amount of wiggle room led them to trample all over you later. Being a soft heart was not acceptable in corporate America.

She'd developed quite the reputation for her no-nonsense attitude. She was actively feared. It suited her perfectly, fear seemed to equate to the perfect blend of work output and professional attitude that she desired.

Until Jessica came along. Georgina shifted uncomfortably in her chair at the unwelcome reminder. Jessica had quickly cut through Georgina's icy exterior. It was so clichéd that it made Georgina want to gag. Initially, she had treated Jessica like any other assistant. That is to say, she treated her terribly. She berated her for the smallest mistake, she deliberately insulted her, and she overburdened her with work to watch her fail.

As time went on and Jessica stood her ground, Georgina had started to feel guilty for her behaviour. An entirely new sensation. Jessica consistently achieved perfection. She accomplished every task Georgina threw her way. She also had the courage to tell Georgina when she felt she was wrong.

Georgina started to treat Jessica differently. For the first time since she had set up shop, she was putting kindness towards a member of staff first.

She'd softened.

And now she was allowing a junior employee to cry in her office.

It infuriated Georgina that she cared for the girl. A few years ago, she would have been the cause of her tears, not the protector of them. Her reputation would be in tatters if people back home knew what she was doing.

"Thank you," Sophie whispered.

Georgina looked into her watery eyes.

"For letting me hide out in here," Sophie explained. "Sorry I'm such a mess. I didn't mean to get myself into this kind of state. It all just came out."

Georgina lowered the lid of her MacBook. "Do you want to talk about it?" she asked again.

"Nothing to talk about," Sophie muttered. "He's been

seeing someone else for a while. He won't admit to it, but I know he is."

"How do you know if he didn't admit to it?" Georgina worried for a moment that she had driven a wedge between Sophie and her boyfriend. Maybe she had planted an idea in her head, and Sophie had seen proof where there was none.

"He goes out a lot, to the same place. And he talks about this one girl a lot. He says she's a friend, but… but I don't think she is. Suddenly, he's losing weight, shaving off that awful beard. He's on his phone all the time. And he hides it. He used to leave it on the table, but now it's always in his pocket."

"Are you sure you're not jumping to conclusions?"

"We haven't had sex in five months," Sophie whispered. "And when he kisses me, it's light kisses. Or on the cheek."

Georgina licked her lips and glanced down at her desk for a moment. Sophie could only be in her mid-twenties. She'd not had sex with her boyfriend in five months, and she considered him to be *the one*. The one she wanted to settle down with forever. She wondered how low her expectations and self-esteem must be to put up with that lack of intimacy. Or if Sophie herself had no desire for intimacy.

"I've embarrassed you, I'm sorry," Sophie said, clearly mortified. "It's just, you mentioned it yesterday and, well, I—"

"No, it's fine, fine," Georgina replied quickly. "I'm just surprised that someone your age, with your looks…" She trailed off, not wishing to finish a sentence that was rapidly becoming inappropriate.

"Well, it wasn't a lack of trying on my part," Sophie admitted. "The truth is, he hasn't loved me for months, he just… just stayed with me because it's easier. While he waited to find someone better."

Georgina shook her head. "I'm sure that's not true. I'm sure he loved you. Loves you, even."

"Maybe, but not enough."

Georgina moved over to the armchair where Sophie sat. Her tear-stained appearance was completed by a wobbling lip. Georgina usually ran away from such a sight, leaving it for someone else to deal with. Someone more competent in matters of the heart. But there was no one else. Sophie was opening up, and she needed support.

She knelt in front of her, placing a comforting hand on her knee. "It's not a reflection on you."

Sophie shook her head. "How can it not be a reflection on me? He… he fell out of love with me. I'm not enough for him."

Georgina shook her head vigorously. "You are an intelligent, beautiful, passionate woman. Maybe he's not good enough for you, and he realised that and got frightened."

"You think so?" Sophie asked.

"I know so." A voice in the back of Georgina's mind screamed at her to stop talking. This road led to trouble. But she couldn't stand to see Sophie distraught. Memories of Jessica swirled in her mind. The similarities between the women were startling. In a few days, Sophie had wormed her way into Georgina's heart, and Georgina had let her in.

She sat on the arm of the chair and pulled Sophie towards her. The shy, bumbling girl seemed to vanish in the swirl of emotions, and she put an arm around Georgina's middle. Georgina held Sophie close as sobs continued to shake her. She used her free hand to softly caress Sophie's hair.

Georgina tried not to think too much about the sensations that were tearing through her. Part of her felt special at being able to offer Sophie the comfort she so desperately needed. But another part of her felt nervous. Why was she helping Sophie? What was it about her that drew Georgina in? And what would she do about it?

They'd sat in a comforting embrace for a few moments, when the door flew open and Kate stepped in. She placed a file on Georgina's desk, only seeing the pair as she turned to leave. She stopped and stared.

Sophie pulled away from Georgina.

"What is going on here?" Kate demanded.

"Nothing is going on," Georgina replied hotly, not appreciating the insinuation.

"I'm sorry, I should go." Sophie wiped at her remaining tears with the sleeve of her cardigan and bolted from the office. The tissue box bounced along the floor.

Kate watched her go before slamming the door closed and spinning to face Georgina. She put her hands on her hips and glared. "What was that?"

Georgina picked up the tissue box and placed it on her desk. "She was upset. She's broken up with her boyfriend," she explained.

"And she came to *you* for comfort?" Kate asked with a smirk. "Or are you pulling her into your clutches?"

Georgina laughed. "My clutches? Are you out of your mind?"

Kate pointed her finger at Georgina. "I've seen the way you look at her. Leave her alone. I won't stand for this."

Georgina folded her arms and smiled. If she'd known she could irritate Kate so easily, she would have done it ages ago.

"I think you're jumping to conclusions," Georgina said. "The girl was crying, I offered her tissues and a shoulder. But, if it *were* more, I don't see what it would have to do with you."

"She's my assistant," Kate fumed. She placed her hands back on her hips.

"No, she's the most junior member of your staff, and I believe you assigned her to me," Georgina replied.

"She is a member of *my* staff." Anger radiated from Kate in waves.

Where is this rage coming from? Georgina mused. *Surely she doesn't have feelings for Sophie?*

"And yet, she comes to me," Georgina replied. It wasn't entirely true, but it was enough to irritate Kate. She felt a lot more at home annoying Kate than she did comforting Sophie.

"I'm watching you," Kate spat.

Georgina opened her mouth to reply but closed it again when she saw Michael approaching her office through the glass door. Kate followed her gaze and turned around.

Michael opened the door. "Sorry to interrupt, but Yannis is here."

"Yannis?" Kate said.

"Do we have a meeting today?" Georgina asked.

Michael shook his head. "He's in Kate's office."

Kate turned to face Georgina. "He does this sometimes."

"Better see what he wants," Georgina said. She had a few clients who would suddenly turn up in the office. It was often not a good sign, but any extra time she could have with Yannis, she was willing to take. She needed to get to know him, understand how his mind worked, his likes and dislikes.

Kate slowly nodded before walking out of the office.

Michael looked at her. "What was that about?" he asked, clearly picking up on the tension in the room.

"I'm not sure," Georgina confessed. "Seems I struck a chord."

"What did you do?"

"Played with her toy."

CHAPTER FOURTEEN

Kᴀᴛᴇ ʙᴏʟᴛᴇᴅ ᴀᴄʀᴏss ᴛʜᴇ ᴏꜰꜰɪᴄᴇ, wanting to put distance between herself and Georgina. The moment she caught her rival embracing Sophie, an unexpected fire rose within her.

She wished she hadn't reacted quite as she had. She feared all she had done was provide Georgina with more ammunition in her attempts to irritate her.

But she'd reacted without thinking, wanting to protect Sophie from Masters. She hadn't even considered that Georgina would attempt to ensnare Sophie, but now it seemed so obvious. Georgina clearly had a type. Kate felt guilty for pushing the innocent girl straight into her clutches. She hoped her reaction would warn Georgina off. The sooner the woman was back in New York, the better.

While she was grateful he had interrupted their tense conversation, Kate was concerned about Yannis's appearance. Yannis turning up out of the blue was a common event, but it was never a good thing. It usually indicated a total change of direction, or full-tilt annoyance with her team.

As she approached her office door, she could see the man pacing anxiously in front of the window. Another indication that she wasn't in for a good meeting.

"Yannis, lovely of you to drop by," she greeted warmly as she walked into the office. "Have you been offered tea, coffee?"

"Yes, yes." He waved his hand to bat away her offer. "I'm fine, thank you. Is Georgina—"

"Yannis, good to see you," Georgina said as she entered the office.

"We need to bring forward our first advertising campaign," Yannis cut to the chase. "Eight months is not soon enough, we need it sooner. Within the next three months."

Kate exchanged a look with Georgina.

"That will be quite difficult. We have a lot of background work to do," Kate admitted.

"Investors are getting nervous, especially considering the... event," Yannis explained.

"You mean fireball," Kate suggested. She wasn't about to let Yannis forget that her staff member had been seriously injured in the incident. "I'm not surprised they are getting nervous."

"It was an accident, we know exactly what it was," Yannis said. He pulled a corroded piece of metal out of his jacket pocket. "This was a spark plug supplied by a third party. The fault came from this, nothing to do with the Atrom engine."

"Presumably you've explained that to investors?" Kate asked.

Yannis nodded and continued to pace. "But they are still asking questions, ridiculous questions. You know what they are like, I need to show them something substantial now. The car is being rebuilt, and without a car, they think we have nothing. That's not the case, but they are too blind to see that. I need to show them something."

Kate looked to Georgina for assistance. They may be vying for the same contract, but surely even she would see the impossibility of what Yannis was asking.

"We'd love to be able to do this for you, Yannis," Georgina spoke up, "but it's just impossible. We don't have a logo, a tagline, a concept. Nothing at all. We're still in the development stage, we have ideas, but nothing pinned down."

"But surely you can get something together. I'm not suggesting a full campaign, just something to wow the investors."

"I'd have to speak with my team, see what we can get together. In fact, Kate and I were just discussing this."

Georgina glanced at Kate, seeking approval to share their idea of splitting the proposals with Yannis. Kate inclined her head.

"We think it would be best, for Atrom, for you," Georgina explained, "to have two options to choose from. Mastery and Red Door can both work on proposals, separately. This gives you the insight of both—"

Yannis stopped pacing and spun to face Georgina. "What do you mean, separately?"

"Upon reflection, we feel that it would be very difficult

to integrate the teams," Kate said. "We think this is best for you. You get two proposal documents, and you choose which you want to go with. It will speed matters up considerably. If we have to integrate teams that don't often work together, which of course we *could*, it would slow the process down."

Yannis's eyes sparkled at the offer of a shorter time-frame. "I see. Yes, yes, that would be better." He folded his arms across his chest and paced quickly in front of the window.

"Excellent," Georgina said, missing that Yannis was still deep in thought. Kate knew better. When Yannis was like this, it was best to let him talk himself out. "Then I will head back to New York soon, and we'll be able to—"

"No, no. I need you here," he said to Georgina. "You can surely liaise with your team from here, at least for the mean-time? I have told our investors that I am working with both of you. I can't go back on that now, at least not until funding is secured. I am paying you for your full time, am I not?"

Kate turned and looked at Georgina. She had to admit, she was enjoying watching Yannis tear a small strip off the woman. Even if it did mean that Georgina would be staying in her office for the time being.

"You are, absolutely. But it would be normal proce-dure for me to work from my own office—"

"But you said you'd be able to work remotely," Yannis interrupted. "Didn't you say that time and distance were not important in any modern business? It seems you are telling me the opposite now."

"I meant I would be able to work from New York and

talk to Kate in London. I meant that a business in New York could easily work with a business in London."

"Then, surely, your being here instead of New York operates under the same principle?" Yannis asked.

Kate regarded him. He was very agitated; the investor news must have come as quite a shock. She wondered how much of his own money was tied up in the project. If he had invested half the amount and the other investors dropped out, he'd lose everything he put in. It would be just like Yannis to throw a ton of money into a project, not considering the possibility of losing it until it was too late.

"I suppose so," Georgina agreed. "As long as Kate is willing to kindly host me here for a while longer?"

Kate turned to Georgina and smiled as warmly as she could muster. "Of course, it's lovely you have you here. The *years* of experience you bring are very welcome." She couldn't help but throw an age comment back in Georgina's face.

Georgina smirked. "Yes, I have been made to feel very welcome. Staying sounds appealing. I look forward to getting to know the team *much* better."

Kate felt a coldness creep up her spine. She again cursed herself for reacting the way she had to catching Sophie in Georgina's office.

Although she wasn't entirely sure what she had walked in on, she knew she didn't like it. Sophie was young, naive, and innocent. Georgina was none of those things. The very idea that Georgina might take advantage of Sophie was enough to make Kate's blood boil.

"So, that is all settled then?" Yannis asked impatiently. "You will be staying in London?"

Georgina nodded. "Absolutely. Until this investor business is sorted out," she turned to look Kate in the eye, "I'll be right here."

CHAPTER FIFTEEN

Sophie walked through hospital corridors with her head hung low. Things were getting out of control at work, and things had gone completely to hell at home. When the work day had ended, she'd rushed from the office, wanting to escape. But the second she was in the busy London street, she realised she had nowhere she wanted to go.

She hadn't told her friends or family about her break-up with Matt yet. And she certainly didn't want to go home. Before she knew it, she was texting Jonathan to tell him that she was on her way to visit him in the hospital. She'd promised she'd come and give him an update on the office gossip, she just didn't think she'd be the subject of all of it.

She paused as she approached his room. She took a deep breath before turning the corner and softly knocking on the open door.

Jonathan looked up at her and smiled. He was looking better; the colour was returning to his face.

"Hey, come in," he said, gesturing to the chair beside

the bed. "How are things going? I've not had any phone calls from you yet, so that must be a good sign?"

She walked into the room and flopped heavily into the chair, letting out a loud sigh.

"Maybe not such a good sign?" he guessed.

"Everything has gone to hell," she mumbled.

"Did Kate fire you?"

Sophie chuckled and shook her head. "No, not yet." She kicked off her shoes, brought her feet up onto the chair, and hugged her knees. "I broke up with Matt."

"Your boyfriend?"

"Sort of fiancé."

"I'm sorry to hear that."

Sophie placed her chin on her knees and looked at Jonathan. She felt guilty, coming to him to cry about her problems when he was in the hospital. But she couldn't stay at work. Seeing Georgina or Kate right now would send her into another crying fit. And going home would mean another fight.

Jonathan was easy to talk to. He was an unbiased third party she could trust to give an honest opinion. He didn't have any agenda, and he wouldn't be judgemental like she knew her parents would. She hadn't called her mum because she knew she'd sigh and sound disappointed.

She just wanted to talk to someone. Someone smart, someone who seemed to have things figured out. Even if that person was forced to listen to her because they were confined to a hospital bed.

"I'm sorry, I shouldn't be complaining. You have it worse than I do."

Jonathan grinned. "Well, broken bones aren't fun. But

neither is breaking up with your boyfriend, or your sort of fiancé. How does that work anyway?"

"It works when your girlfriend is an idiot," she grumbled.

"Hey, come on, you're not an idiot."

"He's been having an affair. But I didn't see it, it took Georgina to see it."

Jonathan furrowed his brow. "Georgina? Okay, you need to explain this."

Sophie sighed. Telling Jonathan what had happened was one thing, actually explaining it was another. She didn't really understand it all herself.

"Georgina asked me out for drinks with her and Michael—"

"Tell me you said no," Jonathan interrupted.

"I did, but only because I was busy."

"She's just trying to pump you for information," Jonathan told her seriously.

Sophie shook her head. She hated the distrust floating around the office. She'd heard of office politics, but she'd never been so deeply entrenched in them. Why people couldn't just get along and not constantly assume the other party had an agenda was beyond her.

"Well, that doesn't matter now. I didn't go. And I mentioned Matt, told her I had to get back home to him. So, she asked me a couple of questions. She, she kinda highlighted some things. Asked questions I hadn't been brave enough to ask myself."

"Like what?"

"Like why we were engaged but no one knew. We'd never made an announcement, I thought it was because we were saving for a wedding. But it was just his way of appeasing me. Delaying things so he could find someone better." Tears started to form in her eyes again. She angrily brushed them away with the palms of her hands.

"You confronted him?" Jonathan asked.

"Yeah, when I got home. I asked all the questions I'd been burying. I could see in his eyes that he was lying to me. He denied everything, but the more he said, the more he incriminated himself. I was so angry." She swiped at her tears again.

"Are you sure, though? I'm not defending him, just asking, especially as he denied it."

"I'm sure. He can't lie to save his life. He told me what I needed to know in his eyes." She recalled Matt's expression when she had started to ask him questions. His eyes had flickered around the room as they always did when he lied. The more she pressed, the more ridiculous his stories and excuses became. Eventually he gave up answering, accused her of already having made up her mind.

Jonathan regarded her sadly. "I'm sorry."

"Wait, it gets worse." Sophie laughed bitterly. "The next day, this morning, I drop off some papers in Georgina's office. I felt so stupid. I'm living with him, sharing a bed with him, and I saw nothing. But she saw it. Just a few questions, and she'd got him all figured out. I thought she'd see it on my face, like I'd seen it on Matt's. So, I tried to hurry out of her office."

Jonathan practically winced at what he assumed came next. "How did that work out for you?"

"She called me back in." She closed her eyes in embarrassment. "I admitted everything, and I cried—oh,

Jonathan, I cried like a baby in her office. She comforted me, and Kate walked in on us. She was livid."

"Kate was?" Jonathan questioned.

"Yes."

"What did she say?"

"I don't know, I just ran away."

"Did she speak to you later?" he pressed.

"A little, but only about work stuff. She was pretty short with me. Yannis showed up at the office. I don't know what was said, but I had an email from Kate telling me to extend Georgina's hotel booking indefinitely."

Working with Kate was difficult enough, but now Sophie had to deal with Kate's anger about catching her and Georgina. Sophie had intended to explain to Kate that it was all perfectly innocent and that Georgina was just offering her comfort. But one look at Kate's stormy expression had told her that the rationalisation wouldn't be welcome.

Jonathan cringed. "So, Georgina's being made to stay in London. No one is going to like that."

"I know," Sophie agreed. "I was kind of happy that Georgina was going home soon. She's been really nice to me, but after I embarrassed myself in front of her, I don't know how I'm going to look her in the eye again."

"Count yourself lucky that she's being nice to you," Jonathan told her. "Her reputation is for eating people alive. Unless…" He looked at her, and his eyes sparkled mischievously.

Sophie frowned. "Unless what?"

"Unless, you're the new assistant."

Sophie knew what he meant. Her encyclopaedic

knowledge of the marketing industry meant that she was well aware of Georgina Masters' relationship with her young assistant.

"No." She shook her head. "No, no, Georgina doesn't…" She laughed. "That's ridiculous."

Jonathan shifted a little to push himself up higher in the bed. "No, it's not. Think about it. Georgina has a reputation for being as mean as they come. But she's comforting you while you cry in her office. If we're to believe rumours, and we totally are, most people crying in Georgina's office are crying because of her. And then are never seen again."

Sophie hugged her legs a little tighter. She knew it was true, but she wasn't about to agree with him. The very idea was too much for her to take in right now.

"And then there's the fact that Georgina is newly single. Having been dumped by her girlfriend, who started off her relationship with Georgina while her assistant. Who happens to be not far from your age."

She called me beautiful, Sophie recalled. *Oh, God… she called me beautiful and passionate.*

"And she invited you for drinks," Jonathan added.

Sophie glared at him. "You were just telling me that was because she was trying to get information from me. Now it's, what? Because she wants to…" Sophie could feel her face flush at the thought.

"Maybe," Jonathan replied. He grinned. "Will you remember me when you're living in some fancy New York penthouse with your millionaire girlfriend?"

"Shut up," Sophie told him forcefully.

He blanched. "Sorry, I'm sorry, that was tactless. You're straight, I get it."

Sophie sighed. Now she sounded homophobic. "I'm… I think I'm bisexual," she admitted. She felt her cheeks heat in a blush.

You think? Why did you say that? She'd never been sure she was one hundred percent straight. She could appreciate a beautiful woman when she saw one. Maybe more than appreciate. But she'd been with Matt for years, so it was never something she'd bothered to explore. But now, now it was all her mind could explore. Was she bisexual? It would answer a few questions, and she knew from recent experience how well she hid tricky questions from herself.

He inclined his head. "I shouldn't have joked about it anyway, I'm sorry. You have to go and work with her, and I know that's not going to be easy."

"What am I going to do?" she implored.

"I don't know," he admitted. "I think you need to see what happens. I'm just joking about Georgina. I'm sure she's nicer in person, the rumours could be wrong. Or she's softened."

"But what if she is flirting with me?" Sophie asked. Now the thought was in her mind, it wasn't going to let go. The very idea of the almost-predatory Georgina flirting with her sent a shiver up her spine. Georgina was an attractive woman. Sophie would kill to have her looks, her figure, her hair. But Sophie wasn't girlfriend material for such an impressive woman, if that was even what Georgina saw in her. Maybe Sophie was reading too much into it, maybe Georgina was simply being kind.

And then there was Kate to consider. Dating the

enemy would certainly put her in Kate's bad books. Sophie got the impression that Kate only tolerated her because Jonathan wasn't around. It wasn't just the thought of losing her job that worried her, she didn't want to disappoint Kate. Working with her idol, despite the difficult circumstances, was a dream come true. She was already learning so much. The chance of losing that, and never seeing Kate again, was a bitter pill to swallow.

"That's up to you," Jonathan said. "You're newly single now. Just see where things take you, there's no rush. But don't let anyone take advantage of you. If you don't want to go for drinks with someone, then don't. Think of this as a new beginning. The new Sophie Young."

Sophie felt a smile on her lips. "Yeah, the new Sophie Young. I think I like the sound of that."

CHAPTER SIXTEEN

"THANK YOU," Georgina said as Michael placed a glass of wine in front of her.

He took a seat opposite her and set his beer down on the table.

"So," he started. "How long do you think we're going to be here?"

Georgina rolled her eyes and shook her head. She looked around the pub. It was located in between the Red Door offices and their hotel: close enough to be convenient, but far enough away that they were unlikely to see any of the Red Door staff.

While the hotel was wonderful, it wasn't the place to have a conversation. Especially when that conversation included sensitive information about stealing business from competitors. Especially since the hotel had been booked by the competitor in question. Walls had ears.

"I don't know," she admitted. "But I'm going to continue to work on Yannis. He was upset today, shaken by this investor situation. He wants to circle the wagons, have a defensive net built up to answer any investor questions. Once this blows over, and I'm sure it will, it will be easy to convince him that our productivity will improve by returning to New York. At the moment his priority is speed, he wants to show he has a commercially viable product as quickly as possible. Once we impress him with the contents of our business proposal, I'll tell him that efficiency requires us to work from New York."

Georgina took a sip of wine. She hoped she could follow through. It made sense to her, but Yannis was a unique individual. She'd never worked with anyone quite like him.

"You really think you can convince him?" Michael asked. "He seems very opinionated, doesn't like to listen to reason."

Georgina chuckled. "That's definitely true. I'm not sure how Kate puts up with him."

"He and Kate seem pretty close," Michael pointed out. "It makes me wonder whether we have a chance to take the Atrom contract from Red Door at all."

He plucked a menu from the holder on the table and looked at it.

"They are close," Georgina agreed. "But that won't last if his beloved sports car project is put in jeopardy."

Michael lowered the menu and picked up his glass. He took a sip of the lager, and as he placed the pint glass back on the table, his eyes were distant. He looked thoughtful, hesitant.

"Out with it," Georgina said.

He smiled. "I'm just wondering if all this is worth it."

Georgina knew it would be coming eventually. Michael was loyal, but he was also a good businessman. He'd happily gone along with her plans to snatch the Atrom account, he'd seen the dollar signs and the opportunity.

But things were changing. Being away from the office for such a long time wasn't ideal. Yes, there was an effective system in place while they were away, but there was nothing like being there yourself. They'd intended to only be away a couple of weeks, now it was an open-ended trip. They were at the mercy of Yannis's mood, a prospect that Georgina wasn't comfortable with.

Michael slid his beer to one side and leaned forward. "I know the Atrom account is worth a lot of money. But can we really split Yannis and Kate? They've been working together for a long time. And, even if we did, do we really want to work with Yannis? He's unpredictable, flighty. One minute he wants one thing, the next it's something different. Is all of this worthwhile?"

Georgina picked up her wine glass and took a small sip. She enjoyed the sweet dryness in her mouth. She had wondered how long it would be before Michael started to have doubts. She couldn't blame him; the same thought had crossed her mind once or twice.

"Especially," she said, "as all of this is a somewhat… personal vendetta?"

Michael shook his head. "It's not that exactly. I felt the loss of the Pink Blossom account as keenly as you, maybe more so. I worked on that account, and when we lost it…

I don't mind admitting that I felt personally hurt. What Kate did was underhanded."

"It was," Georgina agreed. While Pink Blossom wasn't the biggest account that Mastery had lost, it was one of the more visible. The Pink Blossom brand was well-known. All the trade magazines had reported on the loss, citing numerous reasons for the account leaving Mastery.

The damage to the Mastery brand was far more than any damage to the company's bank account. Georgina had slaved away at building her brand; the company was her baby, even shared her name. Defending the company reputation had hurt.

On top of everything, Kate Kennedy had never even acknowledged the matter. Despite the silence, Georgina had always considered it a snub. A silent *I won*.

Georgina hadn't specifically set out for revenge. But she'd always kept her eyes open for any opportunity. A chance meeting with Yannis had been it. She'd pulled out all the stops and schmoozed the man to the very best of her ability, cutting her profit margins and promising the world to land the account. Sadly, she'd only landed the opportunity to work with Kate Kennedy.

It was a start. It had brought her into Red Door. She knew she was perceived as the fox in the henhouse. Her presence had ruffled feathers and was presumably giving Kate sleepless nights. She had to admit, she enjoyed being such a disruptive force.

"It's not ideal," Georgina said. "But you must admit, seeing that little vein in Kate's forehead growing bigger each day is enormously satisfying."

Michael laughed. "It is, it is."

"We've had awkward clients before, we'll have them again. Yannis is no different," Georgina explained. "If we win the Atrom account, wonderful. If we don't, then let's make sure we stress Kate out as much as we can in the meantime. Maybe neither of us will end up with Atrom. At this point, I don't care. I feel like I'm finally able to throw a wrench into Kate's world, and I want to make sure it causes as much trouble as possible. It took us a year to recover from the bad publicity following the Pink Blossom fiasco. A few weeks of us pressing Kate's buttons is fair compensation."

"That's true," Michael acknowledged. "As you say, Kate doesn't seem to be coping too well with our presence."

"Absolutely. Less since she caught me holding Sophie Young." Georgina looked at him meaningfully over the top of her wine glass. She knew she shouldn't mention it, but she had to. If only to share news of Kate's fury.

He raised an eyebrow. "Georgina," he asked teasingly, "whatever have you done?"

She shook her head. "Nothing like that. The girl was in distress. I offered a shoulder to cry on. But you should have seen Kate's face. She was furious. Ordered me away from her."

"Interesting…"

"Very," she agreed.

"But, best to stay away, for your own sake," Michael added.

"Of course." She picked up a menu and looked it over.

"Georgina," he warned.

She looked up at him with a shrug. "What? I agreed."

"Yes, but I know that tone. That's a very noncommittal tone."

She picked up her wine glass and took another sip. "Let's eat," she said, quickly changing the subject as she regarded the menu in her other hand.

Michael regarded her for a moment before shaking his head and picking up his menu.

CHAPTER SEVENTEEN

GEORGINA PICKED up a random folder from the stack Michael had put on her desk.

"How did you get this?" she asked.

He chuckled as he leaned forward and plucked another folder from the stack. "Their strategy to put my desk out of the way, so I wouldn't overhear what they were doing, backfired. They put me in a corner with several filing cabinets that contains printouts of their old presentations."

She smiled and flipped through the folder. "So, the motto is, don't trust you near an unlocked filing cabinet?"

"Definitely not," he drawled.

"Do we know what people Kate is putting on The Bolt project?"

He shook his head. "Nothing has come my way. She's playing things very close to her chest."

"Not surprised." She turned the page and shook her head. She flipped it over for Michael to see. "Look at the lighting on this photo shoot. What were they thinking?"

He turned over the presentation he was reading and showed her. "I can beat that. Three separate serif fonts, anyone?"

She looked at the banner and winced. "Are you sure you didn't find the filing cabinets with the rejects in them? Maybe they saw you coming and these are the decoy presentations?"

"I wish," he sighed.

A knock on the door caught her attention. She saw Sophie through the glass and gestured for her to come in.

"Sorry to interrupt," Sophie said. She handed over a stack of papers. "You asked for the colour palette and the font assets for the last Atrom campaign."

"Oh, wonderful. Very efficient, thank you, Sophie," Georgina said. She took the papers from the girl and placed them on her desk. "How are you feeling today? Better, I hope?"

Sophie awkwardly adjusted her glasses and shifted from foot to foot. Georgina knew she should leave the girl alone, but she couldn't help herself. She couldn't get Sophie out of her mind. Knowing that her interacting with Sophie infuriated Kate just made the act all the sweeter. Although, with Kate out of the office at present, Georgina knew her excuse was flimsy at best.

"I'm much better, thank you," Sophie mumbled.

"Good, I'm very pleased to hear that." She dragged her eyes down Sophie's form. "You're looking lovely today, that cardigan certainly suits you."

Sophie cheeks flushed a deep red, and she stumbled out an acknowledgement.

Michael looked at Georgina and raised a warning eyebrow towards her.

"I-I'm heading out to get lunch for Kate," Sophie said. "Can I get either of you anything?"

Georgina looked at her watch. "Time has flown this morning. What time is Kate due back?"

"In around an hour."

Plenty of time to go through these presentations, Georgina thought.

"I think we're okay for lunch, we were heading out," Michael told Sophie, interrupting anything Georgina might have been about to say.

"Oh, okay," Sophie said. Her eyes drifted towards the desk, eyeing the folders with a puzzled expression. "I'll go then, if you don't need me?"

"I have your number if I do." Georgina winked.

Sophie let out a strangled chuckle before rushing out of the office.

Georgina watched her through the window. The girl really was adorable. All blushed cheeks and nervous gestures.

"You should leave her alone," he said. He picked up another folder and leafed through the documents.

"It's just some entertainment," Georgina reassured him.

"Entertaining for who?" Michael asked. "Are you genuinely interested in her, or are you just doing it to annoy Kate? Or are you rebounding? What I'm asking is, is it fair to Sophie?"

"I really don't know," Georgina admitted. She picked

up a folder, hoping to distract his attention by returning to the task at hand.

"Have you called Jessica?" Michael asked, clearly not dissuaded.

"And why would I do that?" She turned the ad campaign she was looking at to one side and studied it intently.

"Well, I don't know," Michael said. "Maybe because she's the best thing that ever happened to you and you're miserable without her."

Georgina snapped her head up to look at him. "If she was the best thing to ever happen to me, then she wouldn't have left."

He ignored her gaze, instead poring over the presentation papers he held up as a semi-barrier to her anger. "So, you argued. If you'd apologise, as you know you should, then she'd come back to you."

Georgina lowered her own folder. "I will not apologise," she said defiantly.

He shrugged his shoulders. "Your loss."

She fixed him with a piercing glare before picking up the folder again.

"Lucinda's gain," Michael muttered.

"What's that?" She looked at him again, rage starting to bubble within.

He looked up at her and let out a sigh. "Come on, Georgina. You know that Lucinda Waverly has been sniffing around Jessica ever since you two got together. She's bound to act now that word of your split is everywhere. You know how she can be, dog with a bone springs to mind. And Jessica is too sweet to say no. You know as well as I do that Jessica will end up going out with her just to be polite."

Georgina felt her nostrils flare in anger. "I really don't know why you're telling me this, Michael. As if I have any interest at all in Jessica's love life."

He sighed again and leaned back in his chair. "I'm telling you because you are condemning me to act as your new assistant. Why am I here, Georgina? You could have brought anyone, but you brought me. And you won't hire a new assistant, which means I end up doing the work instead."

It was true. Not that she'd for one moment admit it. She'd brought Michael along as a friendly face, someone she could speak to and confide in. Only now he wanted her to speak to and confide in him. And she wasn't ready.

"Well, if you'd not been so insistent on our dating in the first place, then you wouldn't be here now."

Michael's jaw dropped. "You're blaming me for this? You're actually blaming me for your break-up?"

"No." She shook her head. "I'm blaming you for the relationship ever even starting. As you say, I'm to blame for the break-up. But without your interference, neither of us would have found ourselves in this situation." She held up the folder and tried, once again, to change tacks. "The font choice on this menu is truly appalling."

Michael shook his head. "Jessica was a saint to put up with you," he said.

That was true as well. Georgina knew she had treated Jessica badly. The girl deserved so much better than her. One of the reasons Georgina hadn't fought for their relationship, aside from her stubborn nature, was her firm belief that Jessica could do better.

Now she just cursed the fact she'd ever been in a loving relationship with her assistant. If she'd never lowered her defences and let her in, she wouldn't be so miserable and lonely now.

"And that is the last time her name will be mentioned," she said.

"Fine, fine. But I'd keep an eye on Sophie. You may think she's sweet and naïve, but she probably saw these presentations. She might report them back to Kate."

"I'll deal with it," Georgina said. "Now, let's get back to work."

CHAPTER EIGHTEEN

SOPHIE HUNCHED OVER HER KEYBOARD. The muscles in her shoulders throbbed. She knew it was a reaction to stress. Any time she felt stress, her shoulder muscles hardened into concrete. And what she was doing now was certainly stressful.

Kate had ordered her to spy on Georgina and Michael. She'd been very clear that Sophie's continued employment rested on her doing what she was told. When Sophie had seen the old presentation files on Georgina's desk, she knew she had to report it to Kate.

Luckily, Kate was on the phone, and so Sophie had the opportunity to take the coward's way out and email what she had seen. She hated the tension in the office, the spying and the reporting back. Kate was becoming more and more stressed, and she was taking it out on anyone in her path. Sadly, Sophie's new temporary role as Kate's PA had her right in the crosshairs.

She glanced up at Kate through the glass windows looking into her office. Kate seemed to be deep in conversation. Sophie hoped the conversation would last the rest of the working day.

"The presentations were on her desk…"

Sophie jumped at the sound of Georgina's voice in her ear. Her heart rate spiked. Georgina was standing behind her, leaning down and reading her screen. Reading the very email that she was writing to tell Kate about Georgina's actions. But, for some reason, Georgina was smiling.

"This all sounds very serious," Georgina whispered with a nod to the screen. She turned and sat beside the keyboard. "What do you think will happen to me? Off to the tower?"

"I-I…" Sophie stammered. She was mortified at having been caught in the act.

"It's okay, Sophie. I know you're just doing your job." Georgina turned to look at the screen. She pointed her finger to the middle of a sentence. "I'd add a comma here."

Sophie could feel her cheeks heating up in a deep blush.

Georgina turned to look at her and chuckled. "Really, Sophie. It's fine. You've been asked to do this, I get it. I'm a big girl, I can take responsibility for my actions. But it's probably better for you if we pretend that I didn't see it. We'll call it our little secret."

"Oh. Okay." Sophie quickly added in the comma and sent the email to Kate. She checked her screen to see if there was any other incriminating evidence to be found.

"I'm sorry," she said. "It's not something I want to do. I don't agree with it. I wish everyone could just get along."

Georgina smiled. "That's adorable. But that's not how business works, I'm afraid."

"But it should," Sophie argued. "I hate all of these office politics."

Georgina nodded. "I can see it's not your strength. But we have to do what we have to do, to get ahead."

"Yeah, I guess. Still feels horrible. I want to get ahead, but this isn't the way I want to do it."

Georgina folded her arms and looked down at her. "Well, you're not going to get ahead until you can show your worth. You're a little on the quiet side, and that's fine. But if you really want to get ahead then you have to make yourself heard."

Sophie had heard it before. At school, at university, and at work. Everyone told her she was quiet, meek even. People had been telling her to speak up her entire life.

"I know," she admitted. "I don't really get much of an opportunity to make myself heard. And even if I did, I'm worried that my ideas are no good and I'd blow it. I don't want to take a risk and shout out my ideas, just to find out that they are stupid and I've blown my chance."

"I'd be more than happy to listen to your ideas," Georgina offered. "It doesn't have to be about Atrom, that's a little infected at the moment. We can have a more general discussion, and I can give you feedback. If you'd like that, that is?"

Sophie couldn't imagine passing up the opportunity to get feedback from Georgina Masters. She looked nervously towards Kate's office, relieved to see she was engrossed in her phone call.

"That does sound good. Great, actually," she confessed.

"Wonderful. We could discuss it at my hotel, maybe over dinner? It's a little more private than the office, and less noisy than a restaurant."

Sophie swallowed nervously. The offer was taking a turn she hadn't expected. She worried that the heat from her cheeks may set the fire alarms off.

"Dinner with me isn't a requirement for my silence," Georgina reassured her. "If you don't want to have dinner with me, that's perfectly fine. Our little secret will remain just that."

Sophie mentally pictured Kate's rage if she heard that Sophie socialised with Georgina. While the opportunity was amazing, she knew she had to side with Kate. Kate was her employer, and Georgina would be going home soon. As much as it hurt to let such an offer slip through her fingers, she knew she had to.

"I-I… think we better not," she said sadly.

Georgina nodded and offered a small smile. She looked up to Kate's office briefly and then back to Sophie. "I understand. I wouldn't want to be the cause of any further conflict between you and your boss."

"Oh, there's no…" Sophie trailed off. She didn't want to lie. There was already enough deception in the Red Door offices as it was. The unfinished sentence hung between them.

"Sophie, can you come in here, please?" Kate's voice sounded through the intercom on Sophie's desk.

"You better go." Georgina slid from the desk. "I'll see you later."

Sophie watched her leave. She couldn't believe she just turned down career advice from Georgina Masters. Or that Georgina had asked her to dinner. Sophie's mind swam with questions. Did Georgina suggest dinner purely for efficiency's sake, or was it something else?

A smile grew on her face. Again, Georgina's terrible reputation didn't ring true. The formidable woman had been nothing but lovely to her since she arrived. *Or maybe she's just lovely to you,* her mind supplied.

She remembered Kate's request. Grabbing her notepad and pen, she rushed into Kate's office.

"Ah, there you are. Close the door," Kate said without looking up.

Sophie closed the door and walked towards the visitor chair which she had come to think of as her customary spot.

"What did she want?" Kate asked as Sophie sat down.

"Oh, nothing, she… was talking." Sophie adjusted her glasses, keen to avoid direct eye contact.

"Talking?" Kate looked up and chuckled. "With you?"

"Yes," Sophie replied defensively. "Actually, she's really nice."

She wasn't sure what caused her to say it, but she immediately wished she hadn't. Her knee-jerk attempt to get Kate to see that Georgina wasn't the devil himself was quickly regretted.

"Are you ill, Stephanie? Georgina Masters is many things, but nice is most certainly not one of them." Kate glared at her.

"Well, she's nice to me," Sophie mumbled.

"Then she's playing you as much as you are playing her," Kate told her.

"I'm not playing her, you're making me spy on her."

Sophie swallowed. She wasn't sure where this sudden bravery was coming from, but it gave her a chill as well as a thrill. Maybe this was the new Sophie Young.

"Speaking of which, I've read your email. I suppose we were asking for trouble by sitting Michael over there. Draft a memo to all staff that filing cabinets are to be kept locked at all times."

Sophie opened her notepad and scribbled down a note to create the memo and send to Kate for approval. Apparently, the new Sophie Young's outburst wasn't even noticed by Kate.

"Have you heard anything else?" Kate asked.

Sophie held her breath. She had, but she didn't want to say. The tension in the office was rising every day.

"I can see in your face that you know something," Kate added. "Spit it out, Sally."

Sophie winced at the name. She knew Kate was just doing it to push her buttons, but she wasn't quite brave enough to point it out yet.

"I think Michael is going to the pub with the web developers. He got himself invited to their weekly darts match."

"I'll kill them." Kate jumped to her feet.

Sophie stood up as well. "I'll talk to them."

"You? What could you possibly do?" Kate laughed and shook her head. "I want a team meeting first thing tomorrow morning, we need to have a conversation about fraternising with the enemy."

"I think he was just being friendly," Sophie pointed out.

Kate glared at her and slowly lowered herself back into

her seat. "Don't go soft on me. You've only just stopped stammering when I talk to you. Michael is fishing for information. He's not trying to make friends, he's not trying to improve his darts game, he is doing exactly what you are doing. Spying and reporting back. Don't be so naive as to think otherwise. You're dismissed."

"But—"

"Meetings don't book themselves." Kate gave her a final, cold stare.

Sophie nodded. She knew that any argument she made now would fall on deaf ears. She turned and walked out of the office.

At her desk, she opened a new memo template and stared at it blankly. She was desperate to clear the atmosphere, but she didn't know how to do so. Speaking to Kate seemed out of the question, especially lately. Kate seemed temperamental at the best of times, but it was getting worse each day. Sophie knew that the stress was getting to her, but she didn't know what she could do to help. Or if Kate would even accept her help.

Sophie chanced a glance through the office window. Kate was holding her head in her hand as she read something off her laptop screen. Stress was practically radiating from her. Sophie wished there was something she could do, but she guessed she'd be unwelcome anyway. Maybe it was best to steer clear. But she didn't know if she could do that, either; her instinct was to help where she could.

Everything seemed so complicated. On one side, she had Kate. On the other, Georgina. Both presented their unique problems. And Sophie was stuck in the middle.

CHAPTER NINETEEN

"AND, suddenly, I was uninvited from the darts tournament," Michael said. He poured himself another glass of wine and gestured the bottle towards Georgina.

She nodded her head and watched as he topped up her glass. "Well, that was to be expected."

"Normally I wouldn't mind, but I did genuinely want to play darts. I wanted to impress them with my skills. I played up the dumb American thing and suggested I didn't know what darts were."

She chuckled. "Ah, but it's us and them now. You're not in the right group."

He let out a fake sigh. "Who knows, I might have hidden talents. I might be the very best darts player in all of London. And now, we'll never know."

"It's a terrible loss, I'm sure," she drawled with a smirk. She looked at her plate with regret. The food was delicious, perfect ingredients and wonderfully cooked. Yet she couldn't bring herself to eat. Her mind was consumed by a certain person. A person she knew she shouldn't be thinking about.

"So," Michael whispered. "Sophie Young."

Georgina tilted her head up and looked at him. She shouldn't be surprised that he had guessed. He knew her inside out. But that didn't mean she was going to admit anything that would confirm his suspicions. "What about her?" she asked.

"I've seen the way you look at her," he said.

"Don't be ridiculous, Michael." She picked up her fork and stared down at the plate. She'd have to be more careful in the office. She didn't want to get a reputation for undressing the junior administrator with her eyes.

He chuckled. "Fine, fine."

She let out a sigh. As much as it frustrated her to admit, maybe she needed to talk about it. Keeping it bottled up certainly wasn't helping her any. She lowered her fork to her plate and looked around the room to check they weren't being overheard. "I must have a type, Michael."

"A type?"

"Yes. Naive young women with appalling dress sense. That kind of type."

"Corruptible?" he questioned with a waggle of an eyebrow.

"Michael!" she admonished, though she found herself smiling at the thought.

"So, you *are* interested?"

She picked up her glass and looked at the wine as she thought about the question. "She's intriguing," she admitted.

Intriguing wasn't all Sophie Young was. Something was drawing Georgina to her, and she seemed completely unable to stop herself. She knew it was wrong, stupid even.

"Jessica is my friend—"

Georgina glared at him. "Jessica left me. It's over, Michael," she reminded him.

"I know, I just…" He lowered his knife and fork. "This, whatever it might be with Sophie… it's not to get back at Jessica, is it? Because that's not fair to either of them."

Georgina sipped her wine and frowned in concentration, trying to answer the same question she had been asking herself.

"I know. And, despite my annoyance at being lectured, let me assure you that it's not my intention to use Sophie to make Jessica jealous. Besides, Jessica is off in Africa saving starving orphans. I'm sure she won't be calling up to check in on who I might be seeing. Especially considering we are very much broken up. She made that abundantly clear. And, ultimately, Sophie declined my offer of dinner. Which is why I'm here with you and not her. So, maybe this whole conversation is moot."

Michael pulled a face. "Oh, and here I thought it was my charming company."

Georgina lowered her glass and smiled at him. "Maybe a little of both," she allowed.

He returned the smile. "So, she turned you down? Is she back with the boyfriend?"

She shook her head. "No, she thought dinner wasn't appropriate. To be honest, I think Kate is the problem."

Michael picked up his knife and fork. "Yes, I did wonder if there was something going on between her and Kate."

She spat out a laugh. "I didn't mean it like that! Kate treats the girl like dirt. Something going on between them? That's absurd. I really don't know where you get these ideas from."

He gave her a knowing look. "Kate treats her like dirt? A bit like you did with Jessica at the beginning? And you may say it's absurd, but I saw the attraction between you and Jessica long before you did. I have an eye for these things. Lesbian May-December romances, can spot them a mile off."

"May to Dec—!? How dare—"

"Deny it all you like, but Kate looks at Sophie the way you looked at Jessica. And the reverse is true as well."

"Impossible. Kate's…" She trailed off as she considered his words. Kate did seem to have bisexual leanings. And maybe she did employ some of Georgina's behaviours with Jessica. She had pushed the girl in much the same way. But Kate wasn't Georgina, and she knew that gave her the advantage.

"Even if Kate did have feelings for Sophie," Georgina said, "she'd never act on them. She doesn't have the courage to become involved with someone of Sophie's age. She may be one of the big names in marketing here, but she's all about her image. She wouldn't risk the gossip."

"You don't mind the gossip?" Michael enquired.

Georgina grinned devilishly. "They can say whatever they like about me. If my relationship with Jessica taught me one thing, it's that life is made for living."

CHAPTER TWENTY

Sophie closed her eyes and counted to five. It had been the week from hell. Things had gone from bad to worse, and the cherry on top: Jonathan was officially signed off work for another month. Sophie was no longer Kate's temporary PA, she *was* Kate's PA. Except, she wasn't being paid for it.

Georgina and Michael remained in the Red Door offices as Yannis dropped in for impromptu meetings every other day. Georgina and Kate were at each other's throats constantly. Any pretence of kindness had well and truly vanished. Now it was more like outright war.

Every time Yannis visited, he threw Sophie's meticulously planned schedule for Kate out of the window. And most of the time he made sizeable changes to the direction of the campaign. He was a nice guy, but a part of Sophie had started to hate him.

Despite Yannis agreeing to see a pitch from each company and work with only one, he was frantically trying to wow investors. And for that, he needed whomever would give him what he needed at the time. A logo, a wireframe mock-up, a drafted press release. His demands meant Mastery and Red Door were working together on the project. Even if it was the project before the project.

Sophie found herself longing for the good old days when no one knew her name. Even if Kate did call her a variety of names starting with *S*. Even if each grew more outlandish the more frustrated Kate became.

She finished counting to five and opened her eyes. Kate stared back at her, obviously wondering if she had gone insane.

"You want me to lie?" Sophie asked.

"Are you really going to tell me that you've never lied, Sophie?" Kate asked.

"Kate, I—"

"Save it. I want you to go over there and tell Georgina exactly what I just told you."

"Kate, I'm really not comfortable telling—"

"I wonder how comfortable you'll feel when you're unemployed?" Kate asked. Her unwavering stare scared Sophie into swallowing hard.

Sophie was getting to know Kate and her working practices better as the days wore on. She knew that Kate would never actually fire her over such a matter. And she knew that Kate knew that she knew that. But Kate was also well aware that Sophie was still scared of her, and she wasn't afraid to use that advantage. Especially when Kate was as determined as she was at that moment. Sophie's eyes flickered down to her hands where they fidgeted in her lap.

"I'll take your silence to mean that you'll do as I say?" Kate asked. She picked up her pen. "Now?"

Sophie nodded. She quickly stood up and left Kate's office. She was beginning to seriously wonder if Yannis was going to get a campaign out of either agency. Georgina was starting to live up to the rumours of her difficult nature, too.

A couple of staff members from Mastery had been flown over, Georgina claiming that the Red Door staff were unable to provide her with the resources that she needed. But that didn't stop her from ordering Red Door staff to work on projects for her, often without informing Kate first.

As a result, Kate's mood had gone from bad to worse. Sophie had called Jonathan and asked for advice on how to help. She couldn't stand to watch Kate suffer, and she was desperate to support her through the stressful times. Even if Kate did pretend to forget her name and spoke down to her, something in Sophie was determined to help.

He'd joked that Kate maintenance wasn't another facet of the job, but he'd given her some tips. And so, Sophie started scheduling scalp massages and providing Kate with headache medication when she noticed a clenched jaw of pain.

Despite the drama, Kate and Georgina somehow kept up the insane illusion that they didn't want to kill each other when in public. Wide smiles and friendly chuckles would make the average bystander think that nothing untoward was happening. However, just beneath the pleasant veneer, both women were constantly scheming.

They reversed each other's decisions by going directly to the team, or by making Sophie do it.

On top of everything else, Georgina was still being nice to Sophie. And she was the only one. All the Mastery and Red Door staff were too busy to notice her. Everyone was deeply embroiled in office politics, and Sophie was being used by a pawn by more than one party.

But Georgina never asked Sophie what Kate was up to. And she never asked Sophie to lie for her, even though they both knew that if Georgina pressured her to do so, Sophie would cave in an instant.

Sophie half-heartedly knocked on Georgina's open office door. The last thing she wanted to do was to lie, but there really was no other option.

"Come in, Sophie," Georgina called out to her.

Sophie walked in. She fidgeted with her hands as she approached the desk. Georgina was writing and didn't look up at her.

"Kate w-wanted me to tell you that—"

"That the copy for the television ad has been completed?" Georgina guessed. She glanced up at Sophie.

Sophie nodded.

"Presumably, she wants me to look at it and find the deliberate fault or faults therein so she can be assured of my distraction while she makes changes to the website mock-up that I approved this morning?"

Sophie felt her knees go weak. A cold sweat broke out on her forehead.

Georgina smiled. "Don't worry, your boss is only doing exactly what I would do if our positions were reversed. Consider your message passed on. I'll look suitably surprised when the copy changes come to light."

"Thank you so much." Sophie breathed a sigh of relief.

Georgina leaned back in her chair. "Well, I have to admit that I'm only being kind for my own benefit." She offered a lopsided grin. "Hoping that you might have reconsidered my dinner invitation. I'd love to talk more about your career plans. Over a good meal accompanied by fine wine, of course."

Sophie bit her lip. Part of her wanted to. Georgina was the only person in the office treating her with any kindness at the moment, but she knew that the fallout from Kate would be immense. She'd taken on the task of helping Kate deal with the stress of Georgina. Accepting a dinner invitation would make the whole situation worse.

"I'm really sorry, I can't."

Georgina smiled and leaned forward. "I suspected as much, but I had to try."

"I better get back." Sophie indicated the way out of the office with her thumb.

Before Georgina had a chance to reply, Sophie rushed out. It wasn't the first time Georgina had hinted towards a dinner invitation. Each time she did, Sophie felt her resolve crumble a little more.

As she approached her desk, she could see Kate pacing in her office. Kate gestured for her to come in. Sophie let out a deep sigh and walked into the office.

"Well?" Kate demanded as soon as Sophie was within earshot.

"I told her."

"Good. Good, well done, Sophie." Kate grinned for a

moment. Then she looked at Sophie and shook her head. "I'm fairly sure I told you to burn that cardigan."

It wasn't the first time that Kate had made a disparaging comment about her dress or her looks. In fact, they were becoming more frequent the more stressed Kate became. Sophie ignored them. She wasn't about to change a thing about herself to appease Kate. And she was confident that she had the law on her side. Not that she would ever dream of going that far. She was sure that Kate simply employed the tactic as a power play, trying to push Sophie into place.

What Kate didn't seem to grasp was that she didn't need to manipulate Sophie. While Sophie had made it clear that she disliked office politics, she'd also made her position clear. She would side with Kate. Kate was her employer.

Getting closer to Kate had only served to reinforce Sophie's opinions on the woman. Up close, Kate was just as impressive, intelligent, and creative as Sophie had imagined. Working alongside her, seeing how her mind functioned, was incredible. Sophie felt like a sponge soaking up knowledge and ideas.

And the inspiration couldn't have come at a better time. Matt had moved out, and the apartment was a lonely reminder of their sham relationship. Sophie had buried herself in work, taking home as much as possible and using it to hone her own creative instincts and design skills.

Kate's mobile phone beeped, alerting her to a schedule notification. She snatched up the phone and frowned.

"Why do I have a facial booked for this afternoon? I don't know what you were thinking booking it for today."

"But you asked—" Sophie attempted.

"Why would I ask for it today?" Kate shook her head. "Useless," she mumbled.

Sophie flushed with anger. This wasn't the first time that Kate had blamed her for something that obviously wasn't her fault. She understood that Kate was under a lot of stress, but she didn't acknowledge the assistance Sophie was giving her. Instead she took it for granted and continued to push her.

"And my lunch isn't going to deliver itself to my desk. Off you go."

Sophie glared at Kate for a split second before storming from the office. She grabbed her purse and headed over to the elevators.

Sophie hated Kate's habit of taking out her anger on the nearest person who was most likely to take it. Especially as that person was always Sophie herself.

But even when Kate was at her very worse, Sophie still couldn't bring herself to dislike her. Sophie felt a strange pull towards Kate. She had been her idol for many years. As soon as Sophie was old enough to understand how business and marketing worked, she had become fascinated with Red Door and Kate's rise to power.

And yet, Kate seemed to be doing her best to keep Sophie at arm's length. Sometimes they would share moments, just the two of them in the office late at night, Sophie providing headache pills and the solution to a problem that had been bothering Kate. Kate would smile and tell her she was brilliant. All would be right in the world… until a moment later when Kate would realise what she had said and deliver a quick verbal blow, berating Sophie for something else entirely.

Sophie found it infuriating. She was a woman in a male-dominated industry, working for a woman who had managed to climb to the top. To be treated so badly was frustrating. Especially when Sophie had so much respect for Kate.

But Kate was completely consumed, worrying about Georgina and her plans. Kate spoke about Georgina like she was the devil herself.

Which was funny when Sophie considered how scared she had been of Georgina that first day. Georgina's reputation struck fear into the hearts of most juniors within the industry. Sophie had been sure that she would be eaten alive and spat out by Georgina within a few hours of her arriving at Red Door.

Instead, she did her best to keep Sophie out of the office politics. And she was willing to help her get ahead. She'd looked at some of Sophie's designs, spoken with her about her ideas. Georgina had been nothing but kind to her from day one.

The elevator doors opened. Sophie stared into the empty elevator cart for a moment.

Why am I saying no to an opportunity to learn from Georgina Masters? For Kate's sake? It's just a dinner. A chance to learn and better myself. To be better at my job. If Kate won't give me that chance, then I have the right to speak with Georgina.

She turned away from the elevator and walked across

the office. She took a deep breath and raised her hand to knock on Georgina's open office door.

"Georgina?" she asked softly.

Georgina raised her eyebrow in curiosity.

"Is that dinner invitation still available?"

CHAPTER TWENTY-ONE

IN ALL HER years at Red Door, Kate had never been distracted by the view of the city. She'd often used it to impress clients, as real estate in Farringdon didn't come cheap. But the view had never preoccupied her. Until now.

Now, she was happy to stare at the blend of old and new buildings that made up the London skyline. Anything to take her mind off what was happening within her office.

She'd be the first to admit that she had no idea working with Mastery would be quite so demanding. Of course, she had known that it wouldn't be easy. She knew from the start that Georgina was there to try to acquire the Atrom contract.

Now, Georgina was making her presence felt every single day. Her ideas, whispered in Yannis's ear, threw Kate's plans into chaos. Georgina's staff were taking up valuable desk space, and Georgina didn't think twice about ordering Kate's own staff to complete small jobs for her.

Normally, Kate wouldn't have held back, but the situation was fraught. Yannis was on edge, and that made everyone on edge. He demanded more and more each day, effectively sending both Mastery and Red Door into a frenzy to try to provide for and anticipate his needs.

Georgina had nothing to lose. She didn't need the Atrom account. Stealing it away would obviously be a coup for her, but she didn't need it to survive. On the other hand, Kate needed Atrom. And so, her job was twice as hard.

Instead of just being able to focus on the work of creating a campaign for Yannis, she had to manage Georgina as well. She had to investigate and second-guess everything. She had to keep in touch with Yannis, seeking out any information he may be willing to impart about his relationship with Georgina.

Of course, Yannis was oblivious to the all-out war that was happening between the two women. As far as Yannis was concerned, he was building a car and had employed the services of two expert marketing agencies to help him.

On top of everything, Jonathan was out of action, and she was having to manage with Sophie Young as her new assistant.

For some reason, Kate couldn't get Sophie out of her head. She found herself thinking about her, even staring at the girl as she sat at Jonathan's desk. It didn't help that the girl was gleefully leaping over invisible boundaries. Somehow, Sophie knew exactly when to offer headache medication, deliver an extra coffee, book in a massage. It was almost as if the girl knew what she was thinking.

Jonathan was a wonderful assistant; he did everything that Kate asked of him. But Sophie seemed to know the things Kate didn't ask. She knew when a late night was on the cards and to order food to be delivered. She knew when the persistent headache required a change in schedule to give Kate some breathing time.

Kate found it disconcerting. She wasn't used to someone predicting and fulfilling her every need. And so, she pushed Sophie away. She didn't want to become reliant on her kindness. The sooner she could push Sophie back into her nervous role as a junior, the better. But nothing seemed to work. She'd called the girl every name beginning with *S* under the sun, and Sophie just ignored it. She insulted her clothes, her hair, told her to stop smiling, to smile more. Anything to get a reaction. But nothing worked, and Sophie kept up with her self-appointed job description of being Kate's champion and her caregiver.

Kate was caught in a dilemma. She'd considered moving Sophie to another role within the company, somewhere far away from her. But she felt greedy; she wouldn't tell anyone, but she wanted more of the girl's soothing compassion. She was stuck in a circle of promising herself just one more day of care before finally sending Sophie away.

She pressed the intercom button on her phone. "Sophie, come in here, please."

She had to snap out of whatever it was that had her in its grasp. Staring out of the window wasn't going to help her get the campaign back on track.

"Yes, Kate?" Sophie asked as she entered the office. She stood in front of Kate's desk, poised with her notepad and pen, as usual.

"I need you to book the function room in the Winter Garden for the soft press launch. Yannis wants it as soon as possible, like tomorrow. I'm trying to explain to him that if he does that, then no one will come. Not everyone is as excited about his new project as he is. And they presumably have lives." Kate rubbed at her forehead tiredly. "We need to find a compromise."

"Would you like me to tentatively ask the Winter Garden for their availability, and then ask some of the attendees the same thing?" Sophie offered. "I could scope out the nearest date that the space is free, as well as a date when people would be able to attend."

Kate smiled and nodded. "Yes, that would be perfect. This is only a soft launch, just some industry insiders to get thoughts and feedback. It doesn't have to be a big deal; an afternoon event would do if time is an issue. You have the list of attendees."

Sophie scribbled some notes down. Kate looked at her and felt a pang of guilt for the comment she had made earlier about her attire. Sophie didn't deserve that. But Kate simply couldn't stop herself from lashing out.

"Will we be providing food? Should I call the caterers?"

"Yes, Yannis wants this as soon as possible, so he can pay for it. Free food and drink should get a few more people to come along, maybe even cancel existing arrangements."

Georgina walked in through the open door. "Wonderful idea," she said, not concerned about admitting to her eavesdropping.

"I'm glad you agree," Kate said.

"I was literally about to suggest the same thing,"

Georgina replied. "And I'm afraid I have to cancel our meeting this evening."

Kate couldn't say she was unhappy to cancel the meeting. A little less time with Georgina was a welcome thing. She accessed her schedule. "No problem, how is tomorrow at eleven for you?"

"I believe I'm free." Georgina sauntered over to the sideboard to look at the pictures on display. "Send me a request, and I'll accept it if I can."

Kate sent an invite, eager to get it done so Georgina would leave. She hated how the woman strolled into her office uninvited, how she would touch her personal effects.

"It's quiet in the office, so I'm leaving now," Georgina said, still looking at pictures. "That is, if you can spare Sophie?"

Kate looked from Georgina to a blushing Sophie with confusion. "I can spare her, but why would you need her?"

"We're having dinner," Georgina said. She looked at Kate with an almost wicked smile.

"O-oh, I see." Kate hated the shock in her tone. "Well, yes, we're done here. You can go now, if you wish," she addressed Sophie.

Sophie looked from one woman to the other and then gestured towards her desk. "I'll... just..." she mumbled before rushing out of the door.

Georgina watched her leave. She looked over her shoulder at Kate. "I hope you don't mind?"

Kate did mind. She minded very much. But she knew to voice her displeasure would simply give Georgina more ammunition, and Lord knew the woman didn't need any more. There was also the chance that she was simply stringing Sophie along because she knew it would annoy Kate. If she acted indifferent, then maybe Georgina would let Sophie go sooner.

"No, it's fine, obviously." Kate waved her hand with feigned boredom and returned her attention to her laptop.

"Good, we'll see you in the morning." Georgina walked out of the office.

Kate pretended to focus on her screen, but her eyes drifted to Sophie's desk. She watched as Georgina waited for Sophie to gather her things. Together, they walked across the office towards the elevators.

"'We'll see you in the morning'," she repeated Georgina's words in a mocking tone. "Who does she think she is?"

CHAPTER TWENTY-TWO

Sophie nervously fidgeted her hands in her lap. They were in the back of Georgina's car service, heading back to her hotel. Georgina was busily answering emails on her iPhone.

Accepting the dinner invitation had been a moment of madness. One minute Sophie was thinking about how Kate's moods were irritating her, and the next she was saying yes to dinner with Kate's mortal enemy.

She wasn't even sure what kind of dinner it was. When Georgina first asked her to dinner, they'd spoken about Sophie's career in the sector. Georgina was willing to provide guidance and mentoring. But Sophie wasn't that naive. She had caught the wicked smile on Georgina's face.

And of course, she knew about Georgina's previous relationship with her ex-assistant. After the first dinner invitation, Sophie had decided to conduct a little online research into Georgina, to see what she might be getting herself into.

The gossip columns all had different stories, ranging

from Georgina having a midlife crisis to Jessica throwing herself at her wealthy employer. Sophie was surprised to read that Jessica stayed Georgina's assistant throughout most of their relationship. Jessica had even consented to the odd interview. In one she was quoted as saying she enjoyed working with Georgina. They had managed to separate their work and home lives and were happy in both, despite spending so much time together.

She wondered exactly how that would work. How was it possible to live and work with the same person and not want to kill them? Her own working environment with Kate was similar to Georgina and Jessica's. She pictured working a full day with Kate and then going home together. Suddenly, her mind drifted in a direction she was unfamiliar with. A mental image of Kate in a decidedly non-work-related scenario caused her breath to catch.

"Are you warm?"

Sophie turned to Georgina and frowned. "I'm sorry?"

"You're flushed," Georgina commented. "I was wondering if you were a little too warm?"

"N-no." Sophie shook her head. She had no idea where the sudden graphic images had come from. She was supposed to be having dinner with Georgina, and suddenly her brain was having an unexpected adventure of its own. Without her permission. She felt her cheeks flush hotter.

"Sorry, um… yes, maybe a little warm," she replied. Her choices were warm or blushing, and she didn't want Georgina quizzing her on that.

Georgina wordlessly adjusted the heating controls in her door panel. Slightly cooler air started to fill the car.

Sophie sucked in deep breaths as quietly as she could. It was clearly all the stress; her brain was finally having a meltdown. Yes, she admired Kate. But she didn't think of her boss like that.

"I thought we could order room service in my suite?" Georgina suggested. She returned to looking at her iPhone screen. "It will give us an opportunity to talk in private. I'm afraid I'm still paparazzi fodder after my break-up. I wouldn't want you to be dragged into all of that."

Sophie nodded. She looked down at her hands and continued to nervously fidget them. A small voice in the back of her mind had been wondering if Georgina intended to use dinner with her to somehow make Jessica jealous. Having seen some of Georgina's tactics at the office, she certainly wouldn't put it past her. Dinner alone in her room would be terrifying, but at least it put the fear of journalists snapping her picture to rest.

"Sophie?"

Sophie looked up. She realised Georgina hadn't seen the nod. "Oh, yes, sorry. Yes… yes, that's fine. Thank you."

Georgina tilted her head and regarded her with a soft smile before returning her attention to her phone.

Sophie looked out of the passenger window and shook her head. She sounded like an idiot. She just couldn't get her nerves under control. Every time she tried to calm down, her brain reminded her that she was on a date with Georgina Masters. At least, she thought it was a date. They would be alone in Georgina's hotel suite. That sounded like a date.

Suddenly, Sophie began to really worry how much of a

date it was. Would Georgina try to kiss her? Would she expect more from her? She could feel herself beginning to panic. The heat welled up in her cheeks again, and she struggled a little to breathe.

Out of the corner of her eye, she noticed Georgina reach out and adjust the air conditioning once more.

CHAPTER TWENTY-THREE

"WHAT ARE YOU DOING HERE?" Jonathan asked.

Kate blinked in surprise. "Is that any way to greet someone?"

"You hate hospitals," he said. "And you have an autoimmune disease."

Kate rolled her eyes and walked into the room. She placed a plastic bag on the side of his bed and began to unload its contents onto the bedside table.

"Yes, thank you, I'm quite aware of all that. But I'm here to see you, so at least pretend you are happy to see me." She placed a bag of grapes on the table. "I don't know if you like grapes. I don't know if people actually give people grapes when they are in hospital or if that is a myth perpetuated by some conglomerate of grape farmers."

"What's going on?"

She looked at him for a moment before returning her attention to the plastic bag. She'd bought half the shop. As much as she tried to convince herself it was kindness, it was actually just a stalling technique.

She licked her lips and then sat on the edge of the visitor chair beside his bed.

"You're good friends with Sophie, right?"

"Sort of close," he replied.

"Well? Are you or aren't you?" She wasn't about to make a fool of herself for no reason. She'd seen Sophie on her phone, presumably speaking to Jonathan. She'd also heard of the girl's visits to the hospital, so she assumed they'd become close.

"Yes, I'm friends with her. What's this about Kate?"

"I presume you know about her date with Georgina Masters?"

Jonathan slowly nodded.

"What do you know?" Kate fished.

"Nothing. Just that they are having dinner." Jonathan seemed hesitant to say too much. Kate couldn't blame him. She'd been in telephone contact with him every day, advising him of what was happening in the office. He was well aware of her stress levels, he probably thought she'd cracked. She might have for all she knew.

"Where are they having dinner?" she asked. "When?"

"I don't know," he replied. "Now, I suppose?"

She sighed and sat back in the chair. "I thought you were good friends. You don't seem to know anything."

"She sent me a quick text, we didn't go into details. Apparently, Georgina said she was happy to give her career advice, over dinner. This happened a while ago. Sophie said no initially, but for some reason she changed her mind."

Kate snorted a laugh. "Oh, career advice? Is that what

they call it these days? And why didn't she come to me if she wanted career advice? I am her boss."

"Have you made yourself available to her? Or have you just insulted her clothing and called her Sally?"

"She told you that?" Kate sat forward in her chair. "What else has she told you?"

"Nothing I'm willing to tell you. Look, Kate, what's this about?"

She swallowed and broke eye contact, suddenly interested in the terrible pattern of the floor tile. She didn't really know what it was all about. She'd been consumed by some intense urge to find information.

"I need you to report back to me. I need to know what happens on that date."

"I'm sorry, what do you mean?" Jonathan blinked, clearly worried for her mental well-being.

Kate sighed and pinched the bridge of her nose. "Catch up, Jonathan. Sophie is clearly being coerced by that bitter old sea hag. It's no secret that Georgina is happy to play dangerous office politics. Somehow, she has managed to pull Sophie into her plans, so we must look out for her."

"Must we?" he asked.

"Well, I say we, I mean you. Obviously, I can't be asking my millennial assistant about her cougar dates."

"Look, Kate, I'm sure Sophie is just fine—"

"Oh, come on. She's clearly being manipulated. Why on earth would Sophie willingly go on a date with Georgina Masters? She's straight, young—"

"Actually, she's not."

"Not what?" Kate frowned.

"Straight," he clarified.

"Sophie's gay? No, she had a boyfriend." Kate found herself surprised she knew that piece of information. She had members of staff she'd known for years and still didn't know a thing about their personal lives. Just last week she was invited to a twenty-fifth wedding anniversary of a person she didn't even know was married.

"She's bisexual, I think. Not that I think that's any of our business," he explained. "The bottom line is that I don't think she has been coerced by Georgina. She seemed happy about the dinner."

Kate felt all her anger vanish. She had been so sure that Georgina had been manipulating Sophie. Suddenly she felt empty.

"Well, then... I suppose I'm worried about Georgina corrupting her. Sophie is so young and naive. She doesn't know what she's getting herself into," she muttered.

Jonathan chuckled lightly. "She's not as naive as you think she is. If you looked a little harder, you'd see that there is a smart young woman underneath the nervous exterior. I think maybe you spend a little too much time complaining about her cardigans and not enough time getting to know her."

Kate sighed. She had been watching Sophie closely over the last few days, but maybe she hadn't really been seeing her.

"You've not fired her yet, so she must be a reasonable replacement for me," he pressed.

"She's not too terrible."

The truth was, Sophie had slid into the role like it had been built for her. Of course, she was receiving guidance from Jonathan, but the transition had been remarkably smooth.

"She's dedicated to her job, to you," he said. "She really respects you. Even though you're being you."

Kate glared at him. "Careful, I could break your other leg."

He smiled. "Seriously, Sophie only accepted Georgina's offer because she offered. If you offered, she would have been having dinner with you this evening."

Kate spluttered a laugh. "You make it sound like I want to have dinner with her!"

"Don't you?"

She looked at the intravenous drip. "How much pain medication are you on?"

"Sophie's a catch," Jonathan said. "I'm not surprised that Georgina asked her out. She's smart, funny—"

"I suppose you want to date her as well?" Kate sniffed and leaned back in the chair, her arms folded across her chest. "The girl is too much trouble, I may just have to move her back to accounts."

"You're acting like you're jealous," he pointed out.

"It might seem that way to you and your millennial hormones, but… I have a duty of care. As long as Sophie works for me, she's my responsibility. I'm looking out for her well-being, that's all."

"Right, of course." Jonathan chuckled.

"And, if Sophie does side with her new girlfriend during these difficult times of office turmoil, I'll be hearing about it from you. Won't I, Jonathan?" She stared at him.

"Absolutely, Kate," he agreed. "If Sophie tells me anything relevant, I'll let you know."

Kate didn't like his tone. Nor his smile. He presumably thought she was being ridiculous. Maybe she was. But the whole notion of Sophie spending time alone with Georgina terrified her. Terrified her so much that she had come to a germ-ridden hospital.

She swallowed and sat forward. "Anyway, how are you?"

He smiled. "Doing okay, nice to have a visitor. Now, I want to hear everything about the landing page fiasco."

CHAPTER TWENTY-FOUR

"ARE you sure I can't tempt you?" Georgina asked. She lifted the wine bottle from the ice bucket and looked at Sophie.

"I really shouldn't," Sophie said.

Georgina regarded her across the dining table. Ever since they left the office, Sophie had become distant and nervous. More nervous than usual. She had hoped that they'd gotten beyond the nerves, but it seemed that dining alone in the opulent private dining room of her hotel suite had brought them back tenfold. She needed to calm Sophie down before she hyperventilated and passed out.

"I'm not trying to get you drunk," Georgina reassured. "I actually chose a very sweet chardonnay. I noticed you have something of a sweet tooth."

Sophie blushed.

"Just half a glass?" Georgina asked. "Please?"

Sophie nodded. "Okay, but just half a glass."

"Wonderful." Georgina removed the linen napkin from her lap and placed it on the table. She walked over to

Sophie, where she poured out exactly half a glass, not wanting the girl to think she couldn't be trusted. "I think you'll like it. But if you don't, don't feel obligated to drink it."

She placed the bottle back in the ice bucket. Sophie bit her lip as she looked at the glass. Slowly, she lowered her cutlery and reached for the glass. She took a tiny sip. Her eyes lit up, and she smiled.

Georgina sat down. "So. You haven't told me much about yourself."

Sophie's blush deepened. "There's not much to tell."

"Oh, I beg to differ."

Sophie took another sip of wine. She lowered her glass and looked at Georgina. "I was born in Surrey, I'm an only child. My parents were both teachers, they're retired now. I've always loved marketing, I've wanted to work for Red Door for as long as I can remember."

"Because they are the best?" Georgina grinned.

Sophie hesitated and adjusted her glasses. "I suppose so. I'd never really thought about why. Red Door was just always… there. The subject of case studies at university, in the trade journals, in the press. It seemed that wherever I looked, there was Red Door."

"Few people possess the single-mindedness to go after what they want like that, it's a wonderful quality. One I think you undervalue." Georgina picked up her cutlery and continued to eat. "Why didn't you go into marketing after you graduated?"

"Money," Sophie answered simply. "There were a few jobs around, but they were all very low-paid. I'd been working part-time at a law firm to pay my way through university. They offered me a full-time job, and I couldn't really say no. Matt said that it…"

Georgina looked up as Sophie trailed off and stared at her plate.

"Matt said?" she pressed.

Sophie chuckled bitterly. "Matt said that we needed the money. He told me it was ultimately my choice, but I knew what he wanted me to do. He wanted me to take the better paying job. He told me that I could take a salary cut later, when we'd cleared our debts." Sophie reached for her wine glass and took another sip. "But you know what? Those were his debts. Not mine. And it's only now that I'm realising how much he played me. Oh, he was good, he always made me feel like I was making the decision. But I wasn't. He was manipulating me into whatever he thought was best."

Georgina raised her eyebrow at the outburst. She didn't think Sophie had it in her to just blurt out her anger like that. She had to admit, she found it intriguing.

"And all the while he was collecting those damned figurines," Sophie continued. "Despite the fact that we had no money. Every time he got paid a large commission payment, he'd blow it on his hobby. And I felt I couldn't say anything because he'd earned that money. He deserved to spend it on what he wanted. Even if that meant that my car was off the road for three months waiting for new tyres."

Georgina smiled. Sophie's rant was adorable. Of course, she felt terrible that the girl had been treated badly for so long. But she was away from Matt now and processing the time they had been together. Presumably she was revisiting conversations and seeing them in a whole new light.

Sophie's eyes widened. She looked up at Georgina. "I'm sorry, I shouldn't—"

"Why shouldn't you? He was clearly manipulating you. You just broke up with him, and you're processing events." Georgina drank some wine. "Please, continue. I find it fascinating."

Sophie shook her head. "We're… we're not here to talk about my boyfriend. Ex-boyfriend."

Georgina nodded. She didn't want to overstep. Sophie was clearly in a fragile state, and she didn't want to take advantage of that.

"No, we're not. We're here to talk about you. About your career," Georgina said. She lowered her cutlery to her plate and pushed it to one side. "If I could give you only one piece of advice, it would be to know where you want to go. Be precise. Think about what you want, and map a way to get there. That's not to say that your goal won't change over time, so don't hang onto it doggedly. Always check that it is still what you want."

Georgina lowered her gaze to the table. It was a speech she had given many times before. She'd often been invited to lecture on her success. But suddenly she was remembering the time she had given that very speech to Jessica. Out of the recesses of the past, she could see the conversation clearly.

"But I don't know what I want," Sophie replied, shaking Georgina from her memories.

Georgina reached for the wine bottle and topped up her own drink. She gestured the bottle towards Sophie.

The girl considered her wine glass for a moment before slowly nodding and pushing it across the table.

"The first question is to ask yourself what you want to do in your day-to-day job." Georgina poured Sophie another half a glass. "Do you want to be a designer? A developer? Do you want to manage clients?"

Sophie thought for a moment. "Well, I'm not a designer."

"I have to disagree. Some of the things you have shown me have been exceptional," Georgina pointed out.

Sophie blushed. "Well, I know a little, but I don't have the creativity to do it every day. And I'm not a developer. I like managing clients. I like building campaigns, getting the team together and brainstorming. Seeing something come from nothing."

"Maybe a project manager?" Georgina suggested. She placed the empty wine bottle on the room service trolley and put a fresh one in the ice bucket.

"Maybe," Sophie said.

"But that idea doesn't set you on fire?" Georgina chuckled.

"No, I suppose it doesn't."

"How about… managing director?"

Sophie's eyes widened. "M-me?"

"You."

"But… how? I can't! I mean… no, I couldn't run a company."

Georgina smiled at the panic in Sophie's eyes. "I really don't see why not. A managing director organises people, you do that. They liaise with clients, you do that. They present ideas, you've seen that done. They know their limits, you just told me that your design skills aren't perfect, so I believe you can do that, too."

"But how would I own a company? It's crazy."

"You freelance for a while, in your own time, build up a client base. Or maybe someone will offer you a role in a new division of an existing company."

Sophie looked at her curiously. Georgina raised her hands in surrender. "Don't worry, I'm not offering you a job. I may enjoy getting a rise out of Kate, but I'm not suicidal. It's just a suggestion, these things do happen. Company directors are good at spotting talent."

Sophie stared at her half-eaten plate of food, deep in thought.

Georgina watched her with interest. There was no denying it, the girl reminded her of Jessica. She wanted to look after her, protect her, guide her, and more.

She collected herself as sipped her wine. She had brought the girl here to discuss career options, nothing more. Sophie was in a vulnerable state, she had to keep her distance and focus on the work.

"All this talk is keeping you from enjoying your meal," Georgina observed. "You eat, and I'll talk about my favourite subject. Me."

Sophie laughed.

"I knew what I wanted to do from the moment I became aware of the concept of work," Georgina started.

———

Two hours later, and Georgina's best efforts to keep things professional were almost forgotten. They'd eaten dinner and dessert, and Sophie had soon started to loosen up. They'd taken their conversation to the living area and shared a sofa as they talked about the marketing sector.

Sophie's knowledge was impressive. She knew a lot about marketing, more than an ordinary graduate. It was clear that the work was a passion for her and Georgina found that intriguing. She found a lot about Sophie intriguing.

Somehow, they started talking about previous relationships. The wine clouded Georgina's judgement. She had to continually remind herself to keep her distance.

"So, you worked together?" Sophie asked.

"Yes, we'd been working together for a while by that point. The idea of being apart the whole day, after spending all that time together, wasn't pleasant. I suggested it, I didn't think Jessica would agree. But she did. She laid down sound ground rules. She didn't want it to be a secret. She didn't want me to treat her differently." Georgina smiled. "Of course, I didn't want to lose the best assistant I'd ever had."

Sophie nodded. "Sounds amazing, you two must have been formidable."

"We were," Georgina mused. She shook her head slightly. "But that's all over now. We parted amicably, and now she is off, conquering the world."

"I'm sorry you broke up," Sophie said.

"These things happen." Georgina hoped she sounded braver than she felt. "But let's not talk about me all night. You were saying earlier that you're going to be the new Sophie Young?"

Sophie beamed. "Yep. I'm a work in progress. I'm

trying to be braver. Not get so tongue-tied. I think being with Matt made me a weaker person. I mean, I was always a little weak. But I just kind of accepted whatever he told me. And after a while, I did the same with everyone else, too."

Georgina smiled in return. The girl was captivating. She couldn't help but feel proud at helping her out of her shell and into the world.

"And what will this new Sophie be like?"

"She won't stammer so much," Sophie said.

"That's a shame. It's pretty cute."

Sophie edged closer on the sofa to give Georgina a little swat on the arm. "She won't be so cute, either," she joked.

"I don't know, this new Sophie is sounding very bland." Georgina winked.

Sophie ignored her and continued to list her new traits on her fingers. "She'll be confident, brave, she'll have points to make and people will want to listen. She won't... fidget so much. And she'll have... a new wardrobe. And a new look."

"I'm not sure if I can approve of this," Georgina joked. "I won't recognise you."

"I'll still have my notepad and pen."

"Oh, well, then by all means. Go ahead."

"I need to go shopping for new clothes. That will stop Kate from making comments about what I wear."

Georgina bit her lip thoughtfully. She'd been in Kate's shoes. An easy way to bring someone down was to comment on their clothing, make a statement about their hair, forget their name. She rarely saw the other side of the coin, but here it was, sitting in front of her.

"You should change for you, not for anyone else."

Sophie nodded. "I want to change. I want a new haircut. I read an article about women who dump their partner and then get a new haircut. It's meant to be cathartic."

Georgina looked at Sophie's long blonde hair, currently down in soft curls. "You're not going to do anything drastic, I hope? Your hair is beautiful."

Sophie blushed. "Thank you. I-I wasn't sure what to do. I'm still in the early planning stages."

Without thinking, Georgina leaned forward and scooped Sophie's hair up in one hand. She held the handful of hair and regarded it thoughtfully.

"Your hair is thick, you could style it rather than cut it. You have many options," Georgina pointed out.

Her eyes flickered down, and she suddenly realised her face was inches away from Sophie's.

She saw Sophie staring at her. Sophie's eyes were fixed on her lips.

Georgina couldn't help herself. She slowly lowered her lips to Sophie's, giving her enough time to pull away if she didn't want to continue. The girl didn't move. Their lips met in a soft and gentle kiss. Georgina pulled back slowly and smiled reassuringly at Sophie.

She returned her attention to shaping Sophie's hair with her hands. Her hands that were now shaking slightly as a result of the kiss.

Her mind raced. She didn't know if she'd made a mistake

or not. It was ridiculous, but she felt somehow unfaithful towards Jessica. Even though Jessica had walked out on her. She pushed the thought to one side; she shouldn't be thinking about Jessica. Her focus should be on Sophie. Young, sweet Sophie who was trying to rebuild herself after a break-up.

"I think you should go for a shoulder-length bob," Georgina said. "Nothing too fierce, though. Then, if you like it, you can cut it shorter. But if you don't, you still have a lot of hair to work with."

"W-was the kiss… bad?"

Georgina let go of Sophie's hair and looked at her. "No, of course it wasn't bad."

"I've never kissed a woman before," Sophie admitted.

Georgina felt her mouth go dry at the thought. "Well, did you enjoy it?"

"Yes," Sophie breathed.

"Then, I suppose we ought to do it again," Georgina suggested.

Georgina was surprised at the speed with which Sophie reacted. The girl held her face in shaking hands and pressed her lips to Georgina's for the second time. The kiss was pleasant but uninspiring, and Georgina wasted no time in deepening it and sliding her tongue along Sophie's lower lip. Sophie moaned and opened her mouth. Georgina smiled into the kiss as she waited for Sophie to be brave enough to explore with her own tongue.

A few tremulous moments passed, Georgina's hands on the soft material of Sophie's ever-present cardigan as she waited for the girl to acclimatise. Then, Sophie tentatively licked Georgina's upper lip. Georgina responded by pressing her own tongue to Sophie's. She was pleased with the loud moan she received in response.

Despite the alcoholic haze, Georgina knew she had to end things soon. She knew it wouldn't be long before events escalated. She didn't want to go too far until she was certain of Sophie's feelings, as well as her own. Sophie was as pure and innocent as she appeared, and Georgina had no desire to rush her into something she wasn't ready for. She ended the kiss and leaned back with a smile.

"Oh, I think you've kissed a woman before," Georgina joked to lighten the mood. "You're just trying to tease me."

Sophie blushed but smiled widely. "You're being kind."

Georgina took Sophie's hand. "As much as I'm enjoying these developments, I think we should probably call it a night. I've had nearly a bottle of wine to myself, and my ability to say no is severely depleted."

Relief flashed in Sophie's eyes, and Georgina felt pleased with her decision.

Sophie nodded. "I… I really had a wonderful night."

"So did I," Georgina replied. "We should do this again."

"I'd like that."

They stood up together, and Sophie gathered her belongings.

Georgina looked out the window of the hotel room into the darkness. "How will you get home?"

"I'll walk to the station and then get the Underground." She looked at her watch. "I'll catch the last train, I'll be fine."

Georgina watched as Sophie put her coat on. She felt a

lump in her throat. The idea of her walking in the city so late was alarming.

"I'll call you a car," Georgina decided.

"No, I'm fine, really."

"It's late. A car is much better," Georgina argued.

"I don't want a car. I like travelling at night, it's quiet and peaceful. I'm careful, don't worry."

Echoes of Jessica reverberated off the walls of Georgina's mind. She realised she was already trying to take control of Sophie in an uncomfortably similar way. She opened her mouth to argue her point but slowly closed it again. Maybe this was a part of the problem. Her need for control, her desire to be in charge.

"Will you send me a message, so I know you're home?" Georgina asked, deciding that compromise was best.

Sophie looked at her and smiled. "Sure."

Georgina wanted to kiss her goodnight, but she worried that doing so would lead to more. Her thoughts were muddled, but she desperately didn't want to press Sophie into anything.

"So, I'll…" Sophie gestured to the door. The hesitation was back, and the blush was starting to tinge her cheeks.

Georgina placed a soft kiss on Sophie's cheek. "Message me," she told her.

"I will," Sophie promised.

Georgina leaned heavily on the hotel room door as she watched Sophie walk into the corridor. She waited for the elevator to arrive and for Sophie to disappear from sight. Once she had, Georgina entered her suite and closed the door. She rested her back against the door and closed her eyes. She had no idea what she was doing. Her emotions were at war. She couldn't tell if she liked Sophie, or if she was simply trying to replace Jessica.

While her dinner invitation had always been about career advice, she had to admit that she had hoped for more. Now it had happened, she wasn't sure if she was happy about it.

CHAPTER TWENTY-FIVE

Sophie knocked on the hospital door.

"Come in," Jonathan called out.

She opened the door and walked in.

Jonathan grinned at her. She knew she had a wide smile on her face. She'd been happy all morning, thanks to her wonderful date with Georgina the previous evening. The only problem was, she had no one to share the news with. She'd yet to tell anyone about her break-up with Matt. But she did have one person she could tell.

"Please tell me you brought the chocolate croissant," Jonathan begged.

"I brought the chocolate croissant," she confirmed, then looked at him. "But I don't know how you're going to eat it." While some of the plaster casts had been removed, Jonathan's arm was still solidly encased.

"I'll manage. Don't you worry."

She put the paper bag on the table, took out the croissant and coffee, and placed them in front of him. "Is that okay?"

"Perfect." He reached for the coffee with his free arm and took a sip. "You're a life saver."

She smiled and sat on the visitor chair. "So, I wanted to tell you about last night."

"Is this skimmed milk?"

"Yes, does it taste different?"

"No, just checking."

Sophie frowned. She always got him skimmed milk; it seemed strange that he'd ask.

"Anyway," she started, "last night…"

"Could you get me that magazine?" He pointed to the bedside table.

She picked up the magazine and put it on the bed in front of him.

"So, Georgina—"

"Sophie!" Jonathan interrupted, and then shook his head. In a calmer voice, he said, "Maybe you shouldn't tell me?"

"You told me you wanted to hear everything." Sophie frowned. "What's going on? You're acting weird."

Jonathan put the coffee cup down and sighed. "Kate came here, and she kinda asked me to spy on you." He winced. "She thinks Georgina coerced you into a date, and now Kate wants me to report back to her."

"What the hell?" Sophie jumped to her feet and started to pace the room.

"But," Jonathan suggested, "if you don't tell me anything, then I can't tell *her* anything."

"That is ridiculous!" Sophie said as she paced. "I can't believe this. Does she literally think I'm a child? She thinks that Georgina *coerced* me? What does that even mean? Is it so crazy to think that Georgina might actually be interested in me? And what the hell does Kate Kennedy know about my love life? What does she know about me at all? I'm practically invisible to her."

Jonathan toyed with the lid of the coffee cup. "She's just worried about you."

Sophie spun to stare at him. "You're defending her? Oh my God, Jonathan. Come on."

"I know it sounds bad, but this is how Kate does things. She's not good at not knowing information, and she's not good at being sneaky. So, she gets people to find out for her."

"It's called spying, Jonathan." Sophie put her hands on her hips.

"I know," he admitted. "Look, just sit down a minute. You're giving me a neck ache."

She walked back to the chair and sat down, though her hands still fidgeted anxiously. She couldn't believe that Kate had asked her only friend at Red Door to spy on her.

"I can't believe you agreed to spy for her, she's… she's a monster," Sophie whispered.

"She isn't a monster," Jonathan defended.

"She is. She's so… so mean! She won't come here to visit you, she's horrible to everyone. I don't even know why I wanted to work for her." Sophie could feel tears forming in her eyes. Her day had started off so well, and now Kate was ruining everything, without even being there.

"Right, firstly, she can't come and visit me because she

has an immunodeficiency, it's not common information. In fact, it's extremely private so don't tell anyone. But she calls me every day to check I'm okay. She's paying me fully while I recover, and she's even paid me compensation, though she doesn't need to. I know she doesn't show it, but she does care."

Sophie looked at him in surprise. "She's... sick?"

"I can't say too much, I've said too much already."

Sophie put the surprising information to the back of her mind and focused on her anger. "She... she never asks how you are..."

"She doesn't need to, we're in contact all the time."

"You never told me that," she complained.

"You never asked," he replied. "Look, I know Kate constructs this mask, and I know how hard it is to see through it. But I think you do. You know she's not like that really. She's just afraid to show any kindness to anyone, she doesn't want it to be perceived as weakness."

Sophie lowered her head and bit her lip in thought. He was right. Deep down she did know that Kate wasn't as mean as she made out. She'd seen evidence of Kate's kindness while she had worked for her. Kate just kept up an act to keep people at bay.

"But she asked you to spy on me," she whispered angrily.

"She is genuinely worried about you," he said. "I know she has gone about it the wrong way, but she wants to make sure that you're okay. Look at it from Kate's point of view: you're her employee, she's responsible for you. She assigned you to be the liaison with Georgina. Georgina, who has broken up with her young assistant who looks remarkably like you."

Sophie shook her head. "It's not like that."

"I'm not saying it is, I'm saying that Kate is just worried about you. It's not that she doesn't think you're capable, she's worried about Georgina."

Sophie opened her mouth and then closed it again. She hated to admit it, but it made sense. Not that it justified Kate's actions. If she was so interested, then she should ask her herself, not hide behind Jonathan. She couldn't believe that she had come and asked him—

"Wait," Sophie said. "You... you said she came here and asked you to report back on me?"

Jonathan picked up his chocolate croissant. "Did I? I mean—"

Sophie reached forward and snatched the croissant from his hand. "You did. You said she came here. You also said she can't come here because she has an immunodeficiency disorder. So, which is it?"

"Both."

She swallowed. "Kate... came here? Even though it could make her sick?"

"She was worried about you." Jonathan pointed to the bedside table. "Who did you think brought all the magazines, grapes, and cuddly toys?"

Sophie looked at the array of goods. It looked like someone had raided the hospital shop in a blind panic. It looked like Kate had been there.

"She was that worried?" Sophie asked.

"She was that worried," he confirmed.

"Well, she can't treat me like that. Or you, for that matter," Sophie decided. "And this spying has to stop. It just causes trouble."

Jonathan chuckled. "And you're going to tell her that?"

"As a matter of fact, I am."

CHAPTER TWENTY-SIX

KATE GINGERLY TILTED her neck from side to side. She felt the pressure of a trapped nerve constricting under her skin. She was thankful for small mercies, such as being able to take the last meeting of the day in her own office, in its comfortable armchairs.

John from IT rambled on about the new software he wanted to install. Kate made an effort to look like she was listening and actually cared. The upgrade was massively expensive, but she knew it was necessary. However, that didn't stop her from dragging John into her office to explain to her, in detail, why he required the software upgrade.

Giving the impression of understanding every single aspect of her business, no matter how technical or dull, was a fantastic way to save on unnecessary expenditures. All her employees knew that they would have to justify any expense, and therefore would only ask when they really needed something and understood the purchase enough to be able to defend it to her.

She was anxious for the meeting to be over. She was bored and had decided to approve the upgrade long before John opened his mouth.

She was also looking forward to her afternoon catch-up with Sophie. Things had been so hectic that she'd hardly seen the girl throughout the day. Kate was eager to find out what Georgina had been up to, what had happened over dinner. She hadn't yet decided if she would ask Sophie outright or wait to see what she offered up.

After what seemed like an eternity, John finally stopped speaking. His case was made, and Kate made a show of begrudgingly approving his request. He left the room looking victorious, which allowed Kate a moment to close her eyes and lean back in the armchair.

Of course, closing her eyes allowed Kate's overactive mind to scroll through her to-do list at top speed. Yannis had invited the agencies to another day at the track. The very thought of going back was enough to give her a piercing headache. She'd hated being there the first time, and that was before Jonathan was nearly killed. But with Georgina around, she couldn't afford to skip out on the invitation.

She heard a noise and opened her eyes. Sophie stood in front of her, pills in one hand, a glass of water in the other.

"Make me an appointment with Dr Warwick for the morning, eight o'clock if possible," Kate instructed. She took the pills and placed them in her mouth, washing them down with the water.

"Warwick?"

"It's on file," Kate replied, not willing to explain herself.

"I'll make the appointment," Sophie said professionally. She took the glass of water when Kate was finished and placed it on the coffee table. "I need to tell you that Georgina and I are… seeing each other. And, as such, I am not comfortable spying on the Mastery team."

Kate felt her head swim. "I see. Well, that escalated quickly." She wriggled her shoulder to try to release the pinched nerve. "Fine, I will assign someone else to be the liaison between the teams. I'd hate for our multimillion pound deal to affect your love life."

Kate was pleased to see a blush appear on Sophie's cheeks. She may be getting braver with each day, but Kate still had the ability to unnerve her.

"I suggest you be careful, Sophie. You're not the only pretty, young thing she's been seen with."

Sophie nervously fidgeted with her glasses. "Her relationship with Jessica was a legitimate relationship, it's not like it was a fling."

"Oh, I'm sure it was a genuine relationship. I'm sure it left a void that needed to be filled," she emphasised the last word and looked meaningfully at Sophie. "I just find the similarities fascinating."

Kate crossed her legs and picked some lint from her skirt. She looked up at Sophie who was looking a lot less confident.

"Have you booked the Winter Garden?" Kate asked, wanting to change the subject before she said too much.

"Yes," Sophie said. "Monday, as you suggested. All of the details are in your inbox."

Kate nodded. She fixed Sophie with a look. "Then I suppose you should leave for the day."

Sophie nodded. "I'll book your appointment and then I'll go." She turned and left the office.

Kate let out a long sigh as she stood and returned to her desk. She put her glasses on, wincing at her tense back muscles as she did. She began to dig through the heap of emails she had missed while stuck in meetings all day. Seeing the sheer volume that had stacked up caused her to sigh again. If only Sophie weren't liaising between the two agencies, perhaps she could have made a dent for Kate, at least taken care of the spam messages.

Sophie. Kate looked up at the girl. She didn't know why it bothered her so much that Sophie was seeing Georgina.

At first, she thought she was simply angry at Georgina for pushing boundaries. It almost seemed like the woman was deliberately dating Kate's assistant, knowing it would antagonise her. But Kate had to admit that it was more than that.

Not that she wanted to dwell on those thoughts; it was a dangerous area of repressed emotion to dive into. Sophie looked up, and they briefly made eye contact. Kate was the first to break away and look back at her computer.

CHAPTER TWENTY-SEVEN

SOPHIE HAD GIVEN up on taking minutes very soon after the meeting had started. She felt a headache forming behind her eyes and found herself sympathising with Kate who seemed to have the same problem. Sophie glanced at the clock on the meeting room wall, thankful that it was Friday and the day was nearly over. She only had to get through this last meeting and then she could go home and forget about work for two solid days.

She was glad she'd had the foresight to book the entire afternoon for the meeting. As expected, both Kate and Georgina had turned up thirty minutes late. She'd spent those thirty minutes sitting in the meeting room, making awkward small talk with Michael. She had desperately wanted Kate and Georgina to hurry up and show their faces, but now the meeting was underway, she wished they hadn't bothered turning up at all.

They'd manage to race through the actual agenda of the meeting in record quick time. As usual, they were stuck on the last item, any other business. In Sophie's experience, this section was an indicator that the meeting would be over within a couple of minutes, as other business was a rare thing. For Kate and Georgina, any other business was a time to point out everything that their counterpart was attempting to hide by not adding it to the agenda.

"I'm fairly certain I didn't sign off on this amount." Kate placed a sheet of paper on the table and slid it towards Georgina.

Georgina picked up the paper and looked at the dark red circles around its figures. "No, that was precisely what we agreed upon," she replied. "I remember it clearly because it was the same conversation where you suggested that we create an interactive email experience, and I worried that you'd lost your mind."

Kate opened her mouth to reply when Michael handed her his iPad. "Here's the email confirmation from you on those figures."

Kate took the iPad and read the email carefully. "No, this is my confirmation for the first design stage. There have been two subsequent design stages since then." She held the iPad out for Michael to take back. "I find it baffling how you seem to have to revisit the design studio several times, even when using your own people. And we're not even beyond wireframing yet. Maybe if you actually attended the design studio rather than attending lunches with Yannis's investors, you'd end up with something you liked. Rather than finding you dislike it when it heads into development, which is costly and frankly exhausting for the rest of us."

"Perfection isn't always easy to achieve," Georgina said.

"We're not used to putting out substandard work just to satisfy budgets and deadlines. I guess this explains how Red Door can operate with so few staff members."

Sophie heard Kate's slight intake of breath. She knew that Kate was immensely proud of the level of service and the quality of output that Red Door produced. Georgina taking a cheap shot at that was completely false and only served as a way to upset Kate.

She risked a glance at Kate's face and made a mental note to book an osteopath appointment to help with whatever neck and shoulder pain Kate was suffering from. She held herself painfully, and there was a dullness to her eyes. In the short time that Georgina had been at Red Door, she seemed to have successfully sucked the life out of Kate.

Sophie knew that Kate had given as good back, some of the time. And she knew that neither woman was innocent. But it was clear to Sophie that Kate was drained and exhausted. Georgina's continuing harassment of her was now just picking at a carcass.

Kate opened her mouth to reply, but Sophie quickly stepped in with a pleading look at Georgina. "How about we have a look at the previous design stages? See if there is anything we can salvage, maybe fix in post-production. There must be something we can use to move this project on."

Michael looked at her gratefully and nodded. "Yes, I think we might be able to work something out." He turned to look at Georgina. "Georgina, what do you think?"

Georgina hummed distractedly. "I suppose that would do."

"Great," Sophie said happily. "So, that's settled."

"I have yet to see the final copy for the broadsheet ads," Georgina said. She looked at Kate expectantly.

"Well, we can't place it until we know what the photo shoot has produced." Kate took off her glasses and put them on the table. "We need to know what space we have."

"I gave you a word count," Georgina argued.

"And I'm supposed to take your word on that? That's not how we work around here. We get the assets, and then the copywriter looks over what they have to work with. It's called teamwork."

"Oh, is it?" Georgina smirked. "I wasn't aware you'd heard of that, considering how you squirrel yourself away in meeting rooms with your team."

"Oh, not to worry. We're not wasting our time talking about you," Kate replied. "Anyway, back to the matter at hand. Your team will provide me with the final layouts and art assets, and then our copywriter will draw up the ad copy and we'll send it to you for review."

Sophie knew that it hadn't escaped anyone that Kate was not questioning, she was demanding. She anxiously watched to see what Georgina would say in response to Kate's bluntness.

"That's a relief," Georgina breathed. "Is it all right to assume your copywriter works a full day and won't disappear for hours at a time?"

Sophie winced. It was a clear dig at Kate's late arrival to a meeting when her morning doctor's appointment had overrun. Not that Georgina knew that was the reason for the delay.

Kate rolled her eyes. "My personal schedule is not answerable to you."

"It is when I'm left making excuses for you."

"I was two minutes late, I'm sure you coped admirably despite the dire situation," Kate replied.

"And I understand that you won't be available on Monday morning because you're being interviewed?" Georgina huffed out a sigh.

"Yes, it's a piece for the local free daily, it's about financial management in the office. You may want to read it," Kate jabbed.

"Fascinating. You know, I don't need to conduct interviews to increase my reach," Georgina commented offhandedly. "The press are falling over themselves to get to me. But, I suppose that might be because I'm actually of interest. My active social life, you know. The fact I can hold onto a partner for more than an evening."

Before Kate could reply, or punch Georgina, Michael jumped to his feet. "Okay, we need to make those phone calls before the end of the business day," he addressed his boss.

"And I need to confirm the menu with the caterer," Sophie said, rising to her feet as well.

Kate and Georgina remained seated, staring angrily at each other. Sophie wondered if they were about to launch themselves across the table and claw at the other. She looked at Michael, silently asking for assistance. He indicated the door with a tilt of his head.

"I-I'll type up the minutes and get them over to both

of you this evening," Sophie said, attempting to break the deadlock.

"Monday will be fine, Sophie," Kate replied.

"Speaking of Monday, Sophie, I need you to arrange a car for me after the press launch," Georgina requested.

"Already done," Sophie said, pleased that things seemed to be simmering down. Michael used the opportunity to leave the meeting room.

"Wonderful, and then, maybe dinner in the evening. I'll miss you over the weekend. We can finish our... conversation from last time." Georgina stared intently at Sophie.

Sophie couldn't believe that Georgina was being so brazen in front of Kate. She watched as Kate started to gather her things, averting her eyes from the two of them as she did. Once she had everything, she quickly stood up. "I'll see you both after the weekend," she said softly before leaving the room.

Sophie watched her leave before turning to face Georgina. "Did you ask me out in front of Kate on purpose?"

"Yes, of course." Georgina started to gather her things from the table.

"Why?" Sophie could feel anger flaring inside her. She couldn't believe the way Georgina had spoken to Kate. Of course, they had both been arguing, but Georgina had gone too far. And asking her out in front of Kate just seemed inappropriate.

"To annoy her. It can't have escaped your attention that Kate doesn't like us seeing each other." Georgina smiled at the fact.

"She... she's looking out for me." Sophie swiped her notepad from the table. "I wish you wouldn't speak to her like that."

"She's a big girl, she can cope." Georgina stood up. "So, dinner on Monday?"

Sophie clutched the notepad to her chest and stared at her feet. Her mouth contorted as she thought about the things Georgina had said to Kate.

Georgina took a step closer. "I apologise for my petty behaviour." She brushed a stray lock of hair away from Sophie's face. "Sometimes I go too far. It's a hard habit to break. Forgive me?"

Sophie felt her breath catch at Georgina being so close to her. She nodded her head slightly. "O-okay."

"Wonderful." Georgina caressed her check for a moment before stepping around her. "I have some things to tie up, and then I'm back home for the weekend. But I'll see you on Monday at the press event. I'll buy you a drink."

Sophie turned to face her. She adjusted her glasses. "The drinks are free."

Georgina chuckled and shrugged. "Apparently, I'm not very good with financial management." She winked as she left the room.

CHAPTER TWENTY-EIGHT

Kate stared at the form, her pen gripped tightly in her hand. Checking and signing audit forms all morning hadn't helped her headache at all. The words on the form seemed to merge into one large, black-and-white fuzz. She put the pen down and closed her eyes.

She massaged her temples to try to relieve some of the pain. She'd spent the entire weekend working, preparing for the soft press launch at the Winter Garden.

She'd been suffering back-to-back headaches for days, and despite practically bathing in antibacterial gel, she was sure she'd caught something in the hospital the previous week. Not that she was going to slow down, she couldn't afford to. Georgina would jump on any weakness.

The soft knock on the door made her wince. She looked up to see Sophie walk in. "I sent those minutes over to you," she said softly. "Can I get you anything?"

She knew the insinuation was that she looked like crap. She had to get herself together soon, for the launch event. Luckily, she knew that a change of clothes and fresh application of makeup in her office-based private bath-room would hide most sins. She just needed to get through a few hours, and then she could go home and enjoy a hot bath.

"Kate?" Sophie pressed.

She looked up at the girl and blinked. She'd forgotten she was there, the fog in her brain was mixing everything up.

"I'm sorry, what?" Kate asked.

Sophie frowned. "I asked if I could get you anything. Some coffee, maybe?"

"Can you get me some more headache pills?"

Sophie quickly shook her head. "No, it's only been two hours since you took the last ones."

Kate had forgotten she'd taken any. "Oh, yes," she said, pretending that she remembered.

"Kate, should I call your doctor?"

"That won't be necessary." Kate took a deep breath and stood up. "I'm just a little run-down. No need to worry. Now, I presume you have called the caterers, they are aware of the changes to the vegetarian numbers?"

Sophie bit her lip, clearly wanting to pursue the argu-ment. Luckily for Kate, she didn't. "Yes, I checked. I'm heading over there in a couple of minutes to check the screens and do a sound check. Is there anything you need? Do you want me to wait and travel over with you?"

Kate shook her head. "That won't be necessary."

"Kate, I'm worried… are you sure you're okay?"

She met Sophie's eyes with her own. Genuine concern radiated through. Kate thought about denying how terrible she felt, sending Sophie away. But part of her wanted to be honest, to reassure Sophie that she was okay.

"I'm just a little run-down…"

"I don't believe you. Something's bothering you. I see it in your eyes, it's more than just this battle with Georgina," Sophie said.

It unnerved Kate how accurate her assistant could be. "Sophie, I—"

"No, don't deny it," Sophie pushed. "I want to help. But I can't if you don't talk to me."

Kate opened her mouth to issue another denial but quickly closed it again. She was exhausted. That was the only feasible explanation for what she was about to admit.

"Some years ago, I was… I was involved in a car crash. It was a sports car, a super car, I suppose they call them. It came out of nowhere, travelling at a ridiculous speed and sent my car flying. I was okay, some minor injuries, but the memories are still there. Working on this project has reminded me of that time, and I'm having trouble sleeping. That's all."

Sophie's eyes had widened as Kate explained. "So, Dr Warwick…?"

"Is a therapist," Kate confirmed. "I'm working to resolve these issues. I appreciate your concern but really, I'll be fine."

"Is there anything I can do?" Sophie asked. Her eyes were filled with questions and solutions all at once. "I'm going to stop getting you coffee, you need green tea. And I'll look into moving meetings to the morning so you can have a quieter afternoon. And—"

"You're not taking my coffee," Kate joked. "Sophie, I

have medication. I have professional advice. I'll just need some time to get back to normal. As I say, I'm run-down. I'll be fine."

"You're sure there's nothing I can do?"

She opened her mouth to speak when she spotted something over Sophie's shoulder. She slammed her mouth closed again.

Georgina stood by Sophie's desk. Looking into the office with a smirk on her face, her bag in one hand, and her coat over her arm.

"Your girlfriend is waiting for you," Kate commented.

Sophie turned around and then back to Kate. "I can stay if you need me—"

"No, off you go, Sophie. Don't keep her waiting. I'll be there later." Kate took a sip of water. Seeing Georgina's smug face was already fortifying her and making her feel stronger.

Sophie hesitated a moment. "Should I book another appointment with your osteopath?"

"No, I'll do that. I'll see you at the Winter Garden soon." She turned around and picked up her suit bag to let Sophie know that the conversation was over. The last thing she needed was Georgina overhearing anything.

She heard Sophie leave and breathed out a sigh of relief. She wasn't sure why she had shared such personal information with the girl, but she did feel a weight lift off her shoulders having done so. Now she just needed to get through the next few hours and she could go home and rest.

CHAPTER TWENTY-NINE

FROM HER VANTAGE point on the balcony, Sophie watched the public gallery fill up below her. Considering she had never organised an event before, she was proud of the results. Of course, she had called Jonathan about four times a day to assist, but she'd done it. Reporters and influencers had arrived; now it was up to Kate to dazzle them.

The Winter Garden was a sight to behold. A large glass canopy roof covered the spacious event space bringing natural sunlight into the room. Just walking around the venue felt glamourous.

She watched her boss working the room, relieved that she looked a lot healthier now that she was at the event. Sophie hadn't been able to shake her worries about Kate. The whole day she had either been closely watching her or worrying about her from a distance.

She'd been stunned when Kate finally admitted what was wrong. Stunned and gratified that Kate trusted her enough to tell her. Now Sophie's brain whirred with ideas for how to help Kate get some peace and be able to relax. Not that it would be easy with Georgina around.

"You must be Sophie?"

Sophie turned to see a man approaching her with a glass of wine in his hand. "That's me," she replied.

"I'm Elliot Carmichael. I used to work for Mastery, but I'm now with the auto trade desk press, we spoke on the phone."

Sophie shook his hand. "I remember, nice to meet you."

Elliot had been very friendly and helpful in collating people's diaries. Without him, half of the big names that Kate was currently speaking with wouldn't be here.

"It's a great event. Looking forward to hearing more about The Bolt. How did you manage to do all of this so quickly?"

"With a few sleepless nights," Sophie admitted.

Elliot leaned on the balustrade beside her and looked down at the gathering. His eyes seemed to centre in on Georgina as she shook a reporter's hand.

"She doesn't change," he commented. "How's she been at Red Door? A beast, I bet."

Sophie didn't want to gossip, but she did want information. Elliot said he had worked at Mastery, so she wondered how much he could tell her about Georgina.

"She's been... forceful," she said diplomatically.

Elliot laughed. "Yeah, that's Georgina. Well, I hear she's up to her old tricks, striking fear into people now that Jessica's out of the picture?"

"A lot of people talk about Jessica, she must have been pretty special?" Sophie asked innocently.

She was curious to know about Georgina's ex. Stories about Jessica seemed to fill the Red Door office, especially since more Mastery staff had travelled over. But all the gossip stopped whenever she was in hearing distance. She was intrigued to know more about Jessica, especially why she was spoken about in legendary terms.

"All you really need to know about Jessica is that she tamed the dragon." Elliot took a sip of wine. "Georgina was a monster before her."

Sophie swallowed nervously. That wasn't what she wanted to hear.

"Everyone at Mastery can split their working career into two timeframes, before Jessica and after Jessica. Before Jessica, well, those people have more grey hairs and are on medication for their blood pressure and ulcers. After Jessica, those people are still scared out of their minds if they know what's good for them. But they know nothing of the pain that others have suffered."

Sophie turned to look at Georgina. She was smiling and chatting politely with a small group of people. She looked so nice, so sociable and friendly. But Sophie couldn't ignore the amount of evidence pointing towards her fiery side.

"You worked with Georgina before Jessica?" she asked.

"Yes." He let out a long sigh and then shuddered. "Honestly, Georgina changed into a brand new person once she *finally* got together with Jessica."

"Finally?"

"Jessica was her assistant for over a year before they finally got together."

Sophie bit her lip nervously. She wanted to know

more. She knew she shared similarities with Jessica. She wanted to know how deeply they ran. She also knew it was dangerous to fish for information, she might not like what she found out.

"What happened?" she asked.

Elliot took her arm and pulled her towards a couple of seats next to the sound booth, away from prying ears. He sat down and gestured for her to do the same. When she did, he held up his hands dramatically.

"Imagine the scene. Two women. In love. Neither thinking that the other could possibly love her."

Sophie chuckled at his overly dramatic storytelling.

"Hey, are you going to listen to this story, or are you going to giggle?" he chastised with a smile.

"I'm sorry, go on," Sophie encouraged.

"Let me set the scene. Jessica had this boring boyfriend: accountant, grey suits, grey hair, big yawn. One day, she sees sense, and she dumps him. She doesn't even know she's madly in love with Georgina at this point. Georgina, well, she's married to her career. All that she cares about is her job and her business. No interest in settling down, just a string of one-night stands."

Sophie tried to keep her smile on her face, but the story was already making her uncomfortable. She wondered if she had made a mistake asking Elliot to tell the tale. Either way, it was too late now. She could hardly stop him even if she wanted to. Which, in all honesty, she didn't.

"One day, they go to visit this new app developer. The guy made millions from a game he had recently sold, but he gave it all away to the city's public libraries. He has a new idea. Everyone wants to meet him, but Georgina gets an exclusive invitation. She takes Jessica, and they go to this dirty, run-down part of New York to visit this guy. They find the building, get in the elevator and…"

"And?" Sophie tugged on his arm impatiently.

He smiled at her enthusiasm. "The lights go out. The power goes out. They are stuck. In the dark. Together."

She stared at him. "No way."

"Way."

"That's so…"

"Clichéd." He nodded. "Isn't it delicious? I mean, you couldn't make it up."

"What happened?"

He crossed his legs and leaned closer. "The way Jessica tells it, they talked. For the first time in all the time they worked together. They just talked, like normal people. Not like a boss and an assistant. Jessica told Georgina about the break-up, told her that she's looking for a new apartment. You know, just life stuff."

Sophie could feel herself beginning to lightly perspire at the thought of just how similar she was to Jessica.

"They are stuck in there for about two hours, but neither of them notice how much time has gone by. Jessica said that it was like a light bulb moment for her. Suddenly, she realises that there is more to Georgina. She realises that a lot of what she says and does is a front. That she's a normal person. Jessica is intrigued and wants to know more. As they hear the firemen lowering the elevator to rescue them, Jessica asks Georgina out on a date."

"Brave," Sophie breathed.

"As rumour has it, Georgina doesn't speak. So, Jessica clarifies. A date. Not a dinner, not a friendly chat. A date."

"Very brave," she amended.

"Obviously, we know that Georgina agreed. Now, Georgina's version of events has her agreeing to a date and then buying the app from one of New York's hottest new developers. But Jessica claims that Georgina stuttered a confused agreement to the date, she's all blushes and nervously tells Jessica about all of her flaws. Jessica bats each of them away like a boss and then smooth talks the geeky developer. I don't know which version to believe. But the outcome was the same."

Sophie swallowed. For some reason her brain flashed up a picture of Kate. The very idea of being stuck in an elevator with Kate for two hours was enough to bring on a small panic. She quickly squashed the thought.

"Over the next few months," Elliot continued, "Georgina calmed the fuck down. She started to smile at work. The number of people fired each week was cut in half. A woman from account management wore flats in the office and lived to tell the tale."

Sophie laughed.

"I'm serious, she was a monster. The stories you've no doubt heard, they're all true. Georgina was awful before Jessica. But Jessica turned her around and made her human again."

"Why did they break up?" Sophie asked.

Elliot shrugged. "I don't know. I do know that it wasn't Georgina's choice."

Sophie found herself lost in thought. She knew that

Georgina wasn't perfect; in fact, lately she was seeing more evidence of it herself. And even though she wasn't directly in the firing line, she didn't like what she saw. She didn't think she was as strong as Jessica, able to tell Georgina how to act. And she still wondered if she was a replacement for Jessica, which she desperately didn't want to be. She wanted someone to like her for herself, not because she resembled someone else.

"Time to make myself scarce," Elliot whispered as he grabbed his drink and snuck away behind the sound booth.

Sophie looked up and saw Georgina walking towards her.

"Goodbye, Elliot," she called out with a devious grin. She sat beside Sophie. "Having fun?"

"Yes, you?" Sophie asked.

"Terrible. I've been so lonely. My date left me all alone."

Sophie chuckled. "I don't think you've been lonely. Every time I look over you're talking to a new group of people."

"Doesn't mean I'm not missing you," Georgina whispered.

Sophie felt a blush start and attempted to control her breathing. She didn't want to be flustered every time Georgina was near her. She needed to remind herself that Georgina was a normal person, just like anyone else.

"You're cute when you blush," Georgina admitted with a smirk. She leaned in closer so only Sophie could hear her. "What's going on with Kate?"

Sophie frowned. "What do you mean?"

"Something's off, I can't tell what it is. You have to know."

"I… I can't say anything. I mean, if there was something. Which there isn't." Sophie leaned back a little. She was very uncomfortable that Georgina would even consider asking her something like that. Georgina had been her safe haven, the person who didn't drag her into office politics.

Georgina's eyes flittered over Sophie's face. Sophie felt like she was being scanned for information.

"You're very protective of her, aren't you?"

"She's my boss," Sophie defended. "I treat her like I treat anyone else."

Georgina looked amused with Sophie's defence. She folded her arms. "Oh, and how is that?"

"With respect," Sophie answered. She gave a little nod and immediately regretted the gesture, fearing it looked childish.

Georgina bit her lip in amusement and looked away. "I suppose you don't think I'm very respectful?"

"Certainly not towards Kate," Sophie said.

Georgina sighed. "It's business, Sophie. It is what it is. I guess you're not going to answer my question?"

Sophie shook her head.

"Well, I better get back to the crowd. I don't want people to wonder where I am." Georgina stood up. "I'll see you after the event."

Sophie watched her leave. She felt uncomfortable with Georgina's sudden questioning and shook her head to clear the feeling. There was a chance that she was just feeling that way because of her conversation with Elliot. Hearing about the vaunted Jessica had unsettled her a little as she considered the big shoes she had to fill.

She heard people taking their seats in the hall below, and she looked down to see that Kate was preparing to take to the stage. She'd heard the presentation a dozen times already, and she wasn't looking forward to hearing it again.

Her phone started to vibrate in her pocket. She looked at the screen and sighed. It was her mum, who had no doubt heard about her break-up with Matt.

"Shit," she mumbled.

She rushed towards the corridor so she could take the call.

CHAPTER THIRTY

IT HAD TAKEN Sophie an hour to soothe her mum's mood at not being told about the break-up. Apparently, she'd heard through Matt's mum. Sophie felt awful, but she'd been busy with work, busy trying to avoid all thoughts of her ex. She'd apologised several times and then stayed on the phone for another thirty minutes to hear about the colours her mum was thinking of painting the kitchen.

In the back of her mind, she wanted to tell her mum about working as Kate Kennedy's assistant. And dating Georgina Masters. But she couldn't. Not that she was embarrassed, or thought her mum would have a problem. It was more that she couldn't figure out the right way to phrase it. As if she wasn't entirely sure about it herself.

Sophie hated how confused she felt. When she was with Matt, everything was clear and simple. They may not have had the most passionate relationship, and lord knew how many affairs he'd had, but at least life was easy. She didn't have to second-guess herself. It was a new concept for her, doubting your own mind. It seemed that being a new Sophie Young meant re-evaluating a lot of things.

She walked back into the auditorium and could immediately detect a strange atmosphere in the room. Something had happened. People were gathered in clusters and whispering.

"Sophie, where have you been? You missed it," Elliot said as he approached her.

"Something came up." Sophie looked around the room. "What happened?"

"Kate and Georgina," Elliot sighed.

"What now?" Sophie rolled her eyes. She'd had enough of the pettiness between the two women. They were supposed to be adults, well-respected adults. Each at the height of their career and running hugely successful enterprises. And yet they continually acted like children.

"Someone told Georgina that Kate set up a new charity foundation in Japan and has offered Jessica the role of director," Elliot explained.

"Japan? Charity foundation?" Sophie's mind was spinning. She didn't know anything about a new charity foundation. She knew that Kate was very generous with her resources and had contributed a lot to various charities over the years, but a venture in Japan was news to Sophie.

"Jessica never really wanted to work in marketing, it was just a job to her," Elliot explained. "She always wanted to work for a charity, to make a difference in the world. Rumour has it that when an opportunity came up, Jessica jumped at the chance and Georgina vetoed it outright. Apparently, that's why they broke up. I don't know if it's true or not, but that's what I heard."

Sophie felt her eyes widen in surprise. She couldn't imagine Georgina would stop someone from fulfilling their dream. She paused. Actually, if she were honest with herself, she could imagine that. Georgina was extremely single-minded, and she always got what she wanted. The more she thought about it, the more she believed it.

"And now Kate's hired Jessica?" Sophie struggled to catch up.

"Kate's been working on launching a charity in Japan with a friend of hers. It was supposed to be top secret until launch. Didn't you know about it?" Elliot asked.

Sophie shook her head. She wondered how on earth Kate was finding time to run Red Door, fend off Georgina, and establish a new charity. No wonder the woman was burning out.

"Hmm, she must have been keeping it away from Red Door," he said, "I suppose in case of conflicts of interest? I don't know, anyway, it all came out. Georgina was furious. She demanded that Kate fire Jessica. Kate refused, she said she didn't even know anything about Jessica being hired. Her business partner oversaw recruitment. Then she said that she had no intention of undoing it. Then they started properly shouting at each other. It was messy."

Sophie winced. "What happened?"

"Kate said that she was glad to be supporting Jessica and that Jessica must have been lucky to get away from Georgina. Georgina then told Kate that she wouldn't understand as she hadn't been in a real relationship for years, and wouldn't be able to get one now that she's fifty. Did you know she's fifty? Looking good for fifty, mind you—"

"Elliott…"

"Oh, well, Georgina let rip. Called Kate an emotionless has-been. Kate didn't respond to that, she just left. And Georgina left soon after as well. Now your lot are trying to mop up the mess without their illustrious leaders."

Sophie sighed angrily and used her finger to jab her glasses up her nose.

"Thanks, Elliot." She grabbed her stuff and hurried out the door. In the street, she quickly hailed a cab, but when she got in, she sat in the back and paused for a moment. She wasn't sure what to do. Part of her wanted to go and see if Kate was okay, but a bigger part of her wanted to take Georgina to task. Her mind was made up, and she told the driver to take her to the Rosewood Hotel.

All the way there, she considered what she wanted to say. Her anger was boiling over as the cab crept its way through London traffic. She couldn't believe that Georgina had gone off like that. Especially at a press event. It was so unprofessional. So much for her being the expert on business.

Sophie looked down at her phone. She wanted to text Kate, but she had no idea what to say. The intense pull to check on Kate was bewildering to her. She wanted to chalk it up to Kate being her boss, but the care she felt was more than that. She shook her head and looked out the window. She needed to stay focused on Georgina.

"Sophie—"

"Why did you say those things to Kate?" Sophie demanded. She stormed through the open hotel room door, blowing past Georgina to stand with her hands on her hips. "Why are you so mean to her? I know she's not exactly nice to you but… but you two are just… so mean!"

Sophie knew that her speech had wobbled a little towards the end, but she tried to maintain her posture.

Georgina looked her up and down before letting the door go. She waited until it slammed shut before raising her hand and pointing to the sofa.

Sophie took a deep breath and followed her to the sofa, sitting down on the opposite end.

"We rub each other the wrong way," Georgina began. "I know that's no excuse, and yes, I do go too far. But some people are just—"

"You're right. It's no excuse." Sophie was seething with anger. She could understand Georgina was upset by the news of Jessica's employment, but from what she had heard, Kate didn't even know about it. And for Georgina to say that Kate was emotionless, to comment on her age and call her a has-been in public? It was too much. Far too much.

"I realise I went too far," Georgina confessed. "I shouldn't have spoken about the child."

"Child?" Sophie asked in confusion.

"The child she gave up. Come on, Sophie, you could practically write her Wikipedia page, don't tell me you didn't know?"

Sophie swallowed. "Kate gave up a child?" She had no idea. She tried to remember all the articles she had read about Kate, wondering if she had missed something.

"At the start of her career, she was unmarried and Red Door was only just starting to make a name for itself, and—"

"And you announced it at a public event?" Sophie felt her fist tighten in anger. She didn't know exactly what Georgina had said, but it couldn't have been good. At least she had the good sense to look ashamed.

"Well, no, that bit was just between her and me. I think. Things got pretty confusing." Georgina jumped to her feet. "She's given Jessica a job in Japan! I saw red."

"Why didn't you let Jessica take her own career path?" Sophie asked. It was almost off-topic, but it still felt important that she ask. Like it was a key to Georgina's personality that she had to have before they went any further.

Georgina chuckled humourlessly. "Oh, I wondered why you and Elliot were huddled together. Did he tell you that?"

"Is it true?" Sophie wasn't about to be shamed by Georgina. She deserved the truth.

"You mean, did I prevent Jessica from taking a job in New York in a sector she wanted to work in? Yes, I did." Georgina crossed the room and looked out of the window. "Honestly, I don't even know why I did it. I thought it would be the end of our relationship. I told her as much. I didn't want her out of my life. You see, when you're an older woman with someone so young and perfect, you worry that your partner is going to leave you. You think that it can't last. That they'll wake up and realise they're with someone twice their age."

"Did you tell her that?"

Georgina shook her head. "No, I probably should have. But we argued, and then I just couldn't back down."

"Stubborn," Sophie mumbled.

"Yes," Georgina agreed with a sigh. "Still, it's too late now."

Sophie rolled her eyes and stood up. "Of course, it isn't. You need to tell her how you feel."

Georgina chuckled in disbelief. "Are you trying to get me back with my ex? You're a terrible date, Sophie."

"You still love her," Sophie pressed on. "You can't stop fighting for love."

"There's no point in fighting." Georgina shook her head.

"You seem happy to fight with Kate," Sophie pointed out. "Looks like you don't know how to pick your battles."

Georgina regarded Sophie for a few moments. Sophie could almost see the cogs turning as she considered what to say.

"I was… jealous."

"Jealous?" Sophie felt thoroughly confused. "What do you mean?"

Georgina sighed and leaned her head against the window. "I thought that Kate had managed to speak to Jessica… that maybe something was going on between them. That Kate had somehow charmed her and was taking her further away from me."

"That's a bit of a leap," Sophie scoffed with a chuckle.

"Like she'll do with you," Georgina added. She stood up straight and faced Sophie, her arms folded.

"M-me?"

"I was jealous because I thought she was taking Jessica away from me, that she would hold Jessica's heart in the same way she holds yours."

Sophie paused for a second. Her brain started to catch up to the conversation. Suddenly she was spluttering, "T-that... no, you're... no—"

"Sophie, I've seen how you look at her. And how she looks at you. I spend all day every day analysing fine details. I look at marketing and psychology with a fine-tooth comb. I know expressions, no matter how subtle or veiled. So, I... I asked you out for two reasons. One, because I was genuinely interested in getting to know you. And two, because I knew it would bother Kate. I'm not proud of it, but that's the truth."

Sophie didn't know what to think. Or say. She flopped down into a nearby chair. Words entered and exited her mind in quick succession.

"I'm truly sorry if you feel like I used you," Georgina said softly. "It wasn't my intention. As I said, the main reason I asked you out was because I was... *am*... genuinely interested in getting to know you. Upsetting Kate was just a bonus. But even in the short amount of time that I've known you, I can see how you look at her. I can see that I'm a replacement for her—"

Sophie jumped to her feet, horrified that she might have inadvertently hurt Georgina's feelings. "No, that's not the case at all! I... I don't look at Kate that way."

Georgina stared at her curiously. "You don't even know, do you?"

"I…" Sophie stared at the floor. Her heart thudded in her chest. It was the same sensation she felt when she was afraid, or when she'd been caught out in a lie.

"Sophie," Georgina said, "I may be wrong, but I don't think I am. I see how you look at Kate. Hell, I've heard you talk about Kate like she's a goddess. You said you'd never kissed a woman before, and yet you agreed to a date with me. Apologies for the bluntness, but how much experience with women do you have?"

Sophie barked out a laugh. "None. I just… sometimes wondered. I saw pictures of women and I… I don't know, I thought they were attractive, but I didn't know if that was normal. If that was what other women thought. I wondered if I might be bisexual, but I was with Matt. I thought I was going to marry him, so it was irrelevant." She flopped into the chair again. "I'm sorry, I didn't mean to use you."

Georgina kneeled in front of her and took her hand. "I think we used each other a little. No need for apologies. Clearly, my own feelings for Jessica are a long way from being resolved. I don't think I'd realised that. I was wrong to ask you out so soon after my break-up and yours. I hope you'll forgive me for that?"

"Of course," Sophie said. "There's nothing to forgive, you didn't make me."

Georgina squeezed her hand and stood up. "Well, looks like we're both in quite a pickle."

Sophie watched as Georgina crossed the room and

opened the hotel minibar and started to unload the tiny bottles from it.

"What are we going to do?" Sophie asked.

"I'd like to stay friends," Georgina said. She poured a drink into one of the room's glass tumblers.

"Will you call Jessica?" Sophie pressed. "You could do it this weekend when you're back in New York." Now she knew how Georgina felt, she wanted to convince her to talk to Jessica. To resolve their issues and get back together.

"Will you tell Kate how you feel?" Georgina returned.

Sophie felt her cheeks flush. "I don't even know how I feel."

"And if you did?"

Sophie quickly shook her head. "No… no, I couldn't."

Georgina chuckled and sipped her drink.

"What's funny?" Sophie asked.

"Life," Georgina replied. "Think about it. I destroyed my relationship because I was convinced that my partner would realise she was dating an old woman. I kept her at home, locked up in a golden tower, afraid that someone would steal her away from me."

She downed the rest of her drink and quickly replenished it. "And then there's you, the young woman in this equation. Afraid of your feelings for your own old woman, no offence to Kate intended. We're on opposite sides of the same equation. Both feeling the same doubts. Inadequacy, that's not a feeling I'm familiar with."

"I don't know if I have feelings for Kate," Sophie replied.

Georgina pinned her with a glare. "Really? I think you

do know. I think, like so many other things, you're afraid of your feelings. The new Sophie Young may be in the process of being created, but the old Sophie Young is still hanging on tight to all of those fears."

"That's not fair," Sophie defended. She knew Georgina was right, but she didn't like to hear it.

"If I don't say it, then you can just keep on ignoring it. You could spend weeks, months, even years, burying it. Because I think that's what you do, Sophie. I think you are so afraid of being rejected, of being mocked, that you somehow bury all your feelings deep inside you. If you don't acknowledge them, then you don't act on them, and if you don't act on them, then you don't embarrass yourself or feel the sting of disappointment."

Sophie stared at Georgina. She couldn't believe what she was saying. A part of her knew that it was all true, but it still stung to hear it. She did bury things, she always had. People were cruel, they seized upon anything they could to ridicule and hurt others. Sophie had learnt long ago that the best way forward was to fly under the radar. Be bland. Be uninteresting. Or at least appear that way.

"I think you've loved Kate for a long time. I think your fascination with her and with Red Door was born out of more than just an interest in marketing," Georgina suggested. "And I know how Kate looks at you. Remember, I *am* that older woman with feelings for her young assistant. I know the signs. I know the looks."

Sophie shook her head. "She doesn't feel that way about me. Sometimes I think she hates me, the way she speaks to me."

"She hates herself for seeing you as an object of

romantic affection," Georgina explained. "If she's anything like me, and it pains me to admit that she is, then she is trying to push you away. Maybe she's aware of her feelings, or maybe like you, she isn't. But she is trying to push you away, trying to keep you safe."

"Safe?" Sophie laughed bitterly. "Safe from what?"

"Safe from being in love with someone twice your age. Safe from a potential sexual harassment case. Safe from wasting your life being with someone society doesn't think is right for you."

Sophie had heard enough. Her mind was swimming with questions. Questions she just didn't have answers to. She needed time to process what Georgina was telling her.

But in the meantime, she wasn't about to let Georgina off the hook.

"What about you and Jessica?"

"What about us?"

"You love her."

"I do, but maybe my kind of love isn't what's best for her." Georgina sat on the sofa, the tumbler between her hands. "I hold on too hard."

"Maybe you can learn to be gentle?" Sophie suggested.

Georgina shook her head. "I think it's a little too late for that."

Sophie sighed. She turned her head to look out of the window. It was still the middle of the afternoon, but she was exhausted. It was as if ten days had passed in the last hour.

Suddenly, everything was changing again. She wasn't sure she liked the new Sophie Young's life. It was complicated, unsafe, and scary. Things changed at breakneck speeds. She longed for a calm routine. Or at least a quiet few days to herself, where she could figure out exactly what was happening with her.

CHAPTER THIRTY-ONE

KATE HATED WEEKENDS. Unless she was working, which wasn't happening this particular weekend, as she was drunk. After the very public fight with Georgina, she had gone home and ignored the rest of the workday. For the first time in years, she shut off her mobile phone and disconnected from the outside world. She didn't need reminding about what had happened at the press event, nor did she need to be involved in the clean-up process.

It was Saturday, and the living room clock was creeping towards two in the afternoon. Not that Kate cared one bit. She was still dressed in her clothes from Friday's presentation. When she returned home, she had sat on the sofa and started to drink. Hours had turned into a whole day, the longest period of time she had ever been out of communication with her office.

She casually wondered if news of the argument with Georgina had gotten back to Yannis. She wondered if the account was already lost. At this point she would rather it was, just to have a clean break. The last few days had been like waiting for an axe to fall. At least if it had finally dropped, she could get on with her life.

She shook her head. She'd broken her own rules. And all over Georgina Masters mouthing off, saying things that she'd heard said about her countless times before. But somehow it hurt more now, hurt more because it was Georgina saying them.

When the tears started to fall, Kate had assumed that the stress and sickness within her had built up to an unmanageable level and she had cracked. Working with Georgina and the Mastery team had been extremely hard; the office politics and sheer logistics were driving her to the brink. She had assumed that the dam on her emotions had finally burst, that the catty comments from Georgina were the final straw. That she'd been pushed over the edge into a blubbering mess.

It sounded perfectly reasonable. Except that Kate knew she wasn't the kind of person to break under pressure like that. The truth was that she usually thrived on pressure. And during the argument, she had delivered a few beautiful verbal blows back to Georgina. Kate had even smirked when she'd seen Georgina flinch after some of the more scathing remarks hit home.

To an outsider, it may have seemed perfectly reasonable that Kate's current predicament was caused by stress. But Kate knew that wasn't the case. It had nothing to do with the words that Georgina had said. It was Georgina herself.

Kate hated Georgina with a passion. A passion that had grown out of all control in the last few days. Once she realised that simple fact, it had become very clear to her why she hated Georgina. The revelation had come in the middle of a sleepless night. Out of nowhere, with the clarity and speed of a bolt of lightning, she realised she was jealous. Jealous of how Georgina really was the woman who had it all. She hated that Georgina had managed to have a successful career and personal life.

Kate's last long-term relationship was over fifteen years ago. Her marriage was over almost as soon as it had begun, both parties realising that they had made a mistake almost immediately. Since then she had maintained a high emotional wall as a defence against further heartbreak. What followed was a long stream of meaningless dates, many just for show and headlines. Kate had all but resigned herself to the fact that she couldn't have it all. No one wanted to date someone already married to their work.

And then there was Georgina Masters. Good old predictable Georgina Masters. She'd been in a similar situation to Kate for many years. Media outlets would constantly compare them, women in marketing, feared for their famously fierce personalities, top of their game, single. Neither of them having it all, both satisfied with what they had. Until Georgina stepped out with her twenty-four-year-old assistant and created the media storm of the century.

Kate had been so certain that it was a gimmick, but it soon became clear that either Georgina had suffered a massive midlife crisis and subsequent personality transplant, or she was in love with the young woman.

Kate had watched the media reaction with interest. All the while, she felt more and more isolated at the top of her corporate ladder. She was literally the only CEO in the sector to not have a young, beautiful thing on her arm. And it wasn't for lack of desire on her part. She knew exactly why: fear.

While she was alone, drunk, and exhausted, she could finally admit to herself that she was in love with Sophie Young. She wasn't sure when it started, but she was sure that she had somehow become the worst cliché. Falling in love wasn't something she thought she was capable of. Certainly not in such a small amount of time. But, somehow, Sophie had smashed her way past Kate's walls. Kate had denied it for as long as she could, but it had become impossible to deny her feelings.

Obviously, she had done everything she could to avoid this. She didn't want to damage Sophie's reputation or her career. Being the boss that slept with an assistant was one thing, but being the assistant sleeping with the boss was a whole different matter.

One of the things that had helped her to keep her feelings at bay was the secure fact that Sophie was straight and had a boyfriend. Or so Kate had thought. One lonely night at the office she had briefly fantasised about a relationship with Sophie. She'd wondered about the personality hiding beneath the nervous shell. She wondered about her interests, what kinds of food she liked, what they would talk about. But those thoughts were quickly boxed back up when she remembered that Sophie was straight. And, even if she wasn't, she most certainly wouldn't want to be stuck in a relationship with someone twice her age.

Until Sophie had dated Georgina. Apparently simply because Georgina had been brave enough to ask.

Then the agony had set in. Kate had been left to wonder if Sophie could possibly have been interested in her. If things could have been different if she had just had the courage to say something.

Still, it would all be irrelevant soon. Monday would come, and all hell would break loose. Worrying about Sophie was a luxury she no longer had. She now needed to fight for her business life.

———

By Monday, Kate's mood had improved. Somewhere during passing out on Saturday and coming to on Sunday, she'd had time to realise that rock bottom wasn't as bad as she thought. She wasn't quite ready for the scrapheap yet.

And so, she did what she did best, she fixed things. She smoothed out what she could, glossed over what she couldn't. Hundreds of telephone calls and emails had her changing the story. She moved things back on track, singlehandedly. The story was back on Atrom and off her.

Of course, there would still be rumours and gossip floating around, but that wasn't relevant. What was important now was rising above the petty childishness of the last few weeks and getting on with the job at hand.

When she'd arrived that morning, Sophie had offered her a look of pity. Before she could speak, Kate had barked out some instructions that would have the girl running all over London for the next few hours. She'd be able to focus better if Sophie wasn't around.

She was organising the information she had received from her weekend of phone calls when Georgina appeared in the doorway.

"I'm not ready for round two," Kate commented, returning her attention to the papers on her desk. "I left my gloves at home."

"No round two," Georgina said. "I wanted to talk to you about advertising layouts."

Oh, so we're going to ignore it. Act like it never happened, Kate mused.

She cocked her head to the side to regard the woman who had invited herself into the office.

"I wanted to ask your opinion on an offer that's come in." Georgina flipped open the folder she held and started leafing through paperwork.

Kate raised an eyebrow but didn't comment. If Georgina was going to turn over a new leaf, Kate would just enjoy it and not question it.

At that moment, Georgina's mobile started to ring. She glanced at the screen and shrugged before cancelling the call.

"Sorry about that. As I was saying," she pulled out a piece of paper and handed it to Kate, "I think this might be too good an opportunity to pass up, but the timescales are tight."

Kate looked over the offer. "It is a good opportunity," she agreed. "If we can pull together the—"

Georgina's phone started to ring again.

"You might want to get that," Kate suggested.

Georgina sighed in irritation but answered the call. No sooner had she answered, her face paled in shock.

"Jessica?" she breathed. She closed her eyes and fell into the visitor chair in front of Kate's desk.

Kate watched with interest as Georgina's whole demeanour changed.

"Of course, I would… yes… no, I would never…" Georgina argued softly. "No, Jessica, of course… well, I'm sorry you feel that way… no, that's just not the case."

Kate couldn't help but enjoy the uncomfortable conversation Georgina appeared to be having in front of her. She leaned forward and poured herself a glass of water. She knew that Georgina would leave the office if she wanted privacy. It was Kate's office after all.

"Well, I might have told Laura, but that doesn't mean it's the case. How was I supposed to know? It's not like you returned any of my calls. And now you're only calling to accuse me of something I—Jessica? Jessica?"

Georgina looked at the phone and sighed. She lowered it to the desk and stared at it for a moment as if willing it to ring again.

"Problem?" Kate drawled.

Georgina let out a long sigh. "I…" she paused. She looked up at the ceiling for a moment before meeting Kate's eyes. "Do you know that feeling where you just can't say the right thing?"

Kate blinked. She hadn't expected Georgina to want to discuss it.

"Yes," she answered honestly. "Quite often, actually."

Georgina nodded. "When I'm alone, I think of what to say to her. How to say it. And it all goes according to plan. But then, it's like this outside force stops me, and when it comes to the moment, I find it impossible to say what I'd planned."

"It's a defence mechanism." Kate shrugged her shoulders. "In the moment, you can't lower your defences because you're afraid that it won't be enough. That you won't be enough. You're afraid that you'll abandon your stance, apologise, and it won't mean a damn thing. It's easier to stick to your guns and know what will happen than to roll the dice and risk failure."

Georgina chuckled. "Yes, I think you're right."

"But sometimes we must fail, because if you turn around and start thinking, 'What if I'd acted differently,' then how would you feel?" Kate asked. She was unsure why she was helping the woman, but something pushed her on. "What caused the split? Was it because Jessica wanted to start a new job?"

"Partly," Georgina acknowledged. "It was more an overall desire to spread her wings. She always wanted to save the world. I thought giving her more freedom at Mastery would quench her thirst, but she accused me of nepotism. She told me that there were better qualified people lining up around the block for the job I gave her. So then I set up some interviews with top charities in New York, and for some reason she was mad at me for that, too."

Kate laughed. A hand drifted up to cover her mouth. She couldn't believe how naïve Georgina was.

"What's so funny?" Georgina asked.

"Can you really not see why she would be angry?"

"No. I gave her opportunities that other girls could only dream of."

"You took away her self-worth," Kate told her. "You didn't give her the opportunity to do something for herself. To build her own brand. To create her own success. You made her an extension of your own success. If she had taken any of those jobs, she would have always wondered if she had been *given* the job or if she had *earned* it."

Georgina let out a bored sigh. "I suppose that makes *some* sense," she allowed.

"So, let me guess. She went out and found a job by herself?" Kate guessed.

"Exactly."

"And?"

"I told her she wasn't going," Georgina said. "The job she found would have involved spending weeks at a time away from home."

Kate blinked. Had she really spent the whole weekend feeling inferior to this emotional mess of a human being?

"Your own job involves the same," Kate argued.

"Yes, but she's with me when I go. Well, she was when she was my assistant."

Kate shook her head. "So, you handed down an ultimatum and then she left?"

"Yes. She told me that her career was more important to her than me."

Kate frowned. Something didn't ring true. If Jessica really was a charitable soul with a passion to save the world, it didn't sound like she would be career hungry. "Did she actually say that?"

Georgina waved her hand distractedly. "Words to that effect. I forget exactly."

So, nothing like that at all, Kate guessed. She'd had enough of the pity party Georgina was hosting for herself.

"You're an idiot," Kate said.

"Excuse me?" Georgina glared at her.

"You're an idiot," Kate repeated. "You know you're in the wrong. Even you can't be that stupid. You had a loving partner. Then you said things that you clearly didn't mean and now it's over. And why? Because of your petty behaviour."

"How dare—"

"If you had any sense at all, you would phone her and tell her how you feel, how you really feel. Tell her that you think she is brilliant and accomplished and that you were only trying to give her everything because you loved her. Not because you didn't think she could do it herself. Tell her that you are sorry, that you love her, and that you want a second chance, even though you clearly don't deserve one. If you're damn well lucky enough to get her to agree to that, which you really don't deserve, then you should let her choose her own path. Maybe try standing beside her and supporting her. Not in front of her, opening the wrong doors and trying to mould her like she's some kind of prize doll."

Georgina stared at Kate for a few seconds before swallowing hard. "Do you," she whispered, "do you think she'd listen to me?"

"She put up with you for long enough, she must see some redeeming feature in you." Kate stood up. "Besides, I refuse to talk to you about advertising until you call Jessica and tell her that you're an idiot. You're no use to me like this."

"I couldn't."

Kate opened a filing cabinet. "I see. You've destroyed that relationship and you're unwilling to try to fix your mistakes, so now you're permanently trading her in for someone else?"

Georgina remained silent. Kate turned around to see the confusion on the other woman's face.

"Sophie," Kate elaborated. "Your new girlfriend, remember? Sits outside my office, wears glasses."

"Oh, no, that's over," Georgina said. She picked up her phone and stared at the device, seemingly considering her upcoming call.

"Over?" Kate tried to sound uninterested, but she could feel herself radiate with joy at the idea.

"Yes, we both wanted other things." Georgina stood and held up her phone. "I'll go and call her now, since you seem to be refusing to work until I do. If it doesn't go well, I'll blame you, of course."

"Of course." Kate rolled her eyes and returned her attention to the filing cabinet. "Just tell her that you're an idiot."

"It's almost as if you enjoy saying that to me," Georgina said.

Kate shrugged. "Tell her or don't. I don't care either way. Just resolve it so we can get on with work."

Kate heard Georgina leave and sighed. She leant against the filing cabinet. She was relieved that Sophie was out of Georgina's clutches, but suddenly the feelings she had worked so hard to repress were starting to get loose again.

CHAPTER THIRTY-TWO

GEORGINA GRIPPED the phone tightly in her hand. She walked towards her office, her mind churning as she considered what she would say to Jessica.

"Georgina?"

She looked up to see Sophie staring at her expectantly. It was only then she realised that Sophie must have called her several times before she'd gotten her attention.

She shook her head to gain some focus. "Yes?"

"I asked if you wanted me to book the meeting room for your conference call with—"

"Cancel it," Georgina interrupted.

"C-cancel—"

"Yes, I'm not to be disturbed." Georgina stepped around Sophie and continued towards her office. The moment she was inside she closed the door. She closed the blinds on the windows that separated her office from the main office. It was time to beg and grovel, and she wanted privacy for that.

It had been a turbulent weekend. She'd flown back to New York to attend a couple of events that she was unable to get out of. Despite being home, she'd never felt more disorientated. The argument with Kate had weighed heavily upon her.

She regretted the things she had said, not that she would ever freely admit it. No, she had an image to maintain. But she knew she had gone too far. Moreover, she knew she had gone too far in the name of petty jealousy. Jealousy that turned out to be completely unfounded.

Kate hadn't spoken directly with Jessica, but in the moment, Georgina had been certain that she had. And that had ignited a rage within her that she couldn't contain. Suddenly, all her steely dispassion at breaking up with Jessica had melted into a pool of white hot anger. After the event and Sophie's subsequent visit, she could no longer pretend that the break-up wasn't killing her inside.

It was the push she needed to be honest with herself. To realise that Jessica was the best thing that had ever happened to her, and that she was fully responsible for her decision to end their relationship. It also highlighted what she had suspected about Sophie, that the poor girl was just a replacement. She'd felt sick at the realisation that she had dragged Sophie into this situation.

She hadn't really been interested in Sophie at all. She was merely a reminder of Jessica. And proof that Georgina could attract anyone she chose. There was also the uncomfortable truth that she had used the girl's obvious feelings for Kate to make herself available as a handy stand-in. Not to mention using the relationship to irritate Kate.

Even though she had finally been honest with Sophie,

she still felt awful. It wasn't something she often felt, and it was very uncomfortable. Nothing had been particularly resolved. She had cast Sophie free and apologised for her behaviour, but she knew Sophie would do nothing about her feelings for Kate. And she had thought that she would do nothing to repair her own relationship with Jessica.

Until now. It pained her to admit that Kate was right. She was an idiot. She'd held onto Jessica too tightly, and she'd fled, just as any sane person would. But maybe Kate was right that Jessica might give her another chance. If she could just be honest.

She sat down and stared at the phone in her hands. She'd shared a happy relationship with Jessica for some time. Maybe she would listen. She knew she had to try.

Georgina stood at Kate's office door. "Knock, knock," she said, by way of announcement.

Kate looked up and removed her glasses. She seemed confused. She'd probably just read the email that Georgina had sent. The email in which Georgina provided several assets that she'd been holding back, as well as some information that would greatly assist Red Door with their marketing pitch.

"Did you get my email?" Georgina gestured towards Kate's laptop.

"I was just about to read it."

Georgina smirked. It was obvious that Kate was lying. She'd read it, now she was wondering if it was a new ploy.

She was giving herself some time to read, digest, and figure out Georgina's latest scheme.

Except there wasn't one.

"Good. There's nothing in that email that won't wait until tomorrow. I'd like to buy you a drink. A peace offering and a new start, if you will?"

Kate blinked. "Peace offering?"

Georgina nodded. "Yes, I think we need to start over. Bury the hatchet and work out a way to work together for the rest of this awful project. And then never, ever work together again."

"And what brought about this change of heart exactly?" Kate folded her arms across her chest and regarded Georgina suspiciously.

Georgina blew out a breath. "Wouldn't you much rather discuss this over a drink? The workday ended over an hour ago. You can leave the office without your staff thinking you're slacking."

Kate chuckled. "Fine. But only because I'm curious as to what kind of head injury you're suffering from."

Georgina smirked in return. "Wonderful, I'll go and get my bag."

She left Kate's office and walked slowly across the floor, listening out for the sound of Kate telling Sophie she could leave for the day. It was all coming together quite nicely.

A few moments later Georgina waited by the elevator door. She'd glared at a couple employees who had dared to think they would get in the elevator and ruin her precision timing. Miraculously, they had a last-minute desire to take the stairs.

Kate arrived with her bag and coat, and Georgina pressed the call button.

"So, what brought this change of heart on?" Kate asked, apparently eager to know what she was getting herself into.

"Oh, nothing much. Sophie, are you heading downstairs?" Georgina called out.

"Um, y-yes, I suppose." Sophie rushed to gather her belongings.

Georgina stepped inside the waiting elevator and held the button to keep the doors open. Kate stepped inside, and a few moments later Sophie joined them. It was all too easy.

"Oh, you know, I've forgotten my umbrella," Georgina said.

"It's not raining." Kate frowned.

"I heard there was a chance of rain this evening," Georgina explained.

"I hadn't heard that, it's supposed to be dry all week," Sophie added.

"A recent development. I like to keep a close eye on the weather. I don't want to hold you up, Sophie. I'll meet you in the lobby, Kate." Georgina slipped out of the elevator, pressing the button to close the doors as she left.

She looked across the office to the IT technician she had managed to snag earlier and nodded her head. He swallowed and nodded his head in return. She crossed the room and approached him.

"Is it done?" She looked at the gibberish on the computer screen.

"Yes, and I'm going to be fired." He ran his hands through his hair and sighed.

"That's only going to happen if you let them out too soon," Georgina assured him. "An hour and a half ought to do it."

"Kate's going to kill me."

"Kate doesn't need to know that this happened. As far as Kate will ever know, this is a simple elevator malfunction."

"And a telephone malfunction, and an alarm malfunction," he added.

"Details." Georgina waved her hand. "Trust me, everything will work out wonderfully."

She walked back towards her office, feeling very pleased with herself.

In just one day, she had managed to fix everything. After she had grovelled intensely, she and Jessica were on their way towards fixing things. She had explained her feelings, her thought processes in a way she had never done so before. She admitted things that she hadn't even admitted to herself. Once she started, she'd found it hard to stop. They spoke for two hours, Georgina making promises, Jessica giving reassurances.

It was the happiest Georgina had felt in years. And she knew she had a debt of gratitude to Kate. It was so very obvious that Kate and Sophie had feelings for each other. Georgina recognised much of herself in her rival.

Kate was bound by her duty to her staff member. She would never even dream of doing something that could be construed as taking advantage of Sophie. The chance of Kate ever making the first move was out of the question.

It would all come down to Sophie. But Sophie would never admit her feelings to Kate, not under any normal circumstances. Much like Jessica. The similarities were staring her in the face, as was the solution. If it had worked for her and Jessica, then surely it would work for Kate and Sophie.

CHAPTER THIRTY-THREE

KATE PRESSED ALL the buttons on the control panel again. It was the third time she had gone through every single button to no avail. She picked up the elevator phone again and tapped the receiver to try to get a line. Everything was dead.

Sophie stood in the middle of the elevator cart with her mobile out. She held the phone in the air.

"There's never a signal in here," Kate explained. "We're in a metal box, in the middle of the building."

Sophie lowered her arms and looked at the screen.

Kate couldn't believe her luck. She hadn't even wanted to go out for a drink with Georgina. She was just so curious what the woman was up to. The sudden email with all its helpful information was a clear indicator that she'd either lost her mind or been abducted by aliens. Perhaps both.

And now she was stuck in the elevator with Sophie. Sophie, who she had been happily avoiding for the entire day. They'd yet to speak about the press launch, and Kate wanted to keep it that way. She'd sent a short text message in reply to Sophie's eight messages, informing her that she was fine and that the conversation was over.

But still the girl was giving her strange looks. Probably pitying her.

"Georgina will notice that the elevator isn't moving and will call someone," Kate mused. "We'll be out of here in no time."

Sophie softly nodded and put her phone in her bag.

The silence was deafening.

Kate could feel her headache throbbing behind her eyes. This was the absolute last thing she needed. An awkward encounter with her assistant.

"It's weird that the alarm isn't working. Or the phone," Sophie mumbled. "Didn't the engineer check it last month?"

Kate thought back to the stacks of invoices she had recently signed. Sure enough, she could remember one from the lift maintenance company.

"Well, they're sacked," Kate said.

Suddenly she heard a sharp intake of breath. She looked at Sophie curiously. Something was wrong.

"What?" Kate frowned.

She saw Sophie swallow nervously. Sophie had clearly had an epiphany and wasn't about to share it.

She put her hands on her hips. "What?" she repeated.

"Georgina doesn't have an umbrella in her office," Sophie whispered.

"So?" Kate frowned. Then, she began to realise what Sophie was suggesting. "Are you… are you saying that she trapped us in here?"

Sophie slowly nodded. "I think so."

"I knew she was up to something!" Kate dropped her bag to the floor. She stared up at the ceiling, wishing she could somehow glare at the woman who was no doubt standing above them and laughing. "I'm going to murder her."

Sophie lowered her coat to the floor and sunk down against the wall.

"What possible reason could she have for trapping us in here? What can she possibly hope to gain?" Kate fumed as she paced the tiny space.

Kate looked at her watch. "Ten minutes. Ten whole minutes have passed. If she wasn't behind this then she would have raised the alarm by now, and we'd hear men… fixing… whatever sounds you hear when men are fixing whatever it is that needs to be fixed. But we don't hear those things." She stood in front of Sophie and glared down at her. "And why do we not hear those things, Sophie?"

Sophie looked up. She swallowed and shrugged her shoulders.

"Because no one is coming," Kate supplied. "And why is no one coming?"

"I-I…" Sophie stammered.

"Because Georgina hasn't told anyone. Now, why hasn't she told anyone?"

Sophie nervously fidgeted with her glasses. She pressed into the corner of the cart, seemingly trying to make herself as small as possible.

"Because she wants us trapped in here," Kate answered her own question. She looked at Sophie. Sophie who looked more frightened than someone who was simply afraid of Kate's rant. She had the look of someone who knew something. Someone who was in some way to blame.

Kate crouched down and looked Sophie straight in the eye. "What. Did. You. Do?"

CHAPTER THIRTY-FOUR

GEORGINA OPENED the sideboard in Kate's office and smiled. She reached into its dark depths and pulled out a bottle of whiskey, then stood and plucked the phone from between her ear and her shoulder.

"When do you think you'll be home?" she asked.

"Three days at the earliest," Jessica replied with a chuckle. "Exactly like I told you earlier."

"Aw, can't that be shortened?" Georgina felt herself pouting. She turned one of the unused glasses on Kate's table over and poured herself a congratulatory drink. She sat down and put her feet up on Kate's desk.

"No, there are things I need to finish up here. Like I said earlier, I'll be home as soon as I can. But I have obligations here."

"I know, I know," Georgina murmured. This change in dynamic was going to take a while to get used to, but it was more than worth it to have Jessica back. Especially now that she knew the strength of Jessica's feelings for her and the improbability of someone coming between them.

No, now she knew that if the relationship was going to fail, it would be because of her and no one else. Modifying her own behaviour was all she needed to do to remain blissfully happy.

"Besides, aren't you busy trying to poach the Atrom account? Which, by the way, I think is a terrible thing to do," Jessica said.

"I'm not sure if it's worth the trouble." Georgina sipped at the whiskey, appreciating its rich vintage.

"It's all you've talked about for months," Jessica pointed out.

"I'm changing my perspective on things," Georgina replied. "It's the new me."

"I'm liking the new you."

Georgina smiled. "I've missed you."

"I've missed you, too. But remember that we both agreed to take this slowly. I'm not just going to come back and accept things the way they were, Georgina."

"I know, I understand and respect that. Like I said earlier, I will do my best to change."

Jessica chuckled. "Actually, I believe what you said was that you were an idiot."

Georgina bristled slightly. "I thought we agreed not to mention that again?"

"No, I'm pretty sure no such agreement was made. Obviously, I'll be sure not to overuse it. I'll just bring it up when I really need to make a point."

"You're a cruel woman, Jessica," Georgina said with a smile.

"Oh really? And here I was planning to fly to London to see you. Maybe I'll be a few days longer…"

Georgina sat up quickly. "No, please, darling. I want to see you as soon as possible."

Jessica's laughter sounded down the line, and Georgina smiled. She'd missed that beautiful sound.

"I'll be there as soon as I can. Can't have you walking around the city on your own for too long, someone will try to snatch you up," Jessica joked.

Georgina swallowed. "I should probably be honest and tell you that I dated someone."

"Wow, you don't wait around, do you?" Jessica said, her voice was light and teasing. Georgina breathed a small sigh of relief.

"It was very brief, we both did it for all the wrong reasons," Georgina added.

"Did you…?"

"No! No, of course not. Jessica, I… you have to—"

"I believe you, it's okay. Even if you did, we had broken up. Who was she, if I may ask?"

Georgina nervously licked her lips. She hoped she was doing the right thing by admitting what had happened. It would eventually come out anyway, so it was prudent that Jessica heard it from her now. "Kate Kennedy's assistant."

"Jonathan?" Jessica spluttered.

"No, a new girl, Sophie Young."

"Young," Jessica chuckled. "And is she?"

"Twenty-five," Georgina admitted. She took another sip of whiskey.

"You certainly have a type," Jessica said.

"It didn't mean anything. As I said, it was short-lived, and we were both wrong to do it. Both replacements for each other's true affections."

"She has a thing for Kate Kennedy?" Jessica asked.

"Yes, and Kate for her."

"Oh my God, Kate Kennedy has a thing for her young female assistant?" Jessica all but squealed.

Georgina chuckled. "Yes, I've seen the way they look at each other. There's no denying it."

"Sophie dated you as a replacement for Kate? And you dated her as a replacement for me? And presumably to bug the hell out of Kate? Oh, Georgina, that was mean."

Georgina bit her lip. "I know."

"They're just like us," Jessica mused. "We have to get them together."

She had known Jessica would agree with her. Georgina was just proud to be one step ahead. "Already in motion," she smirked.

"What have you done?" Jessica's voice turned cold and serious.

"Jessica, there's no need to take that tone—"

"What. Have. You. Done?"

Georgina swallowed. Suddenly she was reminded of all the times she had incorrectly read a situation and Jessica had to be drafted in to mop up her mess. She had to admit it had happened a few times. Maybe a lot of times. In fact, it was probably most of the time.

She coughed to clear her throat. "I may have arranged to have them trapped in an elevator together."

Jessica sighed, a sigh that Georgina knew meant she had done the wrong thing. A sigh that usually preceded a very exact explanation of what she had done wrong. But first came the shouting.

"Why on earth did you do that?" Jessica yelled.

"It worked for us," Georgina exclaimed.

"Barely!"

Georgina frowned. "What do you mean?"

"Georgina," Jessica sounded exasperated. "Do you even remember that day?"

"Of course I do," she lied. She'd long since forgotten the exact details. All that lingered were the results.

"So, you remember how awkward that time stuck together was? You remember how we eventually started to talk, but I had to push every single step of the way? You remember how I asked you out and you rapidly shot me down with every reason you could think of? You recall perfectly how I fought, fought hard, to get you to agree to go out to one dinner with me? You remember all of that?"

Georgina swallowed. "Well…"

"Oh, Georgina, what have you done? I know you don't want to hear this, but the truth can be painful. Kate Kennedy, she's a lot like you."

Georgina scoffed.

"She is! I'm sorry, but you two are very similar. The real question here is, is Sophie like me? Will she be persistent? Does she know what she wants? Will she go for it with all her heart? Will she be able to stand up to Kate?"

Georgina considered the matter. She knew in her heart that Sophie would collapse like an over-whipped soufflé. Her silence spoke volumes.

"Oh, this is a disaster," Jessica muttered. "Why didn't you wait until you'd spoken to me? You know you don't do matters of the heart."

"I thought I was doing the right thing. I thought they would be together by the time you arrived, and I could tell you that I did it." Georgina got to her feet and started to pace the room. "I thought you'd be happy."

"How did you even do it?"

"There's an IT technician with no balls."

"You made one of Kate's own staff lock her in an elevator?" Jessica sighed.

"Yes. What's wrong with that?" Georgina wasn't sure what was wrong with the situation, but Jessica was sighing a lot. She started to wish that she'd never gotten involved. Matchmaking was obviously a lot more convoluted than she imagined.

"Let them out before it makes matters worse. If they are secretly pining over each other, then trapping them in an elevator might make things worse."

Georgina sneered. "Why do you think that?"

"Because they're both afraid of rejection and have their walls up. If neither has a clue that the other is interested, then they'll be on the defensive. You can't just recreate our situation and assume the same thing will happen. For someone so intelligent, Georgina, you can certainly be an idiot sometimes."

Georgina huffed as she stormed out of Kate's office. "You might be right," she allowed.

"So, let them out."

"I can't."

"Why not?"

Georgina stood by the IT technician's desk. "The ballless wonder has gone home. He didn't want to be around when Kate was released back into the wild."

"So, how were they going to be released?" Jessica asked.

"It's on a timer."

"A timer?"

"Yes, an hour and a half and then it would start up again." Georgina was experiencing a sinking feeling. Her brilliant plan suddenly didn't seem quite so brilliant.

"Well, can you undo it?" Jessica asked.

Georgina looked at the screensaver. She wiggled the mouse. "His computer is locked."

Jessica sighed. "Okay, call maintenance. At least make an effort to get them out before things go bad."

CHAPTER THIRTY-FIVE

KATE WATCHED as Sophie pressed herself into the corner of the corner of the elevator cart.

"Don't make me ask you again," Kate said.

"I…" Sophie trailed off.

"This has a Sophie Young trademarked mess written all over it. What have you done?" Kate asked again. She stood over the girl, her arms folded as she glared down at her menacingly.

"I didn't do anything, I promise."

Kate pursed her lips. She didn't believe her for one second. Sophie was almost hyperventilating. She knew something and wasn't willing to let it go, despite Kate's best efforts. Sophie looked up at her pleadingly, clearly wishing for the interrogation to stop.

"You're seriously expecting me to believe that your girlfriend—"

"She's not my girlfriend," Sophie interrupted.

"Oh?" Kate raised an eyebrow. It wasn't new information, but it was from a new source. "Did she dump you for a graduate?"

"No! We agreed that we weren't right for each other." Sophie broke eye contact to fidget with her glasses.

Kate folded her arms. She took a couple of steps back, giving Sophie some breathing room. She may be angry, but her pressuring Sophie wasn't going to get them their freedom any quicker.

"She was too old for you, I presume?" Kate fished.

"No," Sophie whispered.

"Too… shapely?" Kate raised a questioning eyebrow.

Sophie swallowed. "No, just not… the right person. We wanted different things."

"Clearly she wanted Jessica." Kate leaned against the opposite wall of the cart and looked at Sophie. "But what did you want?"

Sophie cheeks blushed intensely. She looked down at her lap where she nervously twisted her hands.

"That's private," she murmured.

"I… of course, I'm sorry," Kate said. She felt terrible for pushing Sophie when she clearly didn't want to talk about it. "I'm sorry, I shouldn't have questioned you like that. I was just stressed about the situation. I apologise."

Sophie looked up and gave her a small nod of acknowledgement. Her big blue eyes looked so sad, and Kate felt her heart clench. She wanted to reach out, but she knew it was inappropriate.

She took a quick breath. This was the last thing she wanted right now. To be stuck with Sophie Young, virtual puppy. She spun around and tried the alarm button again.

Forty minutes had passed. Kate had given up figuring out why Georgina had locked them in there. She had even given up hope of ever being let out. She sat on the floor with her legs stretched out in front of her. She'd taken her heels off and placed them next to her coat and bag, all neatly stacked up as a barrier between her and Sophie.

Not that Sophie had remained sitting for long. As soon as Kate had stretched out, Sophie was on her feet and pressing buttons on the control panel. Kate watched as Sophie tried every button multiple times in multiple ways. Even some together. She'd taken a panel off the wall and started messing around with the wires inside when Kate couldn't stand it anymore.

"You'll electrocute yourself in a minute," Kate pointed out. "And I'm not good with dead bodies."

Sophie dropped the wires she held in her hands. She turned around and looked at Kate. After a moment of contemplation, she sat down opposite her.

So much for my barrier, Kate mused.

"Maybe we could talk?" Sophie offered.

"And just what are we going to talk about?" Kate asked. She sighed in feigned boredom, hoping to throw Sophie off the idea.

"Um… well, I'm… I'm going to paint my bedroom," Sophie started. "It's sort of a lilac colour. It's nice."

Kate stared at Sophie.

"Okay, um… I… h-have you seen *Game of Thrones*?" Sophie tried again.

Kate reached into her bag for her mobile phone and

stared intently at the screen. She needed space, and this certainly wasn't it. How was she supposed to push aside her feelings for Sophie if she was stuck in a box with her?

And now Sophie wanted to talk to her. Down this path it would only be ten minutes before they were braiding each other's hair and swapping stories of high school romances. She needed to get things back onto a professional level. She couldn't think about the colour of Sophie's bedroom walls or picture her watching television after work.

"Did you get that courier package off to Yannis?"

"Yes, he signed for it at three."

"Good. I need you to send me the latest online advertising stats for the Malloy account."

Sophie picked up her phone and started to type a note to herself. "I'll do it as soon as we're out of here. I'm sure it won't be long."

"It will be as long as Georgina desires. She clearly has something to do with this." Kate looked over her phone and met Sophie's eyes. She couldn't stand that Sophie was keeping something from her. "And you know something. Don't think I don't see that."

"I-I don't know what you mean."

"Yes, you do," Kate pressed. She wanted answers. Time was dragging on and they were no closer to freedom. She had a right to know what was happening. "You sit there, looking so innocent. Like butter wouldn't melt. But you know something and you're refusing to tell me. Still loyal towards her, I see."

Sophie lowered her phone and stared at her. "I have never been disloyal to you. I would never—"

"Oh, come on, you knew that going to her for career advice would push me," Kate accused. "You saw an opportunity to change the balance of power in my office. And you took it."

"I never—"

"You wormed your way into my office," Kate continued.

"Jonathan told me to take over," Sophie argued.

"And then you took the first chance you saw to belittle me in front of my staff!"

"I didn't!"

"And now you know something is up. I'm locked in here for a reason, and you," she pointed her finger, "you know why. But you refuse to tell me. Because you're still involved in something with her."

The elevator cart lurched. Suddenly they were moving again. As soon as the doors opened, Sophie grabbed her things and ran, nearly colliding with Georgina as she did so. Kate got to her feet. She glared at Georgina and the elevator engineer.

"I'm sorry, there was a fault, and for some reason the alarm didn't sound. Miss Masters came to get me," the engineer said.

Kate shooed him away with a flick of her hand, but all the while she stared at Georgina. She grabbed her belongings off the floor and stalked out of the cart.

"What on earth did you do?" she demanded.

Georgina looked to where Sophie was hurrying to the other side of the floor, making a beeline for the stairwell. "You should go after her," Georgina suggested.

"Why don't you? You're her ex-girlfriend after all," Kate replied bitterly.

"Because she's in love with you, you moron," Georgina said.

Kate felt her mouth drop open. She stared at Georgina in surprise. "What?"

"Sophie is in love with you. And I'm pretty sure you feel the same way. You need to go after her, go after her, and tell her you're an idiot."

Kate leaned against the wall as she watched the door to the stairwell close behind Sophie.

She shook her head. "Is this some kind of sick joke?" she demanded.

Georgina shook her own head. "No, no joke. I've seen the way she looks at you. She's all but admitted to me that she has feelings for you. And I know you feel the same about her. I was," she sighed, "I was trying to fix things. Trying to help you. But I'm really bad at this."

"I'll say," Kate agreed.

"Look, let's go and get that drink," Georgina said. "I have some things to explain."

CHAPTER THIRTY-SIX

GEORGINA WAITED for the bartender to pour two large glasses of wine. She stood, anxiously tapping her bank card on the bar. Looking in the mirror behind the bar, she could see Kate at their table. She still looked shell-shocked and confused. Luckily at least, the anger had waned.

Two glasses of wine were placed on the bar, and Georgina tapped her card on the device offered to her. She tucked her purse under her arm and took a deep breath as she carried the glasses over to the table.

"Thank you," Kate murmured.

"Least I can do," Georgina said. She sat opposite Kate, thankful they had the relative peace of a booth at the back of the pub.

"Yes, it is," Kate said firmly.

Georgina blew out a breath. She knew talking to Kate wouldn't be easy, but she owed it to her.

"I'm sorry, about the elevator thing." Georgina waved her hand, trying to dismiss the whole incident. "Actually, I'm sorry about a lot more than just that."

Kate frowned. She sipped at her wine, regarding Georgina suspiciously over the top of the glass.

"I've behaved awfully," she confessed. "It all suddenly seems so petty."

"I've hardly been on my best behaviour either," Kate admitted.

Georgina smiled. "Don't try to downplay how terrible I've been. The things I said to you last week—"

"I'd really rather not revisit that particular scene," Kate said.

Georgina pushed her wine glass to one side and leaned back. "I've always wanted to be the best," she admitted. "Ever since I was a little girl. I wanted to be something. Marketing ended up being the key to it all. I was good at it, I understood it, and I built my career on it. I always thought I was special, unique. I convinced myself that I, and I alone, had established a process of working that was perfection."

She tucked a fallen lock of hair behind her ear. "And then, I heard about you. Kate Kennedy and Red Door. And in the back of my mind, I realised I wasn't so unique. I wasn't so special. You'd done exactly the same things that I'd done. You'd built up an empire in this male-dominated shit fest of an industry that we call home."

Kate looked at her curiously. Guarded but interested.

"I guess I thought you took some of my uniqueness from me. Unintentionally, of course. But then the media started to compare us. We were practically pitted against each other. I opened a new office, you signed a multi-million-dollar deal. You won an award, I had a building named after me at my alma mater. Without even thinking about why, we were in competition."

She snatched up the wine glass and took a fortifying sip. Explaining oneself was more complicated and exhausting than she remembered.

"And then Pink Blossom happened. I remember it so clearly." She plucked a tissue from the pack in her bag and casually wiped at the condensation on the table left by her cold glass. "It was a Monday morning. I had just had a marvellous weekend away. I'd had an idea for a client, I was eager to call them. But when I got into the office, I knew something was wrong. Michael told me that we'd lost Pink Blossom, and I was floored. When he told me we'd lost it to Red Door…"

"You were angry?" Kate guessed.

"Livid," Georgina confirmed. "In my mind, you had deliberately gone behind my back and seized the contract out from under me. It kick-started a chain reaction where the competition turned nasty. Now that I think about it, it sounds ridiculous."

"It doesn't," Kate said. "I've always felt the same. I remember feeling that I'd arrived when the trade press wanted to write about me. I started reading articles about myself, and was shocked to find that the journalist referenced you in the text. Directly comparing us. I was furious. I'd built my company up, I was a success, and there was some journalist, some man, placing a picture of you alongside my article."

"Exactly." Georgina nodded. She was so relieved that Kate understood.

"But I never stole the Pink Blossom account from

you," Kate said seriously. "I may have disliked you, but I would never have done that."

Georgina licked her lips and looked down at the table. As much as she wanted to move on, to finally have this rift over with, it was still hard. The anger at the Pink Blossom account being lost to Red Door was still hot within her.

"I've been friends with Rosie for years," Kate explained. "When she set up Pink Blossom, I had no industry experience that I could offer her. And she was setting up in New York. Neither of us ever thought anything of it. Then, I attended her daughter's wedding, and we naturally started to talk about work. She told me that she was consolidating her businesses in London. She was hoping a grandchild would be on the way soon, and she wanted to be nearby."

Kate twisted her glass around, staring thoughtfully at the liquid. "She told me that she'd seen one of our campaigns for Grantleys and loved it. Asked if we'd be able to do some work for her. Just that, some work. I'd had champagne, it was late, I didn't really think much more about it. The next thing I knew, she was moving the entire account to us."

She chuckled. "I'll admit, I was happy to get one over on you. But I didn't think anything of it, because I hadn't set out to steal an account. I hadn't even known it was happening until Rosie was practically ordering me to write up a contract so she could sign it."

Georgina shook her head. "From where I was sitting, it all happened very differently."

"I can see how it must have looked." Kate sipped her wine. "Positions reversed, I would have thought the same."

"It wasn't the money," Georgina reassured her. "It was the pride. The fact I didn't know. And then the fact that Pink Blossom was such a high-profile account. It was everywhere, we had to do a lot of damage control. Other clients left because of that."

"I never knew that," Kate breathed.

"We haemorrhaged money," Georgina confessed. "Not at first, but a couple of months later. Rumours swirled. It was a terrible time. And at the epicentre of it all—"

"Was me," Kate guessed.

"Was you." Georgina nodded. "I didn't set out to get Yannis and Atrom, but the opportunity arose and I took it. I bent everything into shape to get him to sign with us, but then he got preoccupied by Mastery working with Red Door. Thinking that if he had the two best agencies in the business, it would be marvellous."

"That's Yannis." Kate rolled her eyes.

"And then here I was, and I thought, 'Why don't I just cause mayhem? I might not get the account, but let's just cause trouble while I'm here'. So, I did. I was utterly blinded by this feeling of competition. And I was angry, so angry at myself for losing Jessica. I was so consumed with my desire to beat you, I didn't even notice myself losing the one good thing I had."

"Surely not the only—"

"The *one* good thing I had," Georgina emphasised. It was important to her that Kate understood exactly how important Jessica was. And how important the right partner was.

Kate closed her mouth and nodded.

"I thought you'd spoken to Jessica," she explained.

"That's why I overreacted at the press launch. I heard about the job, I heard about your involvement, I put two and two together and got fifteen."

"I swear to you, I had no idea Jessica had been offered that role. All I heard was that the role had been filled."

"I know, I spoke to Jessica. Too late, of course. By then I'd already said what I'd said to you. I cannot apologise enough."

"It's fine—"

"No, it isn't. I was extremely hurtful and in such a public way. I knew it the moment I'd done it. And then Sophie came to see me and tore a strip off me as well."

Kate's eyes sparkled with amusement. "Sophie? Sophie Young? Nervous cardigan Sophie?"

Georgina laughed. "Yes, that one. She's got quite a temper. She definitely told me what she thought of my actions. Which only confirmed something I had already suspected."

Kate held up her hand. "Please, not this again."

"I saw it from the moment I saw you two together. It gave me an instant flashback to Jessica and me." She frowned contemplatively. "I can't explain it, it's not like you're shooting heart arrows at each other. It's more than that. The kind of connection you can only understand when you've experienced it yourself."

"You're wrong," Kate drawled. She chuckled to herself before taking a sip of wine.

Georgina smiled. "Maybe I am. But I don't think so. I think you feel something for her, and you're terrified of it. I felt the same way about Jessica. I'm too old for her, I'm her boss, I'm hard and acerbic, she's sweetness and light. Everything was telling me that I had to stay away. If for some ungodly reason she did like me, then I knew that I'd destroy her career, break her heart, treat her terribly."

She pulled the wine glass closer, using it as a barrier.

"I'd buried my feelings for months. And then, one day, we got stuck in an elevator."

"Oh my God," Kate said. Georgina didn't have to look up. She could feel Kate's eyes boring into her skull.

"It was over an hour of talking. I just… opened up. Nothing much at first. I spoke about my career, my feelings, my likes and dislikes. She did the same. It was the first time we had talked about anything outside of a boss-employee relationship." She picked up the glass and took a drink. "She asked me out. Very specifically, it was a date. I panicked, blurted out every reason it was a bad idea. Never once did I say I didn't feel that way about her, so I was essentially broadcasting my feelings to her. I was blind-sided by the whole thing."

"You? Blindsided?" Kate laughed. "Now that I'd like to see."

Georgina smiled again. "I agreed to the date. I thought it would be awful. I'd planned for her to walk out the next day, I had HR looking for a replacement. But it never happened. We had another date. And then a standing date every Friday. And then Wednesday and Friday. It just happened so easily. I could never have hoped beyond my wildest dreams for a partner that just snapped into place next to me. It made sense, she'd been watching my every move for months. Anticipating my needs. But I found that I knew her, too. Somehow, in that time, I'd gotten to know about her favourite colour, her style of music, her taste in movies."

At that moment, a waiter bounced up to their table. "Can I get you ladies anything to eat?" he asked cheerfully.

"No," they both replied sternly.

He quickly backed away.

Georgina took a breath, finding her footing again. "I saw the look in Sophie's eyes. I wasn't sure, but I had an inkling. Then I saw the same look in yours. So, I asked her out. It was petty, but I was out to cause havoc. And I was lonely."

"Did you...?" Kate asked meaningfully.

"No." She shook her head. "A small kiss, nothing more."

Kate nodded. "Not that it matters, of course."

"She loves you. She wasn't necessarily aware of it to start with, but she is now." Georgina took a drink. "It's scaring her. I don't know what she's going to do, though I suspect that she's going to run away because that's the easiest thing to do. Now that she's become aware of her feelings—"

"I don't want to be the person who has to guide her through her first crush on a woman," Kate observed. "I'm not the right person to do that."

"I don't think it is a crush. I think she's been infatuated with you for a long time, maybe thinking it was something else." Georgina leaned forward. "I stupidly thought that putting you together in a confined space would have the same result that it had for me and Jessica. Obviously, I neglected to factor in that you are not me and

Sophie is not Jessica. I've made a mess of things, but I want to help."

"Why?" Kate shook her head. "Why this sudden desire to get involved in my love life?"

"Because you got involved in mine, when I needed to hear some truth."

Kate frowned. Then understanding swept over her face. "You called Jessica again."

"I did. I don't think I would have done it if it wasn't for you." It was a lie, she knew she wouldn't have done it. "I owe you, Kate. If there's a fraction of a chance that you can have what I have, I want to help you. I know we're not the same people, but…" She blew out a frustrated breath at Kate's stony face. "Damn it, I know that look!"

"Fine," Kate bit back. "I do have feelings for her. But I'm completely wrong for her, I know that."

"Let her decide," Georgina implored.

Kate shook her head. "She's so young, Georgina."

"She's not as young as you think. There's a bright, mature, passionate woman there."

Kate leaned back and sighed. "I've been awful to her. The things I said to her when we were stuck in the elevator. I can't imagine that it escaped your eagle eye that she ran away from me?"

"It's not like your usual interaction with her is so sunny. She ran because she realised I'd caused the elevator issue and knew it was her move. She panicked. You… were you. The question is, are you willing to try?"

Kate looked up at the ceiling. "Oh, God, I don't know."

"I have an idea, if you're interested," Georgina fished.

Kate looked at her. "What kind of an idea?"

"Something that will help us all out of this very sticky situation. Yannis will be happy. I'll be happy, in New York with Jessica. And, hopefully, you and Sophie will be happy."

Kate licked her lips. Finally, she was breaking down her walls. Finally, she was ready to admit her feelings. "Okay, tell me more."

"Absolutely, but first, let's order. I'm starving." Georgina picked up a menu from the table. "The service in here is terrible."

"It is," Kate agreed. She searched for a member of the staff. "We've been left to waste away."

CHAPTER THIRTY-SEVEN

SOPHIE TURNED in her seat and looked towards the meeting room door for the third time in under a minute. She gnawed her lip and turned back to face Yannis. Not that he noticed, he was fully focused on his MacBook, as he had been from the moment he turned it on.

That was one of the things Sophie liked about Yannis, he wasn't afraid to start up his laptop and get stuck into work no matter where he was. He was often seen in a meeting room, or on public transport, tapping away.

"Are you sure I can't get you a drink?"

Yannis looked up at her. "No, thank you." He smiled and returned his attention to his work.

Sophie swallowed and chanced another glance at the door. She couldn't believe that neither Kate nor Georgina had shown up for the meeting. She looked at her watch; they were now both fifteen minutes late.

She'd seen neither woman that morning. Mainly because she was trying to avoid them after the awkward elevator incident of the previous evening. The morning meeting with Yannis was a perfect opportunity to get away from them. She'd decided to go straight to the meeting and use it as a protective shield against any awkward conversations that might have come up.

But now she was alone with Yannis. No sign of anyone else. And the clock kept ticking by.

She'd rung them, texted them, emailed them. She'd even phoned upstairs and asked someone if they could see them. Both women were nowhere to be found. She looked at her phone again, still no reply from either of them.

"I do have a meeting after this," Yannis commented.

Sophie felt her heart starting to pound in her chest. "Oh, um, I'm sure they'll—"

He returned his attention to his laptop. Yannis was a patient man, but that patience was eventually going to run out. Sophie walked over to the laptop stored under the large television screen on the wall. She figured that she could log in and maybe show Yannis some of the assets she had seen, just to kill time until Kate or Georgina showed up and took over.

She booted up the laptop and used the remote control to turn on the television. She leaned forward and tried to remember the password for the presentation room laptop. She tried a couple of passwords, both incorrect.

It was then that she realised that Yannis was looking at her. He had closed his laptop. His pen and notepad were out, and he was looking eagerly at the screen. With horror, she realised that he had assumed she was about to present.

"Um," she tried to think of a way to backtrack. Or to run away altogether.

"I'm really looking forward to hearing these new

ideas." Yannis folded his arms and leaned back in his chair. His eyes were focused on the dark TV screen, waiting for it to spring to life.

Sophie looked down at the laptop. She still couldn't remember the password. Her hands were poised over the keyboard as she wondered what to do. This wasn't what she had imagined when she was younger and studying to work in a big marketing agency.

But this had always been her dream. To be in a meeting room with a client, presenting ideas. Her eyes drifted to her bag. She looked at the clock on the wall. Yannis's time was limited. If she didn't show him something, then he would up and leave.

"This laptop battery is low," Sophie lied. She shut the lid and yanked the projector cable out of the back. She put the computer back where she had found it and pulled her bag onto the table.

"I'm so sorry that Kate and Georgina are running late, I know they really wanted to be here. But I'm happy to go through the basics of the campaign with you now. I'm sure you'll love what we've put together." Sophie could feel her confidence building as she spoke.

She plugged her own laptop into the projector and quickly accessed her personal folders. Kate and Georgina might kill her for what she was about to do, but it was better than Yannis walking away.

She clicked on the presentation she had created a couple of nights before. It had been a culmination of weeks of work. Sitting in meetings with some of the most creative people in the world, she felt inspired to gather ideas. She spent many hours either at her desk, or at home, creating her own presentations. Using assets from work to develop full campaigns. It was a learning experience like no other.

"These are just some vague ideas, this isn't the finished presentation," Sophie said. She activated the screen and launched the slide deck.

Yannis looked at the screen and then at her expectantly.

She jumped to her feet.

"The Bolt," she started. She felt stupid, standing up and presenting to a party of one, but she knew this was what she had to do. Yannis was here for a presentation, and she'd do just that. She pressed a button on her laptop to move to the next slide.

Yannis sat forward. He stared at the logo on the screen, eagerly taking it in. He frowned, clearly wondering why a large red X covered the logo.

"The Bolt is... the wrong name," Sophie said. "Consumer research, which I carried out personally, has shown that the original name is considered to be unsafe, uncontrollable, and... childish." She took a deep breath. "Financial predictions show that a lack of sales for The Bolt would be disastrous. And a connection between The Bolt and the Atrom brand could cause issues for Atrom itself. A feeling that The Bolt is not safe could translate to Atrom not being safe."

Sophie stepped forward and jabbed a button. "And so, I present to you... Levidi Twelve." Sophie paused and allowed Yannis to take in what was on the screen. She took a breath and looked at the logo she had created herself. It was a little rough around the edges, a little pixelated in places. But the feeling of speed and security came across.

"Levidi, I don't have to tell you, is your mother's hometown. Twelve, the year of your youngest daughter's birth." Sophie took another breath. She forced herself to look at Yannis, trying to see if he thought she'd over-stepped. He was smiling. Hopefully a good sign.

"Levidi Twelve is more than a car," Sophie explained. "It's a passion. It's something that you are setting out to do, something that no one has set out to do before. Bolt may seem cool and fast, but Levidi Twelve is more than that, it's family. It's strength, it's security. It's an ideal that people can buy into. When people see the owner of Atrom Engineering in his Levidi Twelve, they are going to know that it was built to honour his family and his home. They are going to have a deep understanding of the personal meaning of the project."

"Show me more." Yannis waved his hand towards the screen. "What else do you have?"

She didn't know if it was a good sign or a bad one. Was Yannis asking for other ideas or just asking to see more of this one?

She moved to the next slide. She looked up and saw the billboard mock-ups she had created, instantly doubting herself. Her lips were dry, and she could feel herself shake as she walked towards the screen.

She pointed at the mock-ups. "We propose using this sense of family, this sense of home, across the entire campaign. There are a lot of sports cars on the market, but none with an engine as impressive as Atrom's," she added.

Yannis chuckled.

"We need to be different," she said. "We can't be the fastest, or the most expensive, or the cheapest. The market has all these things. But we can be the most inclusive, we bring you into it. It's your car, your project. I suggest we put you into the campaign."

Yannis nodded slowly. His eyes scanned the screen.

It was fifteen minutes later that Sophie finished her presentation. She had gone through all her ideas for the campaign. From billboards and television to online advertising and digital strategy. She'd gone from concepts to specifics, detailing the reasoning behind her ideas and showing mock-ups where she could. She was terrified; Kate and Georgina would surely kill her. In the back of her mind she knew she would never work in marketing ever again. She wondered if the law firm would have her back.

But it had felt invigorating to present to Yannis. It was like a dream come true. She may have never been brave enough to show her ideas to her colleagues, to marketing professionals with years more experience than her. But showing her plans to Yannis, it was easy. Like she was born to do it.

Not that Yannis had given her a shred of indication of his feelings.

She pressed the button to show the last slide in her presentation, the standard thank-you slide that asked for questions from the audience. She turned to Yannis. Her hands nervously twisted behind her back as she watched him furiously making notes on his notepad.

He looked up.

"I am very attached to the name The Bolt," he told her carefully.

She felt her stomach sink. She'd ignored rule one, listen to the client.

"But you are right. And the information you shared on your consumer research was fascinating. I love the concept. Levidi Twelve is something I can take home to my mother, that will make her proud. It's something I want to share with people. I love how you have just understood what I am trying to do here, what my ethos is, what my goals are. This is incredible. I love it all."

Sophie let out a sigh and laughed. "Oh, thank God. I was so worried," she told him.

He smiled. He stretched back in his chair, rubbing his hand over his head. "You don't need to be worried. These ideas are spot on, I'm surprised at the difference between what I was seeing before and what you have shown me today. Are you with Georgina or with Kate?"

Sophie paused. She opened her mouth and then closed it again. She had no idea what to say.

"Neither," a voice said. Sophie spun around as Kate walked into the room. Her eyes went wide in panic.

"Apologies for my delay," Kate continued, "but I see Sophie has presented her ideas?"

Sophie opened her mouth to apologise, to resign, to something.

"Sophie," Kate quickly interjected, "is a consultant. She doesn't work for Georgina or myself, but she works *with* us both. The ideas you have seen here are hers and hers alone."

Kate turned to Sophie and offered her a knowing smile.

Sophie felt herself start to sway. Confusion flooded her senses. She couldn't tell if Kate was being genuine or trying to get rid of Yannis so she could murder her in peace.

Georgina walked in and smiled at Sophie. "Sorry," she said, "trains were delayed."

Sophie looked at Georgina and then at Kate. Suddenly, it snapped into place. She'd been set up. There was a knowing look on both their faces.

"Sophie Young is a bright talent in the marketing world," Kate told Yannis. "She's up and coming and, with Georgina's and my guidance, I can tell you now that she will be one of the best. Georgina and I think that it would be best for everyone if you work directly with Sophie on all creative matters for the Levidi Twelve." Kate turned and smiled at Sophie.

"So, she's not with either of you?" Yannis clarified.

"She's independent," Georgina replied. "Working with both of us."

"But *for* neither of us," Kate clarified, looking at Sophie. She turned to look at Yannis. "I know you have another meeting after this. Let me walk you out and we can go over the details, as I see them working."

Yannis nodded and cleared his things up. "Sophie," he said, "it's been a pleasure." He shook her hand. "I look forward to working with you on this project."

Sophie nodded, unable to speak. She wasn't sure what was happening. Apparently, she was now working directly with Yannis.

He grabbed his laptop bag and hurried from the room, Kate speaking to him as they left.

Sophie fell into her seat and stared at the table blankly.

"Congratulations, you just landed your first client," Georgina said. She pulled out a chair and sat down.

Sophie looked up at her. "Where were you? Both of you?"

"Honestly? We were having breakfast in a delightful little cafe—"

"You deliberately didn't show?" Sophie stood. "You deliberately left me here on my own to deal with Yannis?"

She couldn't believe that they had been having breakfast somewhere while she was having the most frightening business experience of her life.

"Yes. Exhilarating, wasn't it?" Georgina smiled. "Kate and I had dinner last night, we talked. This war between us for the Atrom account had to end. And it has ended."

Sophie blinked. "I don't understand."

"I'm going back to New York," Georgina said. "After a short vacation in London. I want to show Jessica the sights."

"Jessica?" Sophie smiled. "You're back together?"

"We're back together," Georgina confirmed with a grin.

The smile fell from Sophie's face as she remembered the previous evening. She got to her feet. "You locked me in the elevator with Kate."

Georgina winced. "That was a mistake."

"Yeah, it was," Sophie agreed. "What the hell were you thinking?" She put her hands on her hips and glared at Georgina.

"I was thinking that you and Kate would have the same realisation that Jessica and I had. But now I know that was foolish. I could see you looking at each other in that way, and I didn't want you to waste any more time."

"There's nothing between us," Sophie mumbled. She'd thought about it a lot the previous night. She'd known why Georgina had locked them together. She'd known what she had expected, had hoped to happen. As much as she had feelings for Kate, she knew Kate couldn't feel the same way about her. Georgina was projecting her own feelings for Jessica onto Kate. Making wild assumptions that Kate would feel something for Sophie, simply because of the similarities in their situations.

Kate. Suddenly, Sophie processed what her former boss had said. She snapped her head up. "Am I fired?"

Georgina held up a calming hand. "Not exactly."

"Oh my God, I'm fired." Sophie could feel panic racing through her veins. She grabbed her laptop and threw it into her bag along with her notepad and her pen.

"Sophie, wait for Kate to come back, she'll explain—"

"Nope." Sophie swung her bag over her shoulder and grabbed her coat. "I get it, I messed up."

She hurried towards the door, stopping only centimetres before she would have crashed into Kate.

Kate turned to Georgina. "Would you leave us alone, please?"

Georgina nodded and walked out of the room, closing the door behind her.

CHAPTER THIRTY-EIGHT

KATE COULD CLEARLY SEE the panic in Sophie's eyes.

"Am I fired?" the young woman asked.

Kate blinked. "Well, that's not the term I'd use, no."

"Can I leave, please?" Sophie indicated the door behind Kate.

"Not until we talk." Kate gestured towards a chair at the meeting table. She watched as Sophie swallowed. Her eyes darted around the room. "Please," Kate insisted.

Sophie lowered her bag to the floor and moved a chair out from under the table with her foot. She sat down, holding her coat to her chest protectively.

"First of all, Yannis was very impressed with your ideas." Kate took a seat beside Sophie. She ensured there was enough space between them that she wasn't crowding her. "He says that your ideas were original and exciting, high praise indeed from someone like him."

"Thank you," Sophie mumbled.

Kate licked her lips. She knew this conversation wouldn't be easy, but now it was here, she was feeling more nervous than ever. She knew she had to go through with her plan or she would regret it. Or else Georgina would lock them in an elevator again.

"You're not fired. If you want to keep your job here, you are more than welcome to do so," Kate said. "But I have a proposal for you that, hopefully, you will find interesting."

Sophie looked at her and frowned.

"I would like you to consider setting up your own company, as a consultant. If you agree, then you would work directly with Yannis on this project. You would be a liaison between him and Red Door. We would do the work, under your guidance. You'd be under no obligation to use Red Door. If you felt our work was shoddy or our prices too high, you could go elsewhere. You would have that freedom."

"Why, though?" Sophie asked.

"Two reasons," Kate explained. "Firstly, I've been watching you and I know you are talented. Although, you're not very good at sneaking around, which is why I'd seen your presentations. Saving your ideas on the shared drive in a folder called *Sophie* wasn't the brightest idea."

Sophie blushed. She stared down at the floor.

"But, despite your saving process, your ideas are good. Excellent, in fact. I've been watching you develop and learn. I've been sending you to meetings to help you learn more, to see how that would affect your ideas. And I've watched you grow. You're very talented, Sophie. But there isn't an exact position for you to fill here. You're more than a project manager, more than a designer, more than a conceptual editor. You're the whole package. And I don't want to lose that."

Kate stood and walked over to the sideboard. She picked up two glasses and poured water into them. "Sometimes, the best way to keep hold of someone is to let them go. I want to give you the freedom to develop more. In the hope that you will want to remain here, working with us when you choose to. I see a bright future for you. I'd like to help you build that."

She placed a glass of water in front of Sophie and sat down again.

Sophie eagerly took the glass and took a drink. "H-how would this work?" she asked.

"However you'd like it to work. I see a reciprocal agreement. We would keep you on board, on a retainer, and you would be our consultant on certain projects. Georgina has also expressed interest in a similar agreement. Yannis would be another client. You'd be free to source more, I would be happy to help you find further clients. You can work from home, or from here. We can arrange office space for you, if you wish?"

"What's the other reason?"

Kate let out a nervous breath. She took a sip of water.

"You said there were two reasons," Sophie pressed. "What was the other?"

Kate stood up again. This time she walked over to the window, wanting to put some distance between them.

"The second reason is important," Kate said. "But it has absolutely no bearing on what we've discussed. I don't want you to feel that your response will change what has just been said. Does that make sense?"

She looked at Sophie, who looked baffled.

"Not really, no," Sophie admitted.

Kate chuckled. "I'm not explaining this very well. I... Sophie, the truth is that I could never possibly consider dating someone who worked for me. The conflict of interest is too great."

Sophie's eyes started to widen. Kate knew she had to keep talking or she would start to backtrack. She'd come too far to go back now.

She crossed back to her seat, moving it to sit herself directly in front of Sophie.

"I think there is something between us," Kate said. "I think we've both ignored it for a while now, I think we've both done all we can to pretend it isn't there. But it is. At least, I think it is."

Sophie looked like she might pass out. She took a deep breath. "You... want..."

"Sophie, will you join me for dinner tonight?" Kate hoped that she was maintaining a neutral expression on her face. Her heart was hammering hard in her chest.

"D-dinner?"

"Yes, a date. Feel free to say no. As I say, your response to this has no bearing on—"

"Yes," Sophie breathed. "I mean... yes, yes. I..." She trailed off before quickly nodding.

Kate smiled. She'd done it. She'd taken the step and hadn't been rejected like she had in her nightmares.

Sophie had said yes. A very definite yes.

Suddenly, Sophie was launching herself at her. Impossibly soft lips pressed against hers. She let out a gasp, and Sophie quickly pulled back.

"I'm sorry," Sophie whispered. "I shouldn't have—"

Kate grabbed the front of Sophie's cardigan in her fist. She pulled her back and crushed their lips together. She quickly deepened the kiss, trying to express her strong emotions with the action. She pulled back, but only for air.

Sophie's eyes had closed during the kiss, and she seemed to be in a state of bliss. Her lips were stained with Kate's lipstick, a blush on her cheeks, her breathing rapid and uneven.

Kate smirked to herself. "Better than Georgina?" she asked smugly.

Sophie opened her eyes and grinned mischievously. "I don't know, I'll need to try again to be sure."

I adore publishing. There's a wonderful thrill that comes from crafting a manuscript and then releasing it to the world. Especially when you are writing woman loving woman characters. I'm blessed to receive messages from readers all over the world who are thrilled to discover characters and scenarios that resemble their lives.

Books are entertaining escapism, but they are also reinforcement that we are not alone in our struggles. I'm passionate about writing books that people can identify with. Books that are accessible to all and show that love—and acceptance—can be found no matter who you are.

I've been lucky enough to have published books that have been best-sellers and even some award-winners. While I'm still quite a new author, I have plans to write many, many more novels. However, writing, editing, and marketing books take up a lot of time… and writing full-time is a treadmill-like existence, especially in a very small niche market like mine.

Don't get me wrong, I feel very grateful and lucky to be able to live the life I do. But being a full-time author in a small market means never being able to stop and work on developing my writing style, it means rarely having the time or budget to properly market my books, it means immediately picking up the next project the moment the previous has finished.

This is why I have set up a Patreon account. With Patreon, you can donate a small amount each month to enable me to hop off of my treadmill for a while in order to reach my goals. Goals such as exploring better marketing options, developing my writing craft, and investigating writing articles and screenplays.

My Patreon page is a place for exclusive first looks at new works, insight into upcoming projects, Q&A sessions, as well as special gifts and dedications. I'm also pleased to give all of my Patreon subscribers access to **exclusive short stories** which have been written just for patrons. There are tiers to suit all budgets.

My readers are some of the kindest and most supportive people I have met, and I appreciate every book borrow or purchase. With the added support of Patreon, I hope to be able to develop my writing career in order to become a better author as well as level up my marketing strategy to help my books to reach a wider audience.

https://www.patreon.com/aeradley

I sincerely hope you enjoyed reading this book.

If you did, I would greatly appreciate a short review on your favourite book website.

Reviews are crucial for any author, and even just a line or two can make a huge difference.

ABOUT THE AUTHOR

Amanda Radley had no desire to be a writer but accidentally became an award-winning, bestselling author.

She gave up a marketing career in order to make stuff up for a living instead. She claims the similarities are startling.

She describes herself as a Wife. Traveller. Tea Drinker. Biscuit Eater. Animal Lover. Master Pragmatist. Procrastinator. Theme Park Fan.

Connect with Amanda
www.amandaradley.com

GOING UP

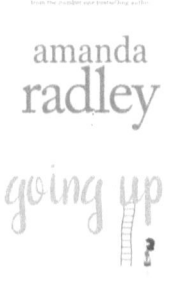

A ruthless executive. A destitute woman. Both on the way up.

Selina Hale is on her way to the top. She's been working towards a boardroom position on the thirteenth floor for her entire career. And no one is going to get in her way. Not her clueless boss, her soon to be ex-wife, and most certainly not the homeless person who has moved into the car park at work.

Kate Morgan fell through the cracks in a broken support system and found herself destitute. Determined and strong-willed, she's not about to accept help from a mean business woman who can't even remember the names of her own nephews.

As their lives continue to intertwine, they have no choice but to work together and follow each other on their journey up.

ALSO BY AMANDA RADLEY

LOST AT SEA

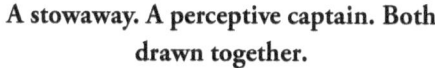

A stowaway. A perceptive captain. Both drawn together.

Annie Peck finds herself in a terrible situation and is literally running for her life. A chance encounter with a surprising lookalike leads her towards a risky solution.

Captain Caroline West knows she is lucky to be one of the few women cruise ship captains in the world. Sadly, not having a standard nine to five job means relationships are nearly impossible and she's all but given up on finding anyone.

Join these two women for an all-expenses-paid cruise of the Mediterranean and find out what happens when an identity thief with a heart of gold meets the rule-abiding woman who could throw her in jail.

ALSO BY AMANDA RADLEY

SECOND CHANCES

Bad childhood memories start to resurface when Hannah Hall's daughter Rosie begins school. To make matters more complicated, Hannah has been steadfastly ignoring the obvious truth that Rosie is intellectually gifted and wise beyond her years.

In the crumbling old school she meets Rosie's new teacher Alice Spencer who has moved from the city to teach in the small coastal town of Fairlight.

Alice immediately sees Rosie's potential and embarks on developing an educational curriculum to suit Rosie's needs, to Hannah's dismay.

Teacher and mother clash over what's best for young Rosie.

Will they be able to compromise? Will Hannah finally open up to someone about her own damaged upbringing?

And will they be able to ignore the sparks that fly whenever they are in the same room?

www.ingramcontent.com/pod-product-compliance
Lightning Source LLC
Chambersburg PA
CBHW021204250626
47155CB00008B/2668